Death in Blue Velvet

The Second Book in the Rhiannon Nolan Series

by

Kathy Buchen

authorHOUSE™

1663 LIBERTY DRIVE, SUITE 200
BLOOMINGTON, INDIANA 47403
(800) 839-8640
WWW.AUTHORHOUSE.COM

First published by AuthorHouse 03/16/05

ISBN: 1-4208-3257-3 (sc)
ISBN: 1-4208-3256-5 (dj)

Library of Congress Control Number: 2005902329

Printed in the United States of America
Bloomington, Indiana

This book is printed on acid-free paper.

as always, for Kelsey and Eddie

Chapter 1

Smoke Gets In Your Eyes

And we came out to see once more the stars.

--Dante's Inferno, Dante Alighieri

Dear Val,

You're my one and only forever and ever.

Luv from Skip

The New Belgium News
Policeman Comes to the Aid of Local Animals

Our Sgt. LeCaptain was called to the aid of a constipated pigeon on Friday afternoon. He transported the bird to the New Belgium Humane Society, where Johnny Brighton saved the animal. Later that same day, Babs O'Reilly called the police to her home, where an angry skunk had somehow got a plastic cup wedged on its head. Sgt. LeCaptain succeeded in removing the cup from the skunk's head without getting sprayed. The skunk then fled the scene.

Only in New Belgium could my nemesis, Sgt. Francis LeCaptain, make front page news with a story like this. I cackled, folded up the paper, and threw it in the back seat of the car. Peering out the window of the Ford, I spied my daughter Tabby's Home Ec teacher, Miss Cooper, open the school door.

1

Miss Valerie Cooper was one of those women who never changed her hairstyle, or indeed, anything about herself. She wore her hair one of two ways; either a teased bubble or a French twist. She still sported powder blue twinsets and pearls, swing skirts, bobby socks, and penny loafers. For a woman in her sixties, she had amazingly good legs. Squinting, I appraised her figure and guessed her to be a disgustingly well preserved size six.

With a rueful sigh I threw my chocolate bar into the glove compartment of the Ford and vowed I would try harder to stick to my diet. I watched Miss Cooper swing down the sidewalk in front of the high school and marveled at how anyone could be so firmly entrenched in the fifties.

Miss Cooper hopped into her classic 1957 Chevy, pink if you please, and slipped on her cat's eye sunglasses. She gazed in the rearview mirror, applied some bright red lipstick, adjusted the visor, cranked the ignition, and roared off to her little white clapboard house on Viola Street. I breathed a sentimental sigh for the fab fifties and my happy childhood spent therein.

"Mom! Hello? Are you like, dead or what?"

Oh, darn, reality intrudes again. In my next life I'm coming back as a Carmelite nun, with no men and no kids to mar the peace and quiet. The only problem is that I would probably be drummed out of the nunnery for being unable to keep the vow of silence. Also, I don't take orders well. Looks like I'm doomed to inhabit the secular world no matter how many reincarnations I have to go through.

My daughter Tabby looked in the car window, bobbed her shock of spiked bright purple hair at me, opened the door, and jumped in the Ford. Her friend Krystal of the black lips and nails and grotesque tongue stud hauled her two hundred pound frame into the back seat.

"I was just looking at Miss Cooper and reminiscing," I said. "And you don't have to be so rude. I see you've died your hair orange again, Krystal."

"Supposed to be pink but I screwed up," said Krystal around the tongue stud. Her real name was Constance but she preferred to be called Krystal. "Coop, Coop, Coop!" she called to Miss Cooper's fast disappearing Chevy. "Miss Fly the Coop is so retro cool. Today

2

in Home Ec class we like, made this cherry pie from scratch like real homemade food, and then the Coop said we could eat it and it was so good!"

"Yeah, lots better than your cooking, Mom," added Tabby.

"Save it," I ordered and eased the Ford out into the bright September sunshine, with the slanting light of a mellow four o'clock sun in my eyes.

"Did you learn anything besides making cherry pies in school today?" I asked, not without apprehension.

"In health class we learned that everyone should use a condom to stop the spread of disease," said Krystal.

"Maybe they should just use will power," I said. "That would be an even better way to stop disease."

"Yeah," agreed Tabby. "Today we studied *Lysistrata* in English. I said I thought it would be great if women worldwide went on strike and there would be no sex anywhere if there were even one teeny, tiny war anywhere on the planet. Don't you think that's a good idea, Mom?" asked Tabby.

"Marvelous," I murmured. "What did your teacher say?"

"She said I was dysfunctional and needed psychological help," said Tabby. "And all the kids laughed at me."

"Yeah, but if you were like, a Greek dramatist, then everyone would say you were a freaking genius," said Krystal. "They just hate you because some day you're gonna be a great punk rock star."

Conversations like this are the reason I don't want to know what is going on in school. I don't think I want to know what is going on, period.

"Anyway, Miss Cooper is like, having us over tonight and she's going to show us how to make baked Alaska," said Krystal.

"Shouldn't you be studying chemistry and algebra tonight?" I asked. "It's the start of your sophomore year and I want you to crank up those grades for college admissions."

"Mother!" cried Tabby. "Is that all you ever think about? No way, Mom, not tonight. The Coop promised to tell us all about her assignation."

"Her what?"

"She's got a date with her long lost true love this weekend and they're going to elope, or possibly even live in sin after forty-four years of being apart. It's like *Wuthering Heights*. It's so romantic! Heathcliff! Heathcliff! It's me, Catherine Earnshaw!" Tabby screamed and swooned over her backpack.

"Coop even showed us his high school graduation picture. She's carried it in her wallet all this time. His name is Skip Winters. He looks dangerous, like Elvin," said Krystal.

"That's Elvis," corrected Tabby. "But really, Skip looks more like a goth Beach Boy, like all blond surfer dude except with a hint of vampire. He was class president and captain of the football team and the Coop was the most popular girl at New Belgium High School. And he's coming back to claim her after all these years! He could never forget her. Oh, geez! I hope someone loves me like that someday."

"Oh, yeah, what a thrill. I'd rather be a nun," I said as we turned the corner. We drove past my handyman Paul Pavalik's farm. Down the lane, Babs O'Reilly, her long bleached blond hair floating in the breeze, tripped across the road on her high heels to get her mail from the box. We waved at her as we passed. She wobbled on her heels, extracted the cigarette stuck in her mouth like a plug, and gave us a wave. We continued on down Red Oak Lane and rolled down the hill towards our house, Raven's Nest.

Home was a three story Victorian farmhouse set on eighty acres directly across the lane from the home of my lifelong best friend, Didi Spencer.

"If Skippy was so crazy about Valerie Cooper why did he leave town for forty-four years?" I asked.

"I dunno, maybe he's a criminal or something," said Krystal.

"Maybe he was marooned on a south sea island," said Tabby, her eyes aglow.

"Or maybe he's a big fat lying scum," I said and pulled the Ford into the driveway. "Or maybe Valerie Cooper is living in fantasy land and there isn't any Skip Winters at all."

Chapter 2

Let's Do the Twist

I fear, too early, for my mind misgives
Some consequence yet hanging in the stars
Shall bitterly begin his fearful date
With this night's revels and expire the term
Of a despised life, closed in my breast,
By some vile forfeit of untimely death,
But he that hath the steerage of my course
Direct my sail. On, lusty gentlemen!

--William Shakespeare, *Romeo and Juliet*, Act. I

Dear Val,

My heart skips a beat whenever I see you walk down the hall in school.

Luv you lots, Skip

Grandmother always said that pride goeth before a fall. Funny how her gaze came to rest on me when she said it. If only I had listened to dear old Grandma instead of hightailing it out the back door as soon as she walked in the front, I could have had less trouble in life. I've always been a trouble magnet, especially where men are concerned. Perhaps if I had taken her warnings to heart, I wouldn't have ended up in my latest pickle.

After I was almost killed while solving my last case, I wasn't too thrilled about doing any more sleuthing, and understandably so. It was pride that drew me into my next case, and sheer cussed pride which prevented me from bowing out when I should have known better.

5

After all, who wants to look bad in front of her daughter? Not Attorney Rhiannon Nolan, twice divorced, once widowed, newly graduated attorney at law, and supermom of three teenagers. Far be it from me to admit to anyone, including myself, that I can't do something all by myself without help, thank you very much.

It all started when I drove Tabby and Krystal over to Miss Valerie Cooper's house that night in early September. Coop's house was a falling down white clapboard surrounded by a picket fence and several big blue spruce trees. A small strip of garden near the door boasted a riot of hardy snapdragons which shone like an eerie rainbow in the soft evening light. The lawn was weedy and there were myriad spider webs on the old eaves and the splintered wood windows.

My guess was that Valerie had inherited the house from her parents and not changed a thing for forty years, a guess which was confirmed when we rang the doorbell and Valerie answered the door. I peered past her at the ancient worn gray carpet strewn with patterned roses. I spied a comfy, sagging gold velveteen couch and chair, a console stereo, and a gold lamp straight out of 1958. Green velvet drapes completed the picture. They looked like they were rotting right on the drapery rods.

"Oh, girls, you came over!" cried an ecstatic Valerie. "Come in, come in! You too, Mrs. Nolan!"

"Oh, I'm just dropping off the girls," I said, feeling like someone's dowager mother barging in on the slumber party.

"No, I insist. Oh, please join us! I've made a divine shrimp cocktail. I almost never get to have company. Wouldn't you like some root beer?" asked Valerie, her face aglow.

She meant it. What would it hurt to play along? The poor lonely old thing belonged in Charles Dickens' *Great Expectations*. She was a modern Miss Havesham, except she had a far sweeter disposition. How did she survive the modern world with its incessant noise and in your face attitude?

"Well, I guess if I'm not intruding that would be fun," I said hesitantly.

"Oh, sharp! Come on in!" said Val.

We stepped into the foyer and I got a good look at Valerie in the light. Her makeup was early Audrey Hepburn and her hair a stiffly teased and sprayed bouffant. A gale force wind couldn't have moved it. She had changed into a blue velvet prom dress with the requisite pearls, silk stockings, and spike heels. The room was softly lit with candles which almost managed to hide the wrinkles on Val's face.

I realized that years ago she must have been quite beautiful. There was something evanescent about her. She had that sparkle, that precious purity of spirit which gets stamped out early in most people. Her smile held that bubbly joy which belongs only to children and a few select adults who never lose their innocence.

In the corner, a plastic rose covered arbor glowed under a pink spotlight. On the battered coffee table, framed pictures of Bobby Vinton, Frankie Avalon, Elvis, and Bobby Darin smiled out at us. Next to the pictures, a stack of yearbooks from the fifties collected dust undisturbed.

"Oh, cool!" cried Krystal. "This is so like, retro."

"Oh, I love the fifties and sixties," Tabby chimed in.

They bounced into the room, exclaiming over the decor. I looked around and realized that the whole scene was no accident. Val wasn't pretending to live in the past; she was firmly entrenched in the reality of it all. Perhaps there was a reason there was no color television, video, compact disc player or computer in the house. Val had taken the A train back to the fifties and there was no way she was coming out alive.

By this time I knew that a relatively large number of God's cracked molds had somehow found their way to New Belgium, Wisconsin. Until now I hadn't realized that Valerie Cooper was one of them.

Oh, Lord, please help me, I prayed silently. I'm not good at dealing with lunatics other than teenagers. It gives me a sick feeling and I'm afraid I'll upset them and drive them into a psychotic episode. I expected Valerie to start humming *Blame It on the Bossa Nova* any minute.

"Help yourself to chips and dip, girls! I'll just get us some sodas and bring out the shrimp. Won't be a minute!" she said with a cheeriness worthy of Donna Reed. She disappeared through swinging doors into what appeared to be an exact replica of my mother's tile floored, scrubbed white kitchen. Leave it to Valerie the Home Ec teacher to be able to do gourmet cooking in such a poorly equipped and out of date kitchen. I had all the latest equipment and I could barely manage spaghetti.

The girls pounced on the chips and then cooed over Val's collection of old records.

"Oh, look Mom! It's Chubby Checker! You used to dance to that one, right?" asked Tabby. "Matt and Jen told me you taught us all how to twist when we were little but I can't remember it."

"Dion, Fabian, Connie Francis, Elvis, Bobby Vinton, Del Shannon, The Platters, The Drifters; Coop has 'em all! She is so cool, just like an old black and white television love story," crowed Krystal.

Miss Cooper bobbed in with a gorgeous plate of shrimp cocktail and hors d'oeuvres. Krystal's eyes grew wide with wonder. Valerie didn't have to tell us twice to dig in.

"We love your house," mumbled Krystal through a mouthful of food.

"It is lovely, isn't it?" said Valerie. I just about choked on a piece of shrimp. "I have two cousins in Jubilee. That's up north about sixty miles. Julia and Pamela are twins, both unmarried like me. They said they absolutely want my house if I ever sell it. But I never will."

"Hey! You promised to tell us about the lover boy," prodded Tabby.

Miss Cooper's eyes misted. She pointed to the old fashioned roll-top desk in the corner. There, enshrined among little bunches of violets, was a framed graduation picture of Skip.

"That's him, that's Skip over there," said Valerie softly. The way she looked at him, I expected his picture to start talking to her any minute. "I've waited over forty years and finally I got my wish. He came to his senses and called me. He's been coming to see me in secret."

Oh, yeah, and the ghost of Gregory Peck comes in secret to see me, too. He tells me that if only he could live again, he would forsake Hollywood fame and fortune for me. Instead of being a star, he would spend his life in New Belgium fulfilling my every desire. Valerie Cooper was definitely in need of reality therapy.

"Another girl came between us when Skip went off to college," said Valerie. "Of course, he looked like Tab Hunter so all the girls were wild about him. But then Melanie Barker got him and ruined him. Sex bomb Melanie and her blond bombshell friend Babs and that rotten Scooter O'Reilly poisoned Skip against me. Babs married Scooter and Melanie married my true love. But his heart has turned again home. He's coming for me Friday night. Skip's coming for me and we're going away. That's why I'm dressed this way. I'm in dress rehearsal for Friday night. When Skip walks in the door, I want to look just the way I did on prom night. Skip doesn't love Melanie. He never really did. He's coming for me at last."

Val's eyes rested on Skip's picture as her voice faded away.

Right Valerie, and the lottery fairy is coming for me on Friday night with the winning ticket, I thought wildly. Some people collect stamps, beanie babies, or autographed baseballs. I collect weirdos. I'm a weirdo magnet. Anyone who knows my ex-husbands and boyfriends can tell you that.

"Miss Coop, wow! Geez!" said Krystal and whistled softly. "What a love story! I hope Skip is like, not too old and crumbly looking."

"Or half dead and crippled so his parts don't work anymore!" Tabby chimed in.

I surreptitiously kicked her. She gave me the teenage look from hell reserved only for mothers.

"Oh, no," sighed Valerie. "Skip is just as handsome as ever, in a more mature way of course. We will have many good years together. God tells me these things. We planned a romantic Hawaiian honeymoon in 1959 and I'm still convinced it will happen."

I started to feel little prickles of panic, just like I did when I got in an enclosed, windowless space. Loonies did that to me, made me claustrophobic. Suddenly Valerie brightened.

"Girls! Let's turn on the dance music," she said. "Come on! This is a party, after all!"

Thank God! At last there was something I felt comfortable with in this museum of dusty love.

Valerie put Fabian on the record player and the four of us began to dance. Valerie kept the tunes coming and I taught Krystal and Tabby the pony, the twist, the mashed potato, the frug, the monkey, the swim, and the jitterbug. Finally exhausted, I threw myself on the couch and laughed until I cried watching Tabby and Krystal trying to do the jitterbug.

The years melted away and I felt young again. I had a flashback of myself as I was long ago; a hundred pound long haired leggy preteen on my way downtown to buy my first Beatles record with my babysitting money. I hadn't had this much fun in a long time. We forgot all about the baked Alaska we were there to learn how to make until Krystal mentioned it.

"I was really looking forward to sampling it," she said wistfully. "But now there won't be time."

"Don't worry, dear. Come over after school tomorrow and I'll whip up a quick batch of my special better than sex chocolate cake and give it to you girls to take home," promised Valerie. The girls started to giggle madly.

"Sweet! We'll be here!" cooed Krystal.

"Time to go," I said. "Miss Cooper has to get ready for school tomorrow and you two must have some homework."

"Oh, geez, you're such a wet blanket," whined Tabby, but I held firm. Tabby, Krystal and I said our good-byes and tumbled out into the fresh September night air. Above us shone a glorious swirl of bright stars. Just before I climbed into the Ford, I glanced back through the open window into the house. Valerie, her eyes closed, swayed gently beneath the rose arbor to the strains of Bobby Vinton's *Blue Velvet*. She was lost in a protective cocoon of fantasy, happy in her bright romantic dreams. The girls heard the music wafting out on a wave of autumnal air.

"That's it!" said Tabby. "That's the song Miss Cooper always hums to herself."

Stay in your happy dreams, Miss Cooper, I thought. *Dreams are so much better than the real world.*

Chapter 3

Dead Man's Curve

O my love's like a red, red rose
That's newly sprung in June;
O my love's like the melodie
That's sweetly played in tune.

As fair thou art, my bonny lass,
So deep in love am I;
And I will love thee still, my dear,
Till a' the seas gang dry.

--A Red, Red Rose, Robert Burns

Dear Val,

We were meant to be together and someday I promise we will be, only this time it will be forever.

Luv U Always, Skip

Nothing makes a girl quite as wacko as unrequited love. Most of us get over it, but I guess for Miss Cooper it was a life sentence. I never could decide if people like Valerie Cooper were saints or lunatics, or maybe a little bit of both.

These are the things I think about when I'm supposed to be doing important things like running a law office and making some money to pay the rent.

I looked up from my desk. My eyes came to rest on my secretary Eunice Dunn, bless her. She of the cherubic face and the twinkling blue eyes had her head buried in the books.

"Will we stay solvent until next week?" I asked cautiously.

"Maybe, but I hope you get that big Stoegbauer case," she said.

"Oh-oh! Sounds ominous. On a lighter note, what do you know about Valerie Cooper?" I asked.

"Cuckoo! Demented romantic fool, but nice, very nice," said Eunice.

"Who is this Skip Winters character and why is Valerie still pining away over him?" I asked.

"Oh, you know about him, huh? Skip Winters was the Don Juan of the graduating class of 1959. I know because I graduated with him and Valerie. They were an item until he went off to college and became a playboy. He showed signs of it even in high school. You know the type."

"Unfortunately, I do, and no, I don't want to talk about it," I said. "Why didn't Valerie marry someone else?"

"Val was the cat's pajamas! She could have had anyone she wanted but she threw her life away pining over that stupid Skip," said Eunice with disgust. "He lives in Maybelle with his wife Melanie and his two grown daughters and their daughters. I think he supports them all on his charm."

"I don't think much of him, then," I said. "I've always found that a man's capacity for love and fidelity is in direct inverse proportion to his charm quotient."

"He's a salesman and I hear he makes top dollar," continued Eunice. "At the moment I think there are two little great granddaughters too; four generations of women in the same house. What fun!"

"You're kidding! Does Valerie know he lives nearby?" I asked. "Does she know he has all those daughters and granddaughters and great-granddaughters?"

"Probably, since Skip makes himself well known throughout a four county area. You see," Eunice said, her voice falling to a whisper, "he's still a playboy!"

"A playboy at his age? Must consume a lot of Viagra," I said.

"I hear he doesn't need it," said Eunice and looked at me over the top of her bifocals. "Dear, all that talent is completely wasted, and none of it on poor Valerie."

So speaks the wise spinster. I couldn't help but giggle.

The legal profession looks exciting on television and film but in reality, it involves a lot of dry, tedious, boring detail. That's why I employ my secretary Eunice. She is painstakingly good at details and also at keeping me on track. In addition to being a bangup secretary, she knows all the gossip, both current and historical, that makes its way through the bush telegraph in New Belgium. Our little town boasts a finely tuned, intricate, and highly developed gossip communications system. It's state of the art, and with Eunice at the helm, there isn't much that gets past the radar.

Eunice lives with her two sisters, Fayne and Maida, who run the Cliffhanger Bookstore on Main Street. None of the sisters ever married, but seven of the eight brothers made up for the sisters' lack of progeny by marrying local women and producing many lively little Dunns. The eighth brother grew up to be a priest.

The eight brothers lived round about New Belgium, including the youngest brother, Father Raymond, who was the priest at St. Paul's Catholic Church. Father Dunn makes a valiant effort to show our younger priest, Father Ryan, how to run a parish, with limited success.

On my lunch hour I drove around aimlessly, trying to decide between a lettuce salad, no dressing, from the drive-through and a diet snack bar which had been moldering away in the bottom of my purse. I tried to make a decision but a third option kept making its determined way through the diet mentality blockade.

Wasn't it Oscar Wilde who said that the only way to get rid of a temptation is to give in to it? Oh Lord, remove these thoughts from my mind, I prayed. Sister Martha always said I lacked self control and she was absolutely right. I need chocolate. Specifically, I need some M&M's. I think my blood sugar is low and I need a quick sugar transfusion. I think I need chocolate right now before I faint. I think I would kill for some M&M's. Well, maybe not kill, maybe just maim. And menopausal craziness is no defense in a court of law, so I'll just have to have some chocolate to soothe the ferocious beast before I do anything nutty. How's that for rationalization?

No! I am not going to give in! I've been doing so well on my low carb, low calorie regimen. But Lord, how long can you go without bread and chocolate? It gets sickening eating nothing but chicken, beef, and fish washed down with sugarless tea day in, day out. As Tabby says, I'm not really into eating dead animal flesh.

I've been eating so much protein I feel overdosed; so much salmon my eyes are turning pink; so many hard boiled eggs with mustard, no mayo that I'm starting to think in terms of ovals. The world is oval, not round. Not just chickens, but everything comes from the egg. The world is one big plastic egg! If I see one more grilled chicken salad, hold the dressing, I'm going to scream. I need taste! I need to taste something sweet right now!

Why have I braked the car to a screeching halt right in the middle of Main Street? Oh, the wheel seems to be turning the car of its own volition right into the Quick Pick. Oh, dear, there are the glass doors. There is sweet, bald Mr. Duffy with the bad dentures. And there, right there in the neat shiny rows of lovely candies, are my dear little M&M's, just waiting for me to buy them.

Shall I get the giant bag with two pounds of heaven inside? How about the one pound bag, or maybe just the king size snack bag? Or shall I be good and get the little bag? Decisions, decisions. Oh, heck, let's go for it.

I walked up to the checkout with my two pound bag of M&M's.

"I thought you were on a diet," said Mr. Duffy.

"What idiot told you that?" I asked.

"Paul Pavalik said you were trying to lose weight and I would be doing you a favor not to sell you any candy," Mr. Duffy said.

"So who elected him pope? Should I genuflect or just kiss his ring? Pavalik walks around under the influence. He's over eighty years old. He has no short term memory left. What does he know? He is a handyman, not a diet doctor. You can't believe everything you hear," I said firmly. "Besides, this is just a one time deal so I have a little stash in the car, just in case I'm suffering from low blood sugar while caught in traffic."

Mr. Duffy looked at me and clicked his dentures.

"Not much traffic to be caught in here in New Belgium," he said wryly.

"Just in case of emergency," I added.

"Won't lose any weight eating chocolate. You have to go low carb," Mr. Duffy advised.

"Oh, would you all shut up about the carbs? I'm a peasant descended from a long line of Irish peasants. I love bread, potatoes, and salt. And I need a few refined carbs to compliment the complex carbs that are, do you hear me, good for you! So crucify me!" I yelled at him.

The corners of Mr. Duffy's mouth drew down.

"Don't have to get so testy about it!" he said reproachfully.

I threw the money on the counter, slammed out the door and into the car, where I tore open the bag and grabbed a handful of carbs, beautiful chocolate carbs. Yum! Ah, heaven. I breathed in the sweet smell of chocolate. And M&M's give you the added bonus of chocolate with crunch. I think it's really the two different textures combined that is my downfall. Sometimes, nothing else will do.

To my undemanding and indiscriminate palate, M&M's are the nectar of the gods. Forget lobster thermidor, steak tartare, caviar, and chocolate mousse. I would rather eat M&M's any day. My only complaint is that there are never enough red ones, probably because I've eaten them all!

I give myself very good advice but I seldom follow it. I tell myself, self, shape up and do things right. Be a better person, parent, lawyer. Be kinder, thinner, more compassionate, and less mouthy. Don't be such a hot tempered smartass. Be cool. Read Milton and C.S. Lewis instead of trashy escapist fiction. But does self listen? No, self gobbles M&M's, cusses at the television, and stands in the checkout line at the grocery store reading *Cosmopolitan* and the *National Inquirer*. Someday I might need to know the latest sex technique and how aliens plan to mate with Hollywood movie stars.

I looked at myself in the mirror. Boy, I looked bad with my mouth stuffed full of M&M's. *Hope nobody is getting this on videotape,* I thought. You have to be careful nowadays. Anything you do can and will be videotaped and used against you. The only place you're safe is in your own home, and sometimes not even there if you have lots of windows and your neighbors own video cameras.

I arranged a series of M&M's on the console of the Ford; red, blue, yellow, green, orange, and brown, in that order. *Life doesn't get any better than this,* I thought as I ate them one by lovely one.

Someone pounded on my windshield and my heart answered with a thump.

"I thought you were on a diet!" Mr. Pavalik leered at me, his aged chimp face drawn back into a grin.

"You almost gave me a heart attack!" I yelled at him, mouth stuffed full of candy and gaping open in what I'm quite sure was an unbecoming manner. He shook his gnarled index finger at me.

"I told Duffy not to give you candy," he said. "You were doing so well. Can't you just say no? You should go to a twelve step program!" he croaked. "You're a chocoholic."

"Twelve step programs are just the modern version of the sacrament of confession, and I've done enough confessing for one lifetime! Why don't you go pound some nails in your hand?" I screamed.

"Temper, temper!" admonished Mr. Pavalik. I turned the key in the ignition, slammed the Ford into reverse, and stomped on the accelerator.

There was a sickening crunch of metal on metal. I looked into the rearview mirror. Oh, dear. Is that a blue and white police vehicle I see attached to my rear bumper? Is that the glowering gaze of New Belgium's finest, Sgt. LeCaptain? He doesn't seem too awfully jovial, but then, he never does when he looks in my direction.

I sighed, put the car in park, and turned off the ignition. It was inevitable that one day I would hit LeCaptain's car. This moment had slunk through the shadows like a jaguar stalking an antelope since the day I moved to town. And now, today, it had finally sprung, gotten me by the throat, and sunk its teeth in. I could do nothing but surrender to fate.

Mr. P shook his head at me and hobbled off to Chuck the red Chevy, his ancient pickup truck. He hustled inside, thumped the dash three times, and turned the key in the ignition. Chuck the Chevy sputtered into life and chugged its way onto Main Street. Fine friend Pavalik turned out to be, leaving me to face Sgt. Francis LeCaptain alone.

"Mrs. Nolan, you have struck my police vehicle," said a gloom infested Eeyore-like voice.

Le Captain loomed into my window, his head a blown up balloon caricature of itself. The cartoon policeman strikes again. Every time I looked at his oval head, his luxurious moustaches, his large dark eyes, and his well oiled, sleek black hair, all I could think of was Agatha Christie's Monsieur Poirot. Oh, Lord help me.

I turned and smiled at him.

"So I have, but I assure you that it was entirely an accident."

"Do you have an insurance company which will still take your money? Because they're going to be demanding a lot of it."

"Is that your pathetic attempt at humor?" I asked him, still smiling.

He ran his hand through his oil slicked hair and wiped it on his blue serge police uniform. Good thing he had the navy shirt on today. It wouldn't show so much greasy stain.

I took out my cell phone and called Eunice at the office.

"Don't expect me in for the rest of the day," I said. "I just smashed into LeCaptain's car and I'm taking the Ford into Stanley Keefer at the garage to have it fixed."

"Lucky you. I'll bet you were good at bumper cars," said Eunice and hung up. Everybody's a card nowadays.

One hour, one ticket, and a lot of argument later, I pulled the Ford into Stanley Keefer's garage lot. My favorite mechanic pulled his head out of the hood of a car and laughed when he saw the Ford.

"What did you do now?" he asked.

"Hit LeCaptain's police car with him in it," I said.

Stan threw back his furry grizzly bear head and roared. Then he went into a giggle which would do any schoolgirl proud. He walked around the car, threw his muscled arms on the cab, leaned his face into his hands, and laughed silently, his shoulders shaking.

"Are you having a palsy fit?" I asked.

He turned and looked at me helplessly, mouth open in soundless mirth.

"Not funny!" I protested. Stan continued to laugh until the tears streamed down his face.

"I wish I had been there to see the look on LeCaptain's face!" he managed to squeak out between gales of giggles.

"Ha, ha! Just fix it!" I ordered and stalked away.

Stan saluted.

"Want a ride home?" he asked.

"Not from you! And besides, I need the exercise," I answered. "I bought a two pound bag of M&M's and blew my diet." I started up the hill towards home.

"I'll give you a discount for frequent customer!" Stan called after me between cupped hands. I ignored him. That's the trouble with this town. It harbors too many smart alecks.

Chapter 4

Only the Lonely

Serene, I fold my hands and wait,
Nor care for wind nor tide nor sea;
I rave no more 'gainst time or fate,
For lo! My own shall come to me.

--*Waiting*, by John Burroughs

Dear Val,

You are the only person who ever understood me, and I like to think I'm the only one who ever really understood you. I was lucky to call you mine, even if it was only for a few years.

Love, Skip

At nine o'clock on Friday night, Krystal and Tabby walked over to Valerie Cooper's house to take back her dessert pan. At precisely nine thirty-one, they came running back up the driveway screaming.

"Mom! Mom!" Tabby screeched. Alarmed, I hurried out the door.

Tabby threw herself into my arms, almost knocking me over. Both she and Krystal were sobbing. Tears of shock and fright ran down their faces.

"Tell me what is wrong!" I ordered.

"Miss Cooper is dead!" Krystal finally managed to choke out.

"What? That's impossible!" I said.

19

Both girls clung to me. I put my arms around them and listened as the story came out bit by bit.

"We went up to the house to give Coop her cake pan," sobbed Krystal. "We waited until nine because we really wanted to meet Skip. She told us today in school that Skip was coming for her at nine o'clock."

"Yeah, we just wanted to meet him and see what he was like, and we thought the dessert pan would be a good excuse to go over there. And we rang the bell several times but she didn't answer," said Tabby.

"The screen door was open and we heard music," said Krystal.

"So we peered inside and saw that she had food set out," said Tabby. "We knew she was there. We thought she just didn't hear us."

"And the record player got stuck at the end of the record the way those old record players did sometimes so we knew she had to be around," said Krystal. She took several deep breaths.

"I walked in," said Tabby, tears streaming down her face.

"Even though I told her not to," declared Krystal stoutly. "I called to her to stop. I knew something was wrong by this time. I was afraid something had happened to Miss Cooper. I called Tabby's name real loud but she went in and looked around anyway."

Krystal glared at Tabby.

"And I saw that Coop had a fresh shrimp cocktail on the kitchen table," said Tabby. "I knew she wouldn't go away and leave that out." She began to wring and twist her hands. "And there was a big suitcase packed with clothes and stuff in the hallway."

"And then we heard the back door slam," said Krystal.

"So we ran to look out the back door but we didn't see anything. It was dark and we didn't see anyone," said Tabby.

"But we knew someone was out in those woods in back of Valerie's house. And then we heard a motor being gunned on the other side of the little woods and someone took off real fast," said Krystal.

"Oh, I can't stand it!" Tabby wailed.

I knew the worst was coming. Krystal put her hands over her eyes.

"We looked in all the rooms and it was like someone had just left," said Krystal. "I could even smell Miss Cooper's perfume. Remember that smelly old perfume she used to wear, Tabby?"

"Yeah, it smelled like Miss Cooper. She always wore that Evening in Paris stuff."

"And then what happened?" I asked with dread. Tabby shut her eyes, recalling the painful moment.

"We went up and looked into the bathroom and the bedrooms but we didn't see anything wrong. And then, and then . . ."

I was afraid she would start to hyperventilate.

"Exhale and get it out," I said. "And then what?"

"And then we went back downstairs to the kitchen and opened the door to the basement steps and we saw her," Tabby said in a choked voice.

"She was laying at the bottom of the steps all crumpled up," said Krystal and started to cry.

"And she had on her blue velvet prom dress and her high heels," said Tabby and gasped, crying soundlessly, the way she had as a toddler when she fell and hurt herself.

"And we knew she was dead!" wailed Krystal.

"Did you see anyone nearby at all?" I asked.

"Only Tiffany Winters strolling her cute little baby," gasped Krystal. "We didn't really see the person take off out the back door and through the woods but we knew someone was there." She opened her eyes wide. "Oh! Whoever they were, they must have heard us too! That's why they took off so fast! And they must have heard me call your name, Tabby."

I didn't want to think about the implications of that. I saw Didi come striding up the drive.

"Hey, what's wrong?" she asked, a look of concern on her face. "I was in the garden and I heard someone crying over here."

I explained the whole thing to Didi and as I did so, I held a girl in each arm and they sobbed onto my shoulders. Didi and I looked at each other with alarm.

"We have to call the police," she said. We shepherded the girls into the house and got them settled in the living room. Then I went into the kitchen and dialed emergency while Didi tried to calm the girls.

It took LeCaptain six rings to get to the telephone.

"Good evening," said a familiar morose voice. "New Belgium Police Department. Sgt. Francis LeCaptain speaking. How can I help you?"

"You can help me by going over to Valerie Cooper's house right away," I said.

"And just who are you?" said my nemesis, the cheese head's Poirot.

"This is Rhiannon Nolan," I said. I heard a deep sigh on the other end of the telephone.

"And just what can I do for you this time, Mrs. Nolan?"

"I told you. You can go over to Valerie Cooper's house and find her dead body at the bottom of the basement stairs."

There was a shocked silence.

"Are you telling me that Valerie Cooper is dead at the bottom of her basement stairs?" he asked.

"That is exactly what I'm telling you," I said.

"Do you know this to be a fact?"

"My daughter Tabby and her friend Krystal were just there to return a dessert pan and they found her," I said.

LeCaptain sighed. I traced the pattern of the lace tablecloth on my kitchen table with my index finger for what seemed like minutes. *He'll find a way to make this look like it's all my fault,* I thought.

"And when they went into her house, they heard the back door slam and the sound of a motor being gunned on the other side of the back yard woods," I said into the silence.

"Stop right there, Mrs. Nolan! I'll call you if I have any further need of your assistance." And abruptly, he hung up.

Typical, I thought, *just typical*. I trotted out to the living room.

"Girls, you stay here," I said to Tabby and Krystal. "Didi and I are going to Valerie's to make sure Sgt. LeCaptain writes everything down in his notebook."

"We are?" asked Didi.

I grabbed my purse and car keys and ran out the door, down the steps, and to the garage. I yanked up the garage door, jumped into the car, and started the engine. When I turned around to back the car out of the garage, I saw three faces in the back seat.

"So what am I, the chauffeur?" I asked. "You two, out!" I pointed at Tabby and Krystal.

"No way, Mom!" insisted Tabby. "We're going."

"You'll just get more upset," I said.

"We can't get any more upset than we already are!" said Krystal around her tongue stud. Two heads of glued up orange and purple spiked hair rattled at me imperiously. Didi opened her wide violet eyes, raised her eyebrows, and shrugged her shoulders.

"Looks like they're going with us," she said.

"Drive, Mom!" ordered Tabby.

I threw the car into reverse, stomped on the accelerator, and we were off.

We made it to Valerie's house within minutes, well ahead of LeCaptain.

"Do you see any yellow police tape?" I asked Didi as we bombed into Valerie's driveway.

"None," she said.

"Good, because I'm going in," I pronounced. I jumped out of the car, bounded up Valerie's steps, and strode into the house with Krystal, Didi, and Tabby close on my heels.

"Stay here in the living room and don't touch anything!" I ordered. I made a quick check of each room. It was just as Krystal and Tabby had said.

The record player was stuck on *Blue Velvet*. A plate of crackers and cheese was placed on the coffee table. There was a fresh plate of shrimp cocktail set out in the kitchen, and all was just as we left it a few nights ago after our dance party with Miss Cooper. The only thing amiss in the house, as far as I could see, was that the door to the basement stairs was ajar. I peered around the door and down the basement steps.

Oh, dear. There was Miss Cooper at the bottom of the stairs, her neck at an impossible angle. She looked small and very still. She was dressed in her blue prom gown and her spike heels. I drew back, sickened at the sight, and bumped into the three of them. I jumped.

"I told you not to follow me!" I screeched. We heard the sound of an ambulance.

"Oh-oh," said Didi.

We all jogged into the living room and sat down in sedate poses, as if we had been sitting there for hours having a friendly chat.

In trooped Sgt. LeCaptain, the coroner, James DeBrall, and Doctor Winston Devlin. DeBrall looked like a ghost himself. He was one of those tall, lanky, gray looking men of indeterminate late middle age. He had a spectral hollow beneath his eyes and a permanent look of displeasure with the world and everyone in it. He hated to be argued with.

Doctor Winston was a tall, handsome man with thick wavy hair and big brown sad eyes which looked out at the world from behind thick old fashioned tortoise shell lenses.

"What are you doing here, Mrs. Nolan?" boomed Sgt. LeCaptain.

"Waiting for you," I said calmly.

"I thought I specifically told you not to come here," he said. I frowned and looked confused. Then I raised my eyebrows and put on my innocent face, the one I had practiced for twelve years of Catholic school.

"I thought you said I should meet you here," was my reply. He narrowed his eyes at me.

"I hope you didn't touch anything," he said.

I held up my hands, palms out.

"Not us! We know better!" I said.

The coroner and Dr. Winston gave us a look which clearly said that they were important men and we were wasting their precious time. They brushed past LeCaptain and went to examine Valerie's body. LeCaptain gave me a nasty look and followed the other two men through the kitchen. We heard them clump down the basement stairs.

After a few minutes, they all clumped back up. Then there was the usual report writing. Valerie had no next of kin, so LeCaptain called an ambulance to take away the body, presumably to the Johanssen funeral home. They were the only game in town and did a bangup wake. Their cousins at Johanssen Florists did the flowers.

While waiting for the ambulance, the coroner, James DeBrall, sat at the kitchen table scribbling busily. LeCaptain paced the floor looking officious. Doctor Winston motioned to us to follow him outside into the inky darkness of the balmy September night. It was now nearing eleven o'clock.

"What happened?" he asked. Tabby and Krystal went through the whole story again, and when they finished, Dr. Winston pursed his lips and squinted.

"She definitely died from a fall down the stairs," he said.

"Was she pushed?" I asked.

"Might have been, especially considering that she obviously expected company and the girls heard the back door slam," said Dr. Winston slowly. "Although I seriously doubt if it really was Skip Winters she was planning to entertain. But the coroner is writing it up as an accident, and without any evidence, you're going to have a hard time proving otherwise."

"You can't be serious!" I said.

"I'm dead on serious. Those high heels Valerie was wearing might have caused her fall, and those old fashioned steps are a danger," said Dr. Winston. "There isn't even a railing, for Pete's sake! Poor Valerie. Why was she wearing those stupid shoes at her age?"

"She wanted her legs to look good for Skip. Any woman could tell you that," I said.

"Skip! You don't really believe all those stories about Skip Winters, do you?" he asked.

"I know high heels are murder, but I don't think they were the culprit," I said evenly. "I think there was someone there who pushed Valerie down the stairs and ran when he heard the girls come in the door. If it wasn't Skip, it was someone else."

"Good luck trying to convince them," said Dr. Winston and inclined his head in the direction of DeBrall and LeCaptain.

LeCaptain lumbered out the door, heaved his bulk down the steps, and wheeled over to us on his little tiny feet in their little tiny polished black shoes.

"Just a minute, girls!" he said. "Before you go, I want to take a statement from you."

25

I rolled my eyes at Didi.

"These poor girls have put in a full day at school and are exhausted with all this upset," I said. "Can't it wait until tomorrow?"

"Just doing my job, Mrs. Nolan," said LeCaptain with an edge to his tone.

"That's probably what the Grand Inquisitor said when he had thousands of people tortured and murdered," I offered. He ignored me, pointed at the girls, and crooked his index finger.

Tabby curled her lip at him. That's my girl.

Nevertheless, she and Krystal trailed up the porch steps and back into the house after LeCaptain and gave their statement. When they all reappeared, LeCaptain asked them to go and sit in the Ford while he talked to Didi and me.

"Is it possible that Tabitha and Krystal would have pushed Miss Cooper down the stairs for a thrill?" he asked.

"Are you nuts?" I yelled at him. "Tabby and Krystal would never do something so insane! What kind of kids do you think they are? They loved Valerie Cooper! They were her friends!"

How had it come to this? Why did I ever have to grow up and leave my parents' home? I had inhabited a Camelot, a kingdom ruled by a good and kind king and queen. And I had voluntarily left it to live in the crazy world outside. I had willingly moved to this godforsaken wilderness of weirdos. I must be nuts!

"Kids do weird things sometimes," said LeCaptain. "Best friends can convince each other to do something neither one would do alone. And I find it hard to believe this back door slamming story. Are you sure Tabby isn't doing drugs?"

Didi grabbed my hand as if to restrain me. She must have known that I was about to punch the cheese head version of Monsieur Poirot in the nose.

I decided not to do that. Instead, I got close enough to him to make him uneasy and said, "Sergeant, you can believe that there wasn't a man in that house who pushed Valerie down the stairs. You can refuse to get fingerprints off that back door like you should be doing. You can believe Val just tripped in her high heels on those steep steps. Or you can believe that Tabby and Krystal are suspects, but let me tell you, those girls would never hurt anyone. And by the way, I insisted Tabby take a drug test when our dear principal accused her of taking drugs just a few weeks ago and it came back negative. Nada! So I guess you better look elsewhere if you're going to accuse someone of taking drugs."

He opened his mouth to say something. I stuck my index finger in his face and said, "Listen up! There is good and there is evil in this world and they are both palpable phenomena. In my little microcosm of the world, I fight on the side of good, and I want you to know that I won't rest until I see that justice is done. Evil should not go unpunished, and if by some strange twist of fate it does, it won't go unpunished in the next world. So put that in your pipe and smoke it, babe!"

"Are you finished, Mrs. Nolan?" asked Sgt. LeCaptain. He looked down his moustaches at me.

"Yes and no," I answered. "And by the way, your nerd pocket pen guard failed to prevent the ink from leaking all over your shirt."

LeCaptain looked down at his shirt and I turned to Didi with a smile.

"Let's go. That man is just a fourth rate Poirot imitation," I whispered as we walked back to the Ford.

"He reminds me of Colonel Klink," said Didi in her low voice and giggled.

"And I think our particular Colonel Klink has klunked," I said. "Valerie Cooper was murdered. Our poor, sweet innocent spinster was murdered and I can't imagine why. And as horrible as that is, even worse for me is the fact that the murderer heard and possibly saw Krystal and Tabby at the scene of the murder, which could endanger both of their lives. And LeCaptain refuses to believe me."

"What are you going to do about it?" asked Didi.

"The first thing to do is find out why Valerie Cooper was murdered, and if I can find out why, perhaps I can find out by whom and bring them to justice," I said.

"Oh-oh, here we go again," said Didi. "Rhi, you are . . ."

"Living proof that middle age can be sexy? I know but I don't like to brag."

We got into the Ford and I started the engine.

"Girls," I said over my shoulder, "LeCaptain thinks you might be on drugs and delusional. You might even have pushed Miss Cooper down the stairs for a thrill."

Howls of protest emanated form the back seat. Tabby hooted with derision.

"He's the one operating on one cylinder," she said. "Maybe he should check the cheerleaders' backpacks if he wants to find some alcohol and drugs."

I looked in the rearview mirror and saw Tabby and Krystal exchange significant looks. I decided to ignore that remark. Selective listening is one of the great arts of parenthood.

"How can you be sure that it was Skip whom Valerie was expecting?" I asked.

Tabby clucked her tongue at me.

"Because, Mom! Today in school, Miss Cooper said to us again, 'Skip is coming at nine o'clock tonight.' And then she showed us the note!" said Tabby. "And she told us a little secret. She said that Skip has been meeting her for six months and writing her love letters. And the biggest evidence was the fact that she was all giggly and goofy, the way people are when they're in love. I saw the note with my own eyes."

"Yeah!" Krystal chimed in.

"And just exactly what did this note say?" I asked as I turned the Ford onto Red Oak Lane and headed for home.

"It said, 'Watch for me at nine. I'll be there come hell or high water.' And it was signed, 'With love from Skip,'" said Tabby.

"And where is that note, I wonder?" I asked. "How do you know that note she showed you wasn't written forty years ago?"

"Because it looked new!" claimed Tabby stoutly. "I would have seen if it was some oldy moldy piece of paper. What do you think I am, an idiot? It looked like it was written yesterday."

"Without that note as proof it will be pretty hard to convince LeCaptain that Val had a date with anyone, much less a murderer," I said. "Wait a minute! Didn't Valerie say that Skip had called her and told her he was coming on Friday night?"

"Yes!" Tabby exclaimed. "She said he had called her when you, Krystal, and I were there the other night!"

"Let's see if we can get Le Captain to look at the telephone log from that night and also from the last few months. If Skip has been calling her, we can find out. I'm sure the phone company can tell us who called her."

Early Saturday morning found the four of us at the police station arguing with Sgt. LeCaptain.

"Examining telephone company records is completely unnecessary. And besides, that is an invasion of privacy," said Sgt. LeCaptain firmly. "And I refuse to take that request seriously."

"Invasion of privacy?" I queried. "I don't think Valerie will mind, since she's dead! She might like us to find her murderer!"

"Mrs. Nolan," explained Sgt. LeCaptain patiently, "You like to see trouble where there is none. Everyone in town knows that you are an excitable type with a volcanic temper."

"They do? I am?" I asked. He ignored me and blathered on.

"I've explained to you that Miss Cooper was a lonely old spinster who lived in dreams. Those dreams consisted wholly of Skip Winters, a man who has been safely wed to his college sweetheart for forty years! Valerie was a wonderful teacher and a sweet person, but she happened to be a little nuts on the subject of Skip Winters, and everyone in town knows it. She even had to do a short stay in the county home because of her delusional problems. It is impossible that Skip Winters would call Valerie, write her, or come to her house to elope with her. It just didn't happen. Poor Valerie slipped on her steep basement stairs, fell, and broke her neck. End of story. That is it! There is no murder."

"But . . ." I began.

"No buts!" Le Captain interrupted. "No one would murder Valerie Cooper! She was the most universally loved person in the county! What motive could there possibly be? It's insane to even suggest that she was murdered. The coroner was adamant that death was due to the fall down the stairs and there was no sign of foul play. And like I told you, if there had been foul play, the first people I would suspect would be Tabby and Krystal, because they were at the scene of the crime and were the first ones to report the body."

He glared at the girls. They gave him the stony stare, followed by the lip curl and a cluck of the tongue.

"Get real!" said Krystal. "Like we would do anything to our favorite teacher. Geez! That is so bogus!"

LeCaptain groaned.

"And now, if you don't mind," he said, "I have better things to do than argue about a nonexistent murder! I have an appointment! Good day!"

And with that, he marched out of the police station and was off to the park, the donut shop, Diane's Diner, and all the other abodes of the lurking criminal element, because he had better things to do.

And so did I!

Chapter 5

Save the Last Dance For Me

We see the ground whereon these woes do lie,
But the true ground of all these piteous woes
We cannot without circumstance descry.

--William Shakespeare, *Romeo and Juliet,* Act V, scene iii

Dear Val,

You are a dream come true. I'll never forget your sparkling blue eyes and the way you looked that night.

Luv U Always, Skip

Early Monday morning, I revved up the Ford and went on my way to investigate crime, feeling just like Nancy Drew in her roadster. I had my yellow legal pad, my Cross pen engraved with my name, and my moxie. What else could I possibly need? All I had to do was get my mojo workin' and bring things back to a state of normalcy in this town.

Normal is important to us in New Belgium. No matter how weird things get everywhere else, the rest of the country can count on us to maintain a normal state of affairs, to go about our quiet way raising the corn, grains, meat, and dairy products; the staples of the diet. We're not ashamed to be lovers of work, mom, baseball, apple pie, and exquisite John Deere tractors humming in the fields. Our small town life isn't much different than a Norman Rockwell painting. As least, we like to think so.

And yet, human nature being what it is, there are those among us who aren't quite right. Some of us are misshapen pots thrown from a lopsided potter's wheel, rather like the pots in Omar Khayyam's *Ruba'iyat.* There are those of us who have rotten, miserable mean streaks which aren't kept in check. And when those unchecked mean streaks crop up, they must be exorcized. They must be surgically removed, cut down, and pulled out at the roots like a weed in grandma's hollyhocks.

Some weeds are just the devil to spot, much less dig out. They masquerade as real flowers, or they grow up so intertwined with the good plants as to be just about inseparable from them. But sooner or later, weeds show themselves for what they are; bad seed, and then they have to be mercilessly dispatched before they spread and endanger the whole darn garden.

Now sometimes flowers will persist in looking like weeds until all of a sudden, they develop beautiful blooms, so you have to be careful not to get too hasty about weeding. And conversely, weeds will persist in looking like they have beautiful bloom potential. It's a fine line you have to walk when you become a gardener, especially when you are a rookie like me. Things can become very confusing, what with the lulling drone of the bee and the distracting beauty of the birds and butterflies flitting about.

But sooner or later, you have to get down to the dirty, sweaty, unpleasant business of getting at the weeds. And there is always the danger of getting stung or bit. Yup, that's the way it is, and all the wishing and whining in the world won't change it, nor cancel out a word of it, as old Omar Khayyam said so long ago.

So you might as well get busy because, like my mom always told me, life is not one big tea party. Sometimes you don't want to do the things that have to be done but you do them anyway. Then you can feel good about enjoying the tea party later. And Dad would chime in that it is best to go to sleep with a clear conscience and sleep the sleep of the just.

I was never sure if he meant sleep or death but it didn't matter. I knew I couldn't argue with such logic. And that's how they got me to do the dishes and my homework and trod the straight and narrow.

I was lost in deep thought and memory and in the middle of negotiating a curve when my cell phone rang out Beethoven's Fifth. I almost swerved off the cliff road. I pulled over and punched the phone to answer mode. There was no way I was going to drive and talk on a cell phone at the same time. I could barely drive with two hands, let alone one.

"Hello?"

"Mom! I have talked to Tabby about you and I just wanted to call you to tell you that you have to let Tabby rebel."

It was my daughter Jennifer calling from Madison where she and my son Matthew both attended university.

"Tabby needs your tacit consent to rebel and establish herself as a self actualized person separate from you. She is in the middle of a life and death struggle for her own identity."

My daughter the psychologist.

"Tabby has enough identity already!" I cried. "Everyone within a thirty mile radius knows who she is!"

Jen ignored me and continued.

"On the positive side, you're doing a really good job of not smothering Matt and I. Letting your young adult offspring pursue their own goals with independence takes great parental restraint."

"That's right, throw in a little praise with the criticism to promote a cooperative attitude. My daughter the professor. Next you'll be giving me bananas when I do something you like."

"Don't spoil it for yourself with your immature attempts at humor, mother!"

"Sorry, Dr. Nolan. I've overstepped my boundaries," I said.

"And I want to tell you about your son. Matt is a chick magnet. The girls keep calling him. It's bugging me."

"How does Kelly feel about that?" I asked. Kelly was Matt's longtime girlfriend.

"She's understandably exasperated and so am I. Gregory can't get through to me."

"Who is Gregory?" I asked.

"He's a professor I might be interested in dating," said Jen. She sounded breezy. When she took that tone of voice, something wasn't quite right.

"A full professor? How old?" I asked with dread. I looked out over the cliff to the rolling gray green waves of Lake Michigan while Jen decided how much she should tell me.

"He is a thirty year old archeologist if you must know."

"Thirty! You are eighteen years old! He's trouble! Stay away from him. He is way too old for you. I don't like him!"

"You haven't even met him!" Jen protested.

"I don't need to meet him. I already know I don't like him. He's a perverted cradle robber. Plus, he has dug his way around the world. How do you know where his spade has been?"

"Mother! You are disgusting!"

"No, I'm not disgusting. I'm just a mom who worries about things like having my daughters seduced by disease ridden date rapists hiding chain saws and axes in the trunks of their Volvos. I'm a mom. In every corner lurks a weirdo is my watchword."

"Mother! You are such a prude!" said Jen.

"Life is tough and you are not dating this dusty professor with the dirt encrusted fingernails! That's an order! He needs to get a real job and stop flirting with teenagers. Now put Matthew on the line!"

Jennifer slammed the phone down and went to roust out Matthew. The phone clunked to the floor and bounced while she screamed at him to answer the phone. After a prolonged pause, a deep male voice came rumbling down the line.

"Yo, Mama!"

"Don't you yo mama me! Keep your sister away from that cradle robber and stop being a chick magnet. And if you and Jen don't tow the line in school, it's dorm city and a nanny for both of you. Understand?"

Tough, aren't I?

"Yup."

"Are you taking care of the house and car and studying?"

"Yup."

"O.K., Mr. Charm. Those girls must like the strong silent type. You better behave and you better keep those grades up. You know that if you slip up, no football team for you."

I heard a crash of glassware and a scream from Jen.

"Yup, gotta go, Mom. Jen just broke the dishwasher again. Love ya. Bye!" Click.

I had visions of Jen walking barefoot and bloody over thousands of tiny shards of glass. Stop it, I told myself. They are fine. They are almost adults. They are mature, capable, well adjusted, and responsible. Sometimes fantasy, coupled with denial, is the only pathway to peace.

I decided to drive over to the high school and take Tabby out for lunch, but when I got to the office, a girl with a nametag which said Brooklyn told me that would be impossible.

"But I just want to take my daughter to lunch!" I cried.

"Sorry, Mrs. Nolan. Security precautions. Nobody goes in by order of the principal. You might be a kidnapper, or a criminal, or a terrorist."

"But you know me!" I protested. "I'm Tabby's mother."

"We can't play favorites," said Brooklyn firmly. "That might lead us into racial profiling, and we can't do that." Where had she learned to talk newspeak? She looked like she graduated Brownie Girl Scouts ten minutes ago.

"It's policy. Can't help it. We don't know where Tabby is and we're not going to get her for you, and you aren't allowed in."

"I know she is in the library," I said firmly. "What is this, a war zone? The DMZ? A brainwash camp? Communist Russia? Nazi Germany? I never heard of such idiocy. I can't go into the high school to get my own daughter in a town this small where everyone knows me?"

Brooklyn looked up at me with the dull acceptance of a bovine animal.

"No, Mr. Weaver's orders," she repeated.

"Oh, tell him to stick it!" I said. "Forget it! I'll tell him myself."

I marched past her and headed for the principal's office. I met Principal Weaver on his way out of the office. Mr. Weaver looked like a corporate CEO. He wore expensive suits which fitted him well. He worked out. He was old enough to look respectable and young enough to look like a movie star. He gelled his hair and vacationed in St. Thomas. His wife and kids were models of all American yuppie living who hung out on soccer and football fields. His kids lived to crush the opposition in every sport they played. He had several framed degrees hanging on his wall. He knew the ins and outs of several graduate schools, and commanded a salary I would be proud to call mine. I thought he stunk.

"Hey!" I said. "Weaver, just a minute!" I told him what I thought of his little no parent rule.

"Mrs. Nolan," he said smoothly, "please come into my office and sit down and let me explain to you how we run our school." *Those teeth must be capped,* I thought. *Such perfection is inhuman.* I followed him into his office.

"Please do," I said, and stayed standing. I folded my arms across my torso and waited for the great one to explain modern education to me. First he gave me an elaborate worst case scenario of what would happen if strict security precautions were not followed. The result would be chaos, anarchy, and the end of civilization as we know it. Then he launched into a well rehearsed public relations statement on what he was doing to keep New Belgium High School in the good graces of modern government and those who hand out the funds.

"Here at New Belgium High School, we have a certain philosophy of education. It includes state of the art technology, a computer for every student, multiculturalism, and zero tolerance for violence of any kind. We want to keep religion out of our schools as befits a strict division of church and state, so we do not allow religious materials in school. We encourage recognition of sexual preference and ethnic diversity."

I wondered if Weaver's sickening flow of the party line was over or if I should jump in. I decided to jump in.

"That's great. Great, fine and wonderful, but do the kids know who President Lincoln was? Do they know that the Liberty Bell is cracked? Can they write a term paper without spell check and solve a math problem without a calculator? Can they spell photosynthesis? Have they ever heard of Emerson, Shelley, Keats, Thoreau, Tennyson, Milton, Chaucer, or even Shakespeare? Can they read anything more difficult than Hemingway? Do they know who Jefferson, Adams, and Franklin were, or do they think maybe they were the dudes who invented the first video game?"

"They receive an excellent education, Mrs. Nolan," the great one said. "Rest assured that in this school system, we test the children with standardized and diagnostic tests every year, and give them extra testing in fourth, eighth, and twelfth grades. We also do a writing assessment every year."

"But do you ever actually teach them anything?"

Mr. Weaver sighed. I was not cooperating.

"Could we talk about Valerie Cooper's death?" I asked him, changing tack. He looked wary.

"My daughter Tabby and her friend Krystal are convinced that you didn't like Valerie and wanted her to retire," I said. "In fact, you tried to force her to retire." Weaver put on a poker face so I pressed on. "Kind of hard to force someone to retire when they have such a good union, isn't it?" I asked, trying to provoke some ire from this smooth Wall Street prototype.

"At no time did I try to force Valerie to retire," he said.

I'd like to yank that hair of his so far out of place it wouldn't settle down for a week, I thought. *Wonder what would happen if someone stole all the clothes in his closet and replaced them with nerd clothes. Bet he wouldn't sound so good then.*

"According to my sources, you tried to force Valerie Cooper to retire."

I watched him clench his jaws. A vein in his temple throbbed. The great one was definitely rattled.

"And were you one of the people who signed Valerie Cooper into the loony bin?" I asked him. I had heard through the grapevine that not too long ago, Val had an enforced rest in the county home for a few days. Even LeCaptain knew about Valerie and her so called delusions. Suddenly, Mr. Weaver grew distinctly aloof. My intuition told me that indeed, he had signed Val into the bin.

"Maybe she wasn't young enough or technologically advanced enough for the new order, hey?" I asked. "Do you think failure to learn how to use a computer constitutes incompetency? Perhaps even lunacy?"

Mr. Weaver's mouth hardened into a grim line.

"I'm afraid I don't understand your point," said Mr. Weaver. I wasn't surprised, since we seemed to speak different languages. "Miss Cooper was a fine, upstanding member of this community and a great teacher. Her death has greatly affected all of us. I'm sure it was a very unfortunate accident, but we all must cope with things as they are. And now if you will excuse me, I must rush off to a meeting," he said.

A likely story. This guy was a big, fat phony. He gave me a vicious look, turned on his heel, consulted his pocket watch, and hurried off like the white rabbit. This one was more adept at dodging the truth than a presidential candidate.

Chapter 6

Why Don't You Tell Him

The blood-dimmed tide is loosed, and everywhere
The ceremony of innocence is drowned.

--The Second Coming, William Butler Yeats

Dear Val,

Whenever I look in your eyes, I know you are the only one alive who can melt this heart of mine.

Love U, Skip

I decided not to get Tabby into trouble and to have lunch with Didi instead. She and I were just about to dig in to our raspberry salads at Eddie's Fifties Diner when the busboy, Buddy, walked by our table. Everyone in town knew Buddy. He was one of our more endearing characters. He wore his usual loopy, lopsided grin.

He bustled by our table as if on a mission, but then, inexplicably, he stopped, looked back at me, and said, "I know something you don't know, Miss Rhi. I seen something bad. Real bad. And it's about Miss Cooper."

I wanted to question him further but he scurried away with a terrified look on his face, as if he were sorry he had brought up the subject of Valerie Cooper.

"I think we'll have to talk to Buddy later," said Didi.

"Sounds like a good idea. How can we get the telephone records from Valerie Cooper's last six months of phone service without going through LeCaptain?" I asked.

"Leave it to me," said Didi. "I have my ways."

"How are you going to do it?" I insisted.

"I know someone who knows someone who knows someone," she said.

"Oh, yeah, one of those methods. You're good at that."

"This salad is to die for," said Didi with relish.

"Yeah, it's great, but it would be even better with chocolate sauce," I said.

After lunch, Didi and I walked around the back of the building to get to our car. Buddy was taking his break just outside the kitchen door.

Didi paused and asked, "Buddy, do you have something you want to tell us?"

"What did you see, Buddy? Did you see something bad?" I prodded. Buddy looked around to see if anyone were near. There was no one in the parking lot but the three of us.

"I seen him in the window!" he cried. "He done something bad! Buddy don't tell no one. No sir! Won't tell no one. Don't cut out my tongue! Don't hurt Buddy. No! Save me, Miss Rhi! Please don't hurt Buddy! I don't see nothing."

To our astonishment, Buddy threw himself into Didi's arms and started to cry. It was a known fact that Beau Dillon, otherwise known as Buddy, liked to peek in windows. Had he seen the murderer? Buddy started to sob and blubber.

"I don't do nothing wrong!" he insisted. "Don't let them hurt Buddy! I don't know nothing!"

I really hate it when people cry. I patted him on the back.

"O.K., Buddy. No one will hurt you. You don't have to tell anyone anything, O.K.?" Buddy continued to cry.

"Don't make Buddy tell!" he managed to gasp out between sobs. I tried to reassure him that no one would make him tell anything. I decided I better take Buddy home before he ruined Didi's angora sweater forever.

"Would you like some ice cream, Buddy?" I asked him gently.

He stopped sobbing immediately and started to sniffle.

An hour later, Buddy was tucking happily into his third bowl of ice cream with chocolate sauce and I was on the telephone with one of my big brothers.

"Ian, please!" I pleaded. "You have to take him and keep him at your house for a month. He's terrified that he will be the next one murdered. He must have seen something and the murderer threatened him. He definitely knows something."

"Threatened him with what?" asked Ian doubtfully.

"Threatened him with getting his tongue cut out, apparently," I said.

"My Lord!" said Ian. "That's inhuman."

"Not really," I said. "It isn't much worse than what you, Sean, Patrick, Ryan, and Michael used to threaten me with."

"We were just kids. That was different," said Ian.

"Yeah, right. In any case, you still owe me for all those English papers I wrote for you in high school. You can thank me for that nice career you have as an English professor, hon. So get your butt up here and get this guy. He's driving me nuts and eating up all Tabby's ice cream. He is plainly terrified and I need to get him out of town. I don't want any more murders. I tried to bribe him with each bowl of ice cream to tell me exactly what terrible thing he saw or thinks he saw but he won't crack."

"It's probably just a ploy to get attention and ice cream from you. You always were gullible," said Ian. "And I'm busy. Why don't you get Ryan to take Buddy in?"

"Our brother the firstborn king, the god of the operating room, the wielder of the great scalpel? You must be kidding me. He isn't unselfish enough."

"Or dumb enough! The things we do for you!" insisted Ian. "Jan won't take him in. She has too much to do now. If I tell her we're taking in Buddy for a few weeks or months until this murder is solved, she'll divorce me."

I wanted to say that would be no great loss but thankfully, I managed to hold my tongue.

"Jan has nothing to do but try out for soccer grandmother of the year and raise money for charity. This will give her a chance to do some real charity up close and personal. Get up here!" I ordered and hung up.

I counted on my ability to boss Ian around and make him do what I wanted him to do ever since our idyllic childhood spent playing cowboys and Indians in Vilas Park. Since I was the lucky one who always got to be the one lone Indian pitted against all my brothers who got to be the cowboys, I quickly developed a deep sympathy for Native Americans.

I read all the Indian biographies I could get my hands on at the library and guilted Ian into representing my interests at the cowboy council of the great white brothers by telling him the story of the Trail of Tears and making him cry. This led to a special symbiosis between Ian and myself. The other brothers weren't nearly as malleable, but Ian always had a soft spot for me. I fed his gerbils and rabbits and did his term papers for him and he pounded on anyone who bothered me, including the other brothers. It was a mutually beneficial arrangement.

Fortunately for me, to this day Ian was a kind soul beneath the crust. That afternoon he showed up in his silver Lexus to whisk Buddy away to safety in Madison. Buddy sat in the front seat of the Lexus hugging his cardboard suitcase and grinning from ear to ear.

"This is better than the smelly old bus!" he said in delight. "Mr. Ian will take good care of me, right?" he asked.

"Yup, he sure will. You get to eat all the ice cream you want, and his wife and kids and grandchildren will play soccer with you, too," I promised. Ian clenched his jaw and rolled his eyes. "All day," I added.

"I never had a friend to play ball with before," said Buddy wistfully. The rapture on his face was almost heartbreaking. I reached through the window and gave him a high five.

"Have fun!" I called as I waved them off. "You won't regret this Ian! Mom and Dad would be so proud of you."

Might as well drag out the big emotional warheads while I'm at it, I thought.

Ian waved and grimaced at me in the rearview mirror. Then he flipped me the bird. I smiled. Such brotherly love is truly uncommon in today's dog eat dog world.

That evening, Didi and I went to Valerie's funeral service together. It was a sad, dismal affair punctuated with the weeping of the local women and of Val's female students. Just about the whole town turned out to stand together in church and then in the soft rain at the cemetery to bury their beloved spinster. She may have been a bit odd, but the townspeople loved her and showed it with an outpouring of emotion.

The two chief mourners were Valerie's cousins, Julia and Pamela, from Jubilee. *Retro must run in the genes of this family,* I thought. *Where do these people come from?*

Julia was dressed in a 1950's style shirtwaist dress, old fashioned raincoat, and spike heels. She sported cat's eye glasses with rhinestones, a charm bracelet, and a French twist hairdo. Pamela had progressed as far as the mod sixties and decided to stop there. She wore white lipstick, a geometric haircut, knee high velvet boots, a gold velour miniskirt and zip-up gold velour fitted jacket over a white knit turtleneck, and hoop earrings. She wore lots of black eyeliner and false eyelashes. If it weren't for the wrinkles, she might have stepped out of a 1966 copy of *Vogue* magazine.

As Julie and Pamela sniffled and dabbed their noses with lacy handkerchiefs, Eunice leaned close to me and whispered in my ear, "Skip is right over there behind that big oak tree."

I looked quickly but failed to get the infamous Skip in my sights. He had faded into the mist and the rain and disappeared. His wife Melanie was notably absent from the gathering.

On the other side of the oak tree, I saw "that rotten Scooter O'Reilly" as Valerie had called him, leaning against the tree smoking a cigarette. Babs was talking to Scooter out of the side of her mouth in the way some women do when they don't want anyone to know that they are fighting with their husband. He looked mulish and insolent, the way some men do when they are trying mightily to make their wife even angrier than she already is.

My guess was that Babs wanted Scooter to come up and join the prayer group and Scooter wanted nothing to do with it. Babs glared at him, set her jaw, and marched up to the prayer group.

She shouldered her way into the center of the group and started to pray loudly, with a voice which carried easily over the soft murmurs of the others. Babs must have learned voice projection and studied it well, because her voice would have placed first in any cow calling contest.

In my opinion, she didn't give a fig about Valerie Cooper, but the day called for grief and piety and Babs gave her all. We said prayers for Valerie and then disbursed into the soggy dusk. Tabby and Krystal went to the drive-in with some other students from Valerie's Home Ec class. Didi and I went out for a sandwich.

We drove silently through the soft rain to Diane's Diner. I had bought a pair of huge velvet dice and hung them from the Ford's rearview mirror in honor of Valerie. They swung softly to some pretend love song from the fifties. Didi and I ate a sad, soggy sandwich and went home.

Later, just before sunset, the skies cleared and a brilliant rainbow burst through the clouds. Didi and I enjoyed a quiet hour on the porch and by mutual consent, did not talk of Valerie. We sipped vanilla latte and read from a book on raising teenagers which my middle child, Jennifer, had sent me from Madison.

"'The emotionally immature mother will attempt to control her adolescent daughter,'" I read. "'Failing that, she will try to compete with her in her own arenas.' I hope I don't do that!" I said.

"Very bad," commented Didi. "I'm so glad that Jen is a psychology major. That way, we can learn all about raising children."

"You know," I said, "when my Dad was getting his advanced degree in counseling, we had to listen to this stuff every night at the dinner table. I thought my mother would go insane before Dad got that degree."

"Yeah, and isn't it nice that Jen takes after her grandfather?" asked Didi. "I seem to remember your mother sighing a lot with relief the day we all went to your Dad's graduation."

Jen had told me that this book would help me do a better job of parenting Tabby. I had my doubts. Jen had also sent me two tapes to listen to in the car. I was beginning to think that Jen took her future job of child psychologist a bit too seriously. I resumed reading.

"'The controlling mother will monopolize her daughter's time or over schedule her time,'" I read. "'She will push her daughter to join every club and extra curricular activity, and will expect her to excel academically, athletically, and socially.'"

"Sounds like too much work to me," said Didi.

"Whew! I'm sure that's not me," I said. I continued to read aloud.

"'Adversely, the permissive mother allows too much freedom, while the neglectful mother washes her hands of any responsibility.'"

"Didi, do you think I'm too permissive? Too controlling? Am I too hard on Tabby? Or not hard enough? No matter what I do I'm doing it all wrong!"

"Welcome to motherhood," said Didi laconically.

"There is no way a mother can be right!" I protested. "Once a year, at Mother's Day brunch, we can feel good about ourselves. The rest of the year, we are the ones who make our kids a case for the couch. It's all our fault!"

"Could have told you," drawled Didi. "Didn't I tell you that years ago?"

"Listen to this!" I said. "It says, 'As you face a declining sexuality and aging, your daughter feels the start of her most intensely sexual years.'"

"Thanks, we needed that," said Didi.

"There's more," I said. "It says here, 'You must face your own mid-life menopausal demons at the same time that your daughter bears the weight of her burgeoning sexuality. She will take her cues from you. Are you secure about your body, about your sexual self?'"

"Oh-oh," said Didi. "Could be trouble." She grabbed the book and read, "'At school, she is faced with issues of sexual disease, violence, date rape, teen pregnancy, AIDS, alcohol, and drug use. Problems are rampant in the teen world and these are issues she must confront and deal with.'"

"Thanks," I said. "If I wasn't sleepless before, I sure will be now."

"Wait, there's more," said Didi. "'Adolescent girls are particularly vulnerable to a vicious form of social pecking order; ostracism, humiliation, the controlling behaviors of a very few girls at the top of the socially elite scale in every high school. Who can say who lives and who dies on the popularity parade? Cruel taunts, emotional or even physical pain are not unusual.'"

"Well, I know who that is at New Belgium High School. I'll bet it's that Bailey Wilson," I said. "She looks like a social pecker. You just wait! Next time I see her, I'm going to pop her one right between the eyes!"

Just at that moment, Tabby and Krystal walked up the drive and onto the porch. I ran to Tabby and threw my arms around her.

"Tabby!" I said. "I'm here for you honey! Don't worry! We'll get you through this!"

"Mom!" said Tabby, struggling out of my grasp. "You're so embarrassing! How did you know I got in-school suspension?"

"What?" I asked. "What did you do now? Throw spitballs at the math teacher?"

"I painted political slogans on my punk rock shirt which the principal found inappropriate. Then they found the cell phone I'm not supposed to have in school. I swore at some of the football players because they were throwing erasers at my hair. And then I called the football coach a chauvinist pig, and now I have to sit in a little room all by myself for three days thinking about choices, or some such drivel."

Didi laughed.

"Not funny!" I glowered at her. To Tabby I said, "Why must you do these things? Why?"

"Couldn't help it!" said Tabby. "He's so useless! Going over to Krystal's to do homework and make vegan pizza and plot the downfall of our patriarchal society. Later."

She and Krystal gave me the peace sign and trailed off while Didi giggled and I sighed. Some days, it just doesn't pay to be a mother.

I felt a headache coming on. I needed a distraction.

"Didi, are you ready to do a little investigating?" I asked.

"Sure thing. Where are we going?"

"I think a visit to old Emily Kutchen is in order. It seems as though Valerie's best friend should be a good place to start this investigation," I said.

"You'll have to go alone then," said Didi. "I'm not walking in that house."

"Why ever not?" I asked. "She isn't the wicked witch of the west. She is just a harmless old woman."

"Uh-huh, that's what you think," said Didi. "I have it on good authority that she drinks sloe gin fizz all day and doesn't bathe but once a week. I'll gag if I go anywhere near that house."

I laughed. "Ridiculous!"

"I'm telling you she smells, and that house smells like dead cats."

"Oh, all right, Miss Sensitive, I'll go alone then," I said. Didi went home to feed Kelly, her Irish setter, and I hopped in the Ford. I popped in the tape Jen had sent me and headed for Miss Emily's house.

The tape delivered my parenting instructions in a slow patient voice, as if the psychologist were speaking to a person who was both a foreigner and an idiot.

"Your daughter is in the middle of a crucial life stage. She is about to break away from her childish self and form new social bonds. She will soon break free of her chrysalis and try her fragile wings for the first time. Remember, her developmental task is to break the bonds of your control."

Oh, goody. This was even better than reality television.

"Your daughter may exhibit rude, irritable, contradictory behavior. She may act like a little girl who wants to be mothered one minute and the next, seem to be a highly sophisticated independent young woman." Tell me about it. "At times, nothing you do seems appropriate or acceptable to her."

Yeah, like all the time. I had enough for one day. I switched from Parenting for Dummies to Motown. Ah! Now that was much better. I think that parents need frequent short breaks from parenting so they get to feel like a real person instead of a dim bulb for a change.

Ten minutes later, I knocked on Miss Emily's front door. I heard her shuffling to the door and prepared myself. Two locks and a deadbolt opened laboriously. Crikey! You'd think we lived in New York City instead of the back of beyond. The door opened and a blast of stale hot air, old lady mustiness, the smell of old, unwashed flesh, and sour liquor wafted out into the light, borne on a wave of Loretta Lynn music. Oh, dear, Didi was right, as usual.

Chapter 7

Splish Splash

That time of year thou may'st in me behold
When yellow leaves, or none, or few, do hang
Upon those boughs which shake against the cold,
Bare ruin'd choirs, where late the sweet birds sang.

--*That Time of Year*, William Shakespeare

Dear Val,

There were never two people more perfectly suited for each other than you and me.

Love U forever, Skip

"Hi, Miss Emily, I've come to see you about Valerie Cooper," I said faintly, trying not to inhale. She peered at me like a bear looking out of its cave after a long winter's sleep.

"Oh, it's you, the scarlet woman. Saw you at the funeral this evening. Come to see me about Valerie Cooper, have you?" she asked. "Well, I guess I'll have to talk to you," she said grudgingly.

That's our famous Midwest hospitality. Gee, nothing like making a body feel welcome.

"Come on in," she said in a booming voice. Must have lungs like a bellows. I followed her into the living room, reeling from the smell of stale sweat and booze.

Miss Emily Kutchen, retired grade school teacher, her wrinkled lips a crooked splash of plum pink, turned and smiled at me like the cat who ate the canary. She probably colored outside the lines in kindergarten and the present state of her lipstick testified that her aim had not improved with age.

Her big, farsighted brown eyes looked huge behind their thick trifocal lenses. She wore a voluminous flowered polyester muumuu which did not quite hide her legs lined with bulging varicose veins, legs which, from my point of view, would have been better covered in stockings. Better for the rest of the world, anyway. Her feet were encased in white, furry slippers with little kitty faces on them.

If I live to be as old as Emily, please Lord, don't ever let me buy kitty face slippers. Then I realized with a start that Miss Emily wasn't too much older than I was, except she acted like she was ninety and on a good day, I could regress to twelve with a great deal of success.

Emily sat and gestured imperiously for me to do the same. I removed a set of wicked looking knitting needles and some purple yarn from an overstuffed orange rocker. It clashed nicely with the green shag carpeting and the drapes. They were a perfect match to the burnt sienna in my much prized second grade box of crayons. Between the dizzying wafts of booze, stale sweat drenched air, and old lady smells, not to mention the disharmonious clash of color, I felt quite sick. I visualized a giant pristine glacier and tried not to breathe.

"Stanley Keefer's mother is afraid you're going to ruin her boy, you being a loose woman and all." Emily believed in starting things on the offensive.

"I am not a loose woman!" I protested. "Besides, I'm a respectable widow the last time around. Stanley and I are just friends."

"A likely story," sniffed Miss Emily.

"We haven't even been out on one date!" I said.

"Mr. Pavalik tells us you have been married three times and that you blatantly seduced our innocent Sgt. LeCaptain!"

"Innocent?"

"Robbed him of his virginity! Do you deny it?" she said with a caw of triumph.

"Yes, I deny it! I wouldn't touch that man with a ten foot pole!" I vowed. "And how do you know he is a virgin?"

But Miss Emily was one of those old ladies who does not hear, much less acknowledge, anyone's agenda but her own. She squinted at me.

"Mr. P says the sexual tension between you and LeCaptain is just about as good as a romance saga, but I guess you've dumped him now, though. Mr. P says now that you've conquered poor Sgt. LeCaptain and robbed him of his virginity and his good name, not to mention his heart, you're after Stanley Keefer."

"What?" I screeched. Emily ignored me and continued.

"Guess you think you'll just take Stanley's life savings he earned from working his fingers to the bone at the garage. Well, I can tell you, sister, Agnes Keefer is putting all her money in trust for Stanley as an inheritance. So if you marry him and divorce him, you won't get a dime!"

There was that self satisfied smirk on her face again.

Wait until I saw Pavalik! Can you do time for beating up an old man?

"Stanley and I haven't even been out to dinner and you already have us married and divorced," I said.

Emily nodded her head in self-righteous glee.

"Plus Agnes Keefer told Stan to make you sign a prenup, and don't even think of palimony or alimony because that don't cut the mustard up here like it does down there in the big city where you come from!"

She paused for breath, folded her hands on her lap, and ground her false teeth.

"Guess I took the wind out of your sails, huh?" She smiled at me, showing her unnaturally large and white dentures.

Why did it seem that all the crusty old crows this side of the Mississippi River found their way to New Belgium, La Follette County, Wisconsin, population three hundred sixty three, where they congregated in colonies? What phenomenon of nature drove them north when they should be flocking south to Miami where they could burn their old carcasses to splendid wrinkly perfection in the equatorial heat?

Lord, if I can stop myself from strangling this one, I'll say five Hail Marys and go to confession too. But what will I say when I kneel down in the confessional? Bless me Father, for I have sinned. It's been thirty-eight years since my last confession. I can't count the number of times I ate meat on Friday. Is that a mortal or a venial sin? I can't remember. I started out with kicking my five brothers in the lucky charms when they made me mad, and I quickly progressed to much worse sins. In fact, I have committed almost every sin you can think of, so just put me down for the complete list. Oh, and did I happen to mention that I am seriously planning to strangle one hateful old crone?

I guess that's tantamount to murder. After all, if you think of a sin it's as good as done. As least, that's what Sister Martha used to tell us. Boy, I committed a lot of fornication at a very young age! Just think of all those impure thoughts! Yikes! Guess I'll have to do some time in the old purgatory hole.

I sighed.

"Could we move along?" I asked. "Tell me about Valerie Cooper, please."

"What do you want to know?" asked Miss Emily in her big, booming voice. "You think someone threw her down the stairs, don't you?"

She took a big drink from the thermos by her side. I was willing to bet it contained one very strong sloe gin fizz. Yuk!

Miss Emily leaned closer and hissed, "Well, so do I!" I exhaled to repel the strong odor of sweat and gin. "I think Skip came back and murdered her for her money!"

"What money?" I asked. "She didn't have any money."

"Says you!" Emily insisted. "Her parents left her a pretty penny when they died. Yes, a pretty penny."

"If they did, I don't know where she put it all," I said. "She sure didn't spend it on the house."

"Hmpf!" said Emily. "There's some that know how to save for a rainy day. Fancy houses and law offices! And college in Madison! I guess the community college ain't good enough for you and those kids of yours!"

I decided to let that one rest and pursued a different angle.

"My secretary Eunice said that you, Ethel, and Valerie were great pals," I said. "Tell me about the three of you."

"Ethel Saunders, Valerie Cooper, and I were friends all our lives, don't you know?" She wrapped her gnarled middle and index fingers together and held them up for me to see. "Just like that, we were! Closer than close! And every summer we traveled. We went everywhere together; out west to a dude ranch, California, Florida, Paris, Belgium, London, Hawaii, Australia, Washington D.C., you name it!"

She stared at me with unfocused eyes.

"What happened?" I prompted.

"Those two had a fight over the computers. Valerie wouldn't learn the computer program at school and Ethel had her put away for a stay in the nut house."

"That's crazy!" I said. "You can't put someone away for refusing to operate a computer." I had heard this story but somehow I hadn't quite believed it. Now I did.

If not learning a computer program qualified one for the loony house, what would they do to me? I had been known to pick up the printer and throw it against the wall. Guess I should be in a padded cell.

"They put Val away. Principal Weaver tried to force Val to retire because she clung to the old ways and wouldn't change, but she resisted. So he signed to have her put away for a rest."

So it was true, just as Tabby and Krystal had said. Weaver didn't like Valerie and had actually helped put her in the loony bin.

"And Miss Hussey, the computer teacher, hated Val for not learning the school's computer program, so she gladly signed too," said Miss Emily.

Ever since I met him, I thought that there was something seriously wrong with Principal Weaver, and I was right.

Miss Emily continued. "But don't you see, it wasn't really about the computers. It was all about Skip Winters. Ethel believed Val was stark raving crazy over Skip and lost touch with reality, and she was right!" Miss Emily nodded her head.

"What's so special about this Skip character?" I asked.

Miss Emily sighed and shook her head.

"He used to flirt with all of us. I knew he was just flirting and that he really loved Valerie, but Ethel never got over it. She couldn't stand all that talk about Skip. She couldn't bear knowing that Valerie waited for Skip, dreamed about Skip, lived and breathed for Skip.

And here Skip was married to that bombshell Melanie. And running around on her too, if what we heard was true!"

She clucked her tongue and took another long pull on the thermos.

"It all went sour and somehow, we weren't friends anymore." Her eyes grew large with unshed tears. "And we ended up lonely and all of us lost without each other. The world just passed us by," she added, her booming voice shrinking to a whisper. She was silent for a moment.

"We shouldn't have let Skip come between us," she added. "Life was so much fun before the fight."

"You could have stayed friends with Valerie," I said, "even if Ethel didn't."

"No," she said, her eyes focused on the past. "It was all ruined. It wouldn't have been the same. I had my sisters and Ethel had her other teacher friends at the high school and Valerie had, well, nobody I guess." A tear slipped from the corner of her eye.

"Poor Valerie," she whispered. I waited for a moment and was just about to ask about Skip when she surprised me by snapping to attention.

"The money!" she bellowed like an army sergeant.

"What money?" I asked, startled.

"Valerie's money, you dummy! You have to look for it. I'll bet you my right arm Skip took the money and threw Val down the stairs!"

"Are you telling me that Val might have had a small fortune buried in the basement in a pirate's chest?" I asked.

"I'm telling you I don't know where it was! Maybe under the mattress. Maybe in the bank. Maybe stuck in the fireplace, but mark my words." She pointed a gnarly finger at my face. "Skip didn't come back after all those years to get Val for a love-in! He came to get her money! He's probably down at the casino right now spending it all!" She slapped her knee and reached for the thermos.

Well, golly gee, that Skip sure was one nasty character. The portrait I drew of him in my mind was starting to look more and more like the painting of Dorian Gray. I drew a little notebook from my bag and wrote, "Find money and Skip!"

I took my leave of Miss Emily, promising to look for Skip and the ghostly chest of gold, or whatever it was. I stepped out into the evening and inhaled deeply, trying to rush some clean air and oxygen to my brain. I heard something behind me and turned.

"You're not so bad," Miss Emily said to me, giving me her huge denture smile. Then she added, "For a tramp, that is," and slammed the door in my face.

Ya gotta love this place. It's just so full of endearing characters. It's Mayberry gone berserk. Where is Aunt Bea when you need her? *These people are badly in need of Prozac,* I thought and gritted my teeth. And speaking of chemical aid, I needed some chocolate badly. I dug in the bottom of my bag and came up with a red M&M candy. Just what the doctor ordered. I popped it under my tongue and let it melt while I stood on the step and contemplated.

The cell phone rang.

"Hello?" I said.

"Hi, dear. It's Eunice. I have a message from Didi about the telephone company. It seems that Skip has been calling Valerie for months. Got it?"

"Oh, yes, I've got it," I said. "I'll see you in the office tomorrow. Thanks, Eunice."

No matter how I looked at it, I had to find Skip. Oh, goody. Where was I supposed to find this aging Tab Hunter look-alike? Better consult with Eunice. She knows everything, and what she doesn't know she can find out by bush telegraph.

Chapter 8

Leader of the Pack

I saw the green Spring
Wading the brooks
With wild jay laughter
And hoyden looks.

I saw the grey Spring
Weeping alone
Where woods are misty
And buds unblown.

Red were the lips
Whence laughter leapt;
But oh, it was Beauty
Herself that wept.

--*The Grey Spring*, Alfred Noyes

Dear Val,

I'll never forget our prom night. Just to hold you in my arms again would be ecstasy.

Love, Skip

The next day, just as I thought she would, Eunice located Skip through the Dunn sisters' bush telegraph people finder service. She called her sisters Fayne and Maida at the Cliffhanger bookstore. Maida was the location expert. She gave me the directions to Maybelle over the phone. I wrote them down and tucked them in my pocket, knowing that I would get lost a couple of times, make about three wrong turns, and end up where I should be about an hour over schedule. But hey, I never said I was perfect.

I got into the Ford and checked the rearview mirror. Oh, boy! I needed a good haircut. Usually I chopped it off and colored it myself, but I needed a treat. I decided to drop in at Katie's Kurly-Q for a hairdo before I began my sleuthing. Katie was a large fortyish lady who looked like a Sumo wrestler in drag. Almost everyone in town had their hair done by Katie, except for Didi and her country club friends. They went to Mr. K's in Shelbyville and paid an exorbitant price to be pampered while they were shorn of hair and money.

Within minutes, I settled back in Katie's swivel chair and closed my eyes.

"Give me the Rod Stewart look," I said. "Make me cool, tousled, and sexy." Katie chuckled.

"Right," she said. Perhaps I failed to detect the note of sarcasm in her voice.

Fifteen minutes later, I looked in the mirror and gasped.

"I said I wanted hair like Rod Stewart, not a plexiglass bubble! What year is this, 1962? What have you done to my hair?" I cried. "It looks like a bubblegum dispenser! I never knew you hated me! What did I ever do to you to deserve this?"

Katie wielded the hairspray can like a sword and cut off my wail with a cloud of chemical glue. I inhaled and choked.

"Jumpin Joseph on a pogo stick!" I finally managed to croak out. "I didn't say I wanted to look my age!"

Katie slammed the hairspray on the counter and crossed her arms over her ample chest.

"You're too old for that rocker stuff," she said firmly.

"I'm younger than Rod Stewart," I said in my own defense. "I'll show you who's old."

I grabbed the comb off the counter and started to tease up strands of the plexiglass bubble. Then I sprayed the strands so they stood straight up.

"There!" I said. "How much do I owe you?"

Katie ripped the plastic apron off my neck and slammed it down on the counter.

"Nothing!" she said. "And don't tell anyone you had your hair done here! I have a reputation to maintain!"

"Fine by me!" I retorted and stomped out.

I was so upset about my hair that I retreated home before going to find Skip. I needed to talk to Didi. On the way up the driveway I met Tabby and Krystal.

"Hey!" said Krystal around her tongue stud. "Cool hair! Guess what! Tabby got a threatening note! It was just sitting on the front porch. Look!"

She thrust a sheet of cutout magazine print letters under my nose.

"Tabby, you will die soon," I read. "Quit nosing around in my business. I saw you and the fat girl."

"Cool, huh?" said Krystal. "I'm the fat girl, but I'll show them. I'm going on a diet."

"Definitely not cool," I retorted. "We have to get to the bottom of this Valerie Cooper business and fast."

I was now more convinced than ever that Valerie had been murdered and the murderer had seen and heard Krystal and Tabby at Valerie's house before he made his getaway.

"Tabby, I don't want you going anywhere. Get in the house and stay there," I ordered.

"What? You are nuts if you think I'm staying under house arrest for the rest of my life!" yelled Tabby. "I have to live! I have to love! I have to create! I'm an artist!" She tossed her shock of bright purple punk rock hair. "Plus all that, we're going to meet Todd, Brandon, and Trevor at Eddie's Fifties Diner."

"Gimme gimme shock treatment!" I quoted from Joey Ramone, father of punk rock. "It's not my fault I am the mother of three teenagers! I have a duty to perform! I'm just protecting you! It's my job! You're not going out to meet boys with a maniac on the loose!" I yelled.

"Mom, you are so not cool! I refuse to be jailed in the house! I'm going wherever I want with whomever I want! And you can't stop me! And look at that ugly hair! You are so fashion challenged and geeky! Why can't you just be like all the other moms?" Tabby screamed, her purple spiked hair rattling, her black goth poet blouse waving in the breeze. "You always have to be different! Sometimes I really hate you!"

She stomped away in her four inch heeled black punk rock lace up velvet shoes. Krystal gave me a curled lip grimace and followed. My heart sunk. I didn't have enough energy to fight anymore. I hung my head and trailed slump shouldered up the stairs into the house where Didi stood in the foyer.

"I heard," she said.

"Look at this!" I said and handed Didi the death threat note. She gasped and turned pale. "We have to get this to LeCaptain as soon as possible."

I tossed the note on the coffee table, threw myself in a chair, and hid my face in my hands.

"As if that will do any good! The cheese head Poirot wouldn't know a clue if it jumped up and hit him in the eye. Tabby hates me," I sobbed. "She's a rebel and I'm an embarrassment. I'm a failure, a washed up old bag, a freak, an anachronism in a generation X world. I give up!" I said. "I can't take it anymore!"

"Oh, grow up!" said Didi. "Everybody's kids hate them. So what? The world stinks. People stink. That's life. You always were a naive idealist. Get over it!" My head came up from my hands, my eyes narrowed.

"Oh, O.K. Miss Hardball! Whatever you say, Green Beret! I guess I can't have feelings! Just wait until the next time you complain about anything, you prima donna princess!"

I stood up and ran up the stairs to the second floor bathroom. I looked wildly in the mirror. No one should have to endure a hairdo like this. I dug deep in the back of the medicine cabinet for the pain pills my son Matthew had gotten from the doctor for a broken hand three years ago. I knew there was one pill left. I had been saving it for the right moment, and that moment was now. I popped it and took a drink of water. I would soon feel ready to be the mother of three teenagers again. I turned around and there was Didi.

"You didn't just take that last pain pill, did you?" asked Didi.

Sometimes your best friend can know you too well. I looked at her defiantly. Then I picked up Tabby's extra midnight blue hair spray canister and shook it in her face. Didi's violet eyes grew wide. She turned around and beat it downstairs. I sprayed deep midnight blue all over my head of auburn plexiglass bubble hair. I thought the resulting dark blue coif matched my blue eyes rather well. Then I took the pick and teased and pulled my hair into a glory of blue spikes. Finally, I took the regular hair spray and glued it up but good.

For a finishing touch I took Tabby's black lipstick and applied it liberally. If you can't beat 'em, join 'em. I peered into the mirror. Actually, I didn't look so bad as a freaked out punk rock middle aged mom. I looked kind of like a goth Phyllis Diller. Me and Joey Ramone, baby. In the words of the father of punk rock, "I wanna be sedated," and now I am! I'm not only sedated, but I look pretty darn good in blue hair and black lipstick. Wow! I've got a whole new attitude!

I dragged out the nail polish and did my nails blood red. Then I went into my room and picked out a black muscle tee shirt, black jeans, and my black suede orthopedic shoes. Why not join the rest of America and dress in black, the power color? We look like a nation of professional mourners for hire. What are we mourning anyway, the death of sanity?

I added some silver bangle jewelry and lots of blue eyeshadow, black eyeliner, and mascara. A deep dig in the closet produced my old black leather jacket, which amazingly enough, still fit me, probably because I bought it five sizes too big thirty years ago.

I looked in the full length mirror. Now that's entertainment! I was way beyond generation X. I was runnin' with the big dogs now! I added a gold cuff earring, tucked a skull kerchief into my tee shirt, grabbed my black leather handbag, and I was ready to hit the streets of New Belgium.

But was New Belgium ready for me?

When I sauntered down the stairs, Zoro, my Siberian husky, growled at me and Didi's mouth fell open. I spoke baby talk to Zoro. He came over and sniffed at me. Satisfied that it was really me, he relaxed and flopped down on his rug.

Someone banged on the door. It was Stan.

"Come in, Stan," I called. Stan's usual uniform of tee shirt, flannel shirt, jeans, and boots was in place, but his face looked in disarray. Where was the warm grizzly bear grin?

"I just came to tell you that Mr. P and Phoebe Keith both told me you had an affair with Sgt. LeCaptain," Stan said accusingly. "How could you do a thing like that? I thought you and I, well, you and me were, you know. And how can we be you know when you and him were you know already? And what the heck did you do to yourself?"

"Stan," I began, "I don't know what you're talking about. Francis LeCaptain and I were not ever, nor are we now, well, you know. Mr. P and Phoebe Keith and all the old bags in this town don't know anything about anything. And I'm in punk rock rebellion."

Stan looked about to cry.

"Huh!" he said, and stomped out. This was sure shaping up to be one great day. I turned to Didi. She shook her head at me.

"Rhi, you're a Miss Marple in the making. You have a new law career and your own law firm to worry about. You're working out at Shapely Lady three times a week, and you have a teenager at home and two more in college. You cannot possibly have a mad, passionate affair with Stan the car repairman. How will you find the time?"

"I guess I'll just have to stop recycling," I said. "That should save a few minutes."

Didi eyed my punk rock do.

"Nice hair," she said. "What happened? Did they call you as an extra for *Night of the Living Dead*?"

"Eat it, Grandma!" I yelled at her and jogged out the door and down the steps to the Ford. Stan had just burned out of the driveway and headed for town. My guess was that he would go to the Pickle Jar, drink three beers, and then go and bury his head in a car engine for two days. I had to get the truth through his head, but that was a task which had to wait for another day. Today I was super punk rock Miss Marple.

I noted with satisfaction that Didi, in her fancy fashion clogs, had trouble keeping up with me. She should just give in and wear orthopedic shoes like Miss Marple and I do.

"Bus is leaving! Next stop, Skip's house!" I called out. Didi ran to hop aboard, and we were off in a cloud of hair spray.

Chapter 9

I'm a Tiger

"O where ha'e ye been, Lord Randall my son?
O where ha'e ye been, my handsome young man?"
"I ha'e been to the wild wood: mother, make my bed soon,
For I'm weary wi' hunting, and fain wald lie down."

--*Lord Randall*, Anonymous

Dear Val,

They have all taken everything from me. You're the only one who ever truly loved me. I was mad to leave you.

Love, Skip

Following my secretary Eunice's sister Maida's directions, we eventually wound our tortuous way to Maybelle, where we located Skip Winters' sprawling home set back from the road on four acres of cutesy country landscaping. I didn't mind the autumn harvest theme, but the ceramic dwarves combined with the shepherdess statues and the cherubs in the fountain were a bit much. Maida had warned us that Melanie spent her time doing ceramic statues.

"Just follow the dwarf trail to her house," she had said.

"Looks like art deco cheese head to me," I commented. Didi sniffed. She had excellent aesthetic sense and bad taste made her physically ill. We walked up to the door and Didi rang the doorbell.

The infamous Melanie answered the door. The first thing I thought about her was that they must have pulled the skin a little too tight on her last face lift and shoved her brains up into the attic. Even after all these years, she still exuded a strong sex appeal but her eyes seemed a little vacant, as if she couldn't or simply wouldn't focus on the present moment.

"Hi! I'm Attorney Rhiannon Nolan and this is Didi Spencer. We're trying to find Skip Winters," I said. "Any chance he might be at home?"

"I'm his wife. What you want him for?" was the desultory answer. Her eyes took us in and calculated our usefulness.

"I'm the attorney for Miss Valerie Cooper's estate," I lied smoothly. "Perhaps you've heard of her unfortunate death."

"Hasn't everyone?" she murmured and squinted at us. I got the feeling that Melanie needed glasses and refused to wear them.

"I'm looking into Valerie's background to clarify a few things in the dispersion of her assets."

I felt Didi raise an eyebrow at me. At the mention of money, Melanie grew a little friendlier. Maybe she figured Val left Skip a pot of gold for old time's sake and she should get her half.

"Skip is gone but you're welcome to come in if you want," she said, showing her beautifully capped teeth. She led us into the foyer and from there into the living room. She picked up the cigarette she had burning in the ashtray and took a drag.

"Make yourselves comfortable," she said and gestured to an overstuffed couch. We smiled and sat. The house seemed large and overflowing with females, who wandered in and out of the room on waves of cologne. Catching each wave as it ebbed and flowed, Melanie introduced us to her two daughters, Amber and Bobby. Then came her four granddaughters, Tiffany, Taffy, and the twins, Brandy and Candy. Taffy belonged to Bobby. Tiffany, Brandy, and Candy were Amber's daughters. And last but not least, there were the two toddlers, Emma and Olivia, who were Melanie's great granddaughters, age two and three respectively.

Emma pointed at me and my electric midnight blue spiked hair.

"Mommy, is she a bad stranger?" she lisped.

"Hush, now," said Tiffany.

Olivia took one look at me, screamed, and hid behind her grandma Amber's legs. I tried not to be offended. I didn't think I looked that scary, but I guess when you were a member of this sorority of ultra-feminine perfection, you expected a certain standard, even at age three.

What I saw when I looked around was four generations of people with legendary good looks and absolutely no ambition to get anywhere but the nearest beauty parlor. Melanie, her two daughters, their four daughters, and the little tykes looked ready to walk on the set of the classiest of afternoon soap operas.

Hair was dyed, curled, moussed, and gelled. Nails were manicured and polished. Fingers were jewel encrusted. The makeup was worthy of Elizabeth Arden, and the clothes could have stepped right out of the Spiegel catalog. Everything matched everything else in sight. The whole house and all the people in it were color coded and blended in decorator colors. The entire family was one gene pool of all American model good looks. And they were all depressingly skinny, even Melanie the matriarch.

All this for a family play date in the back yard? I looked down at myself. I felt quite sure that not one of these women worked. Yet they looked ready for a Hollywood movie set, while I, who had slaved all my life, looked like their punk rock maid. Something was wrong with this picture.

I sighed and plunged ahead with my agenda, which was to adroitly find out as much about Skip as I possibly could.

Apparently, Skip hadn't been seen in days but that wasn't unusual. Melanie didn't seem at all upset by his absence. There are families where the males seem eclipsed by the women, and this was one of them. Skip was outnumbered nine to one. It would appear that he was a peripheral entity. My guess was they saw him as a useful financier and not much more. Perhaps he was in hiding, or maybe they had expunged him for not matching his underwear to the window treatments.

One of the living room walls was completely covered in pictures of beauty pageants, proms, baton twirling contests, pom and cheerleader squad pictures. Three generations of sorority sisters smiled their beatific smiles. Three generations of cheerleaders rampant beamed out at me. My question was, what lurked beneath the surface of their all American girl glory?

There were Babs and Melanie together in an old faded photograph with Skip and Scooter. Skip really did look like Tab Hunter, and Scooter had also been good looking. He looked like he might have been Skip's younger brother, but he lacked Skip's well defined jaw line and his perfect smile.

Nowadays, Scooter worked driving truck for Diamond Packing Company just outside of town. He had never made it through college. His intellect only went as far as the goal line of the football field. Today, Scooter still had all his hair. It was dull blond and greased back into a ducktail, just as he had worn it in high school. He now had skinny legs in blue jeans, steel toed work boots, and always sported plaid flannel shirts which he wore one size too big to cover his ample belly. His face was lined and creased. His one good feature was his glowing warm brown eyes with their long, thick lashes. Other than his eyes, he was unremarkable.

Wait a minute! Scooter was always in Skip's shadow. Didn't he ever get sick of that arrangement? Was he perhaps aware, as Skip's best friend, that Valerie had scads of ready cash somewhere? Might he have thought that he should have or somehow deserved that cash? Maybe he was heartily sick of being Skip's lifelong sidekick and egotistical Babs' unremarkable husband. The lure of money might have goaded him to change all that.

Skip was the one people noticed, loved, worshiped, lionized, and believed in. Scooter had been the perfect blank dark backdrop to the meteor which was Skip. Skip got the honors, the trophies, the scholarships, and the girls. He was the all American boy whom heroes and Hollywood movies were made of. And Scooter? He was the dependable buddy in the shadows.

I looked at another photo and saw that there beside Scooter was Babs. She had indeed been a busty blond knockout, the type of girl every boy drooled over. She had been a perfect typecast Hollywood blond bombshell, a blowsy bleached blond with false eyelashes and fake stick-on nails, the kind you bought for a buck at the dime store. Now she looked like an aged Jean Harlow who had taken a few too many nips at the whiskey bottle, but thanks to tight jeans, stiletto heels, and lots of surgical help, she still looked sexy, though the flower of youth had long since faded.

In the photo, her mouth was painted a bright red. Her eyes were heavily shadowed with liner and mascara, like Joan Crawford's in those old movies. Babs looked much the same today as she had then, except hard as nails.

And then there was Mel, with her pale, creamy skin and long dark hair. Back then, Melanie had definitely looked like a sex bomb in a cleavage showing skin tight hot pink sweater and matching stretch pants, so tight they looked like a second skin. And there were those Cyd Charisse go on forever legs. I could see why Skip fell for her. No boy could have failed to notice her, no matter what the competition.

I took a look around and decided that Melanie was one of those women who studied the catalogs and wanted everything to be picture perfect. I guessed that she spent most of her life making sure that her family looked like the Brady bunch. Her carefully created extended nuclear family was designed to look just like the cutesy ones on television.

But were they? It seemed to me that this family was just a little strange. It was Petticoat Junction with a twist.

Little Emma and Olivia both screamed with hysterical glee as they chased the three cats in circles around the entire house.

Melanie's granddaughter Candy sat in an armchair, watching television with the sound off, lifting hand weights. By the look of her triceps, I decided I wouldn't want to mess with her. Her twin sister Brandy crouched on the floor doing stomach crunches at an alarming and seemingly indefatigable rate.

Melanie's daughter Bobby sat in the corner polishing one of her guns, and from the looks of the gun case on the wall, guns were a very big thing in her life. She looked up at me from under long, carefully coated lashes with a look which I thought coldly calculated to scare me, and she was doing a good job. I sincerely hoped that none of those guns were loaded.

Bobby's sister Amber sat just to my left in a big, deep armchair. I glanced over her shoulder at the catalog she leafed through. It was a catalog of personal protection equipment; mace, stun guns, burglar alarms.

"Mom," said Amber to Melanie, "I think Brandy and Candy could use some of this stuff in their course at police science school."

"Are you and Candy studying to be police officers?" asked Didi, smiling brightly at Brandy.

"Candy is but I just like locks and stuff," she said. "I'm taking the class to familiarize myself with it. I like reading about cops and robbers. Mom used to be a locksmith so I guess it's in my blood."

I glanced at Amber. Somehow, she looked capable of lock picking, in a very all American girl sort of way.

"Probably a dominatrix," I whispered in Didi's ear. She lifted an eyebrow at me to indicate that she thought they were all weird. The only seemingly normal person in this sea of odd female pulchritude was Tiffany. Tiff sat in the light streaming in through the window, knitting a pink sweater for little Emma. With her gentle classic features, she could have been a medieval Madonna.

"Emma!" she called. "Come here, honey. I want to see if this fits you." Emma ran in screaming, pursued by the cats and Olivia.

"Grandma great has a secret!" lisped Olivia at me.

"Hush, hush!" admonished Melanie. She frowned sternly at Olivia while Tiffany tried to distract her with a candy.

"Secret! Secret!" screeched Olivia in the way children will carry on exactly when you desperately want them to be quiet.

Bobby, at a sign from Melanie, scooped up Olivia and carried her off screaming at the top of her lungs.

"Be nice for Grandma," called Taffy.

Tiffany smiled at me apologetically and measured the arm of Emma's sweater. Emma swiped the sucker she was carrying on the couch and held it out to the cat.

"Go take that candy in the kitchen," said Melanie to Emma. Emma stared at her with big eyes, raised her chubby little fist, pointed her index finger at Mel and said, "No! No! Naughty!"

Emma was summarily banished to the kitchen by Tiffany. Brandy picked up the weights and started to work her biceps.

A minor emergency of burned chocolate chip cookies called most everyone to the kitchen. Brandy alone remained, pumping iron in the corner. She finished her biceps crunches and turned to me with a shy smile.

"Little Olivia is yours, isn't she?" I asked. "She's a lovely child. She could be a child star or a model with those looks. And such a sweet disposition."

And I'm a big fat liar. I could feel Didi give me the look which said, "That's a crock." I ignored her.

"You're going to have to beat the boys off her with a stick," I gushed. "What a looker she'll be!"

Had my flattery been too obvious? Apparently not, for suddenly Brandy grew ten degrees warmer and very chatty.

"Olivia is going to be all of us rolled into one," she said fondly. "And that secret she was talking about was just Grandma telling us today that she has a trip planned for all of us. I don't know why she wants it kept secret. Grandma will soon come into tons of money somehow but she wants it kept hush-hush. She calls it her secret stash. She has promised us all a trip to Europe soon. Won't that be sweet?" she asked on a rising note of enthusiasm.

I got the feeling that Brandy had inherited all of her grandpa's looks and charm without the brains and the low cunning.

"This may be a delicate question," I said, "but why don't any of you get married? There must be lots of men interested in you. You, Tiffany, Taffy, and Candy are all drop dead lookers. And there is no shortage of men around town."

"You'd be surprised," said Brandy wistfully. "I just heard on television that eleven percent of men are gay. That's one in ten, isn't it?" Not quite but close enough.

"I don't think they could have gotten that statistic from LaFollette County," I said. "Most of the young men I've observed here seem intent on doing a perpetual James Dean imitation."

"Who is James Dean?" asked Brandy. "Is he that new guy on Young Malibu?" I looked askance at Didi.

"Soap opera," she said.

"I don't want to get married anyway," said Brandy with a sigh.

"How come?" asked Didi.

"Because marriages always end in divorce. Grandma is the only one who can stay married because Grandpa is so wonderful. I mean, look at Aunt Bobby. She's divorced. Mom's divorced too. I guess we all decided not to bother with marriage. Besides, why should we? Grandpa takes care of everyone anyway."

"Does anyone besides your grandpa work?" asked Didi.

"Oh, we don't have to work," said Brandy. "Grandma wants us to stay home and raise the children, and anyway, Grandpa's such a great salesman. He works for Keller Farm Equipment and makes a ton."

Brandy looked toward the kitchen, weighed something in the balance, and then said quickly, in a conspiratorial whisper, "Grandma Mel is really glad that Valerie Cooper is dead."

"Why?" I asked, stunned.

"Because Grandma and Grandpa always fought about Val. Ever since I can remember, Grandma Mel and Grandpa Skip had regular fights about Valerie Cooper. They didn't fight about anything else, not money, not the other women Grandpa Skip had on the side . . ."

"Wait! You mean that you know about those other women?" I asked, incredulous.

"Well, yeah! Who doesn't? Nobody cares about those other women, including Grandpa. It's just something he does, like playing croquet."

"Only with a different kind of mallet," said Didi.

Brandy giggled.

"Grandpa Skip is just one of those ultra-top performance men," she said. "He is like a . . . ." Her face screwed up with the effort of trying to put her thoughts into words.

"Like an alpha male?" I prompted. I was well acquainted with the habits of alpha males.

Her face brightened.

"Exactly! He is like a king or a president. It's just accepted that he has women on the side. He has, like, an obsession with sex." She giggled again. "Even though he's old, he's still a stud. Can you believe it?"

She launched into a crescendo of giggles. We could believe it, all right.

"I see," I said.

What I saw was that the women in this family were mercenary and the lone male was chronically unfaithful. Sounded like a prescription for disaster. What I saw was that lots of people think we can conveniently explain away any kind of unacceptable or immoral behavior with a few pat psychological formulas.

Apparently, no one but me suffered any longer under the delusion that men had free will and as such, can be held responsible and accountable for their actions. We were all hostage to our emotions, primitive and otherwise, incapable of one shred of decency or self control. And if someone else was hurt beyond repair, well, too bad. Only the strong survive, right? Everybody lies, right?

Gee, God, I just couldn't control my nasty bloodthirsty obsessions. My medication wasn't working too well. My shrink said I shouldn't be held accountable. Hey, what do you mean, I'm responsible? Come on, you can't be serious!

"Yeah," Brandy resumed. "That's how we got Moustache Mary. Grandpa denies it, but everyone in town knows that Mary is his kid. Hard to believe, huh?"

"No kidding," I said. "Amazing things, gene pools."

My secretary Eunice had already given me the scoop on Moustache Mary. She was the product of one of Skip's forays into the stranger side of infidelity. Mary's mother, Charlotte Chantelle Charpentier, or Char-Char as she was commonly known about town, was of French origin. She had retained a sizzling sexuality well into middle age, they say, even though at present she looked pretty fizzled to me. She was small, dark, and hirsute, and she never shaved. She had that European sex appeal; earthy, natural, and totally unrepressed. Even her hairiness was appealing, or so Skip must have thought when he had that mad, passionate affair which produced Mary.

Charlotte Chantelle Charpentier looked like an effeminate hairy man dressed as a woman, which made her a real gender bender and Skip's only lapse from his determined pursuit of the ultra feminine all American girl. Maybe it was the hair that fascinated him. It surely fascinated me. It grew in luxurious dark profusion on eyebrows, nostrils, lips, cheeks, arms, legs, on every uncovered and presumably also on the covered places on Char's body. I, for one, was thankful they were covered.

Eunice told me that Char-Char was sufficiently captivating to hold Skip's interest for over a year, quite a feat in Skip's love biography. Moustache Mary was the product of their passionate love affair.

Moustache Mary grew up hating Skip and everyone else, too. Skip had ignored her all her life. He couldn't bring himself to admit that he had sired such a creature. Mary isn't beautiful, or even cute. She has none of the looks of either parent. All she inherited was her mother's anti-social disposition and her hirsutism. Mary runs the locks on the river and legend has it that if she doesn't like you, you can be stuck forty-five minutes waiting to get through. Since she doesn't like most people, it takes everyone a long time to get through the locks. They call her the troll of Bridge Street.

The burned chocolate chip cookie emergency was over. Everyone trooped out to the living room, and Brandy promptly clammed up. It was time to go.

I gave Melanie my card and asked her to call me if Skip dialed in his location.

"If you can think of any reason why there may have been some recent contact between Valerie and Skip," I said, "I would appreciate it if you could give me a call. I would like to talk to Skip about Valerie."

All of a sudden, the air grew distinctly frosty. All the feminine chatter ceased abruptly, and there was an unpleasant silence. Oops!

"Are you casting aspersions on my husband?" Melanie said menacingly, her eyes narrowing. "Skip hasn't even seen that weirdo Valerie since high school. Why would he have anything to do with that pathetic old bag?"

Why indeed, when the bush telegraph has it that he runs around with every woman he can get within a four county radius?

"Valerie Cooper was a certified wacko and an ugly old cow," said Melanie. "Skip laughed about her all the time. Said she was a bad joke. And you're a joke too, punk rock grandma. Why don't you just make like a tree and leave?"

Next she'll be telling me to cool my jets.

She smirked and I was reminded of Tina, a girl I had known in high school. Tina had been cute, fashionable, popular, and generally envied, but inside, she had the heart of a witch. Her favorite game involved cutting other girls' reputations to shreds. I wouldn't be surprised if it were battery acid, not blood, which flowed through Melanie's veins. It was a certainty that she lacked the milk of human kindness.

I stood up straight and raised my chin. It wasn't easy to look superior in my punk rock garb, but I gave it a good try.

"Maybe Skip liked Val more than you knew," I said lightly, giving her a little smile. "Maybe the flame never really died. Sometimes love is funny that way."

Bingo! I saw the look of a long held secret fear in her eyes and knew I had scored a hit. That was just one tiny shred of revenge on Valerie's behalf in exchange for a lifetime of loneliness. I smiled, shrugged, and turned away, but not before Melanie's face scrunched up into a surprisingly ugly mask for one who had maintained her marvelous good looks for so long. I don't think her plastic surgeon would like that look marring his beautiful sculpture. Mel gave me a gesture which I think has an Italian origin. I laughed and turned away. Didi followed me to the door.

I gave Mel a parting shot.

"Valerie left a large estate and according to her will, Skip might have an interest in it," I said. "But if you can't cooperate, fine by me."

I saw a gleam in Melanie's eye and she made a contrite gesture just before I slammed the door shut and walked away. Let her think about that one for a while.

"You are one big fat liar," Didi breathed into my ear in her low voice.

"Serves her right," I said as I headed for the Ford. "I'm not taking that stuff from anybody, least of all her."

"Your mother was right about you," said Didi.

"Yes, I guess I was the only royalty in the family because she always called me the Queen of Sheba when she wasn't calling me the snip."

"There was a reason for that!"

"Yeah, I had attitude before it was fashionable."

The door slammed behind us and Tiffany appeared at our side.

"If you really want to speak to Grandpa, try the Drake and Hen Inn on Highway A," she said, and then, as quickly as she had materialized, she slipped away into the pearly dusk.

"Thanks!" I called.

Didi raised her eyebrows at me. Fifteen minutes later, we stood in the foyer of the Drake and Hen, watching four couples sway to the music on the darkened dance floor. It was only early twilight, but at the Drake and Hen, any time was the right time for a boozy, smokey cloud of let's play pretend. I peered through the murky haze at the dancers.

Didn't they know they looked completely ridiculous? I wish I could look so ridiculous.

I glanced around the bar and sure enough, there was Skip. He was unmistakably the same handsome man of Valerie's dreams and the one who had stared out from his high school photo at me the night Tabby, Krystal, and I did the jitterbug at Valerie's house. And brother, did he look good! He had the same blond, blue eyed, surfer boy good looks that he had back then. A little age and a little fading had only served to add a hint of mystery to the masterpiece that was Skip. I tried not to stare at him but it was difficult to tear one's eyes away from such a work of art.

Didi and I sauntered over to the bar and sat. I ordered a whiskey and cola.

A middle aged salesman type slid onto the leather barstool next to me. He reeked of beer, cigarette smoke, and adultery.

"Hi, gorgeous, who are you, a punk rock grandma?" he asked.

"Hi, I'm Rhi Nolan, and I'm here to make your life complete but first I need you to divorce your wife and give me all your money," I said. He laughed, melted away into the smoky haze, and went in search of someone who could appreciate mediocrity.

I looked over at the dance floor and sighed. If only someone would ask me to dance. It had been too long. As if on cue, Skip walked up to us. I presumed he would try to flirt with Didi since she, like him, was not only a well preserved blond hottie, but also a sex magnet. But to my surprise, Skip smiled at me.

"Wanna dance, punk?" he asked. Is this the best introductory line this guy can think of? I thought he was supposed to be so smooth. Huh!

Be careful what you wish for. I hesitated a second before saying, "No, I can't dance."

I was the best dancer in my high school class, but of course, that was back in the dark ages.

"Aw, come on. No one will ever know you danced with some old guy in some bar in the back of beyond," said Skip.

Can't argue with that one. He grabbed my hand and dragged me out on the floor. Oh, well, I'll consider it research. Let's see if the Skipper still has it.

We swirled and twirled around a few times and then Skip settled down into a rolling slow step. O.K., so he still has it. O.K., so my red alert beware button is flashing. I got the feeling Skip had closed his eyes and was pretending that I was someone else, perhaps someone he was in love with. So I closed my eyes and pretended Skip was Mick. It was easy since they were roughly the same height, weight, and build.

Ah! That was much better! What could one three minute fantasy hurt? Mick had been one dead sexy article, although he had also been some other not so nice things. Since Mick had died in a small engine plane crash three years ago, I had lived a totally romantically deprived life. This made a nice change.

There had been one tweedy old law professor who had expressed an interest when I was in law school. Trouble was, my taste in men didn't run to tweedy old highly evolved and civilized law professors. It ran to men marked trouble with a capital T! Red alert! Panic button! Type T high risk alpha male here!

Why had I married not one, not two, but three wild men by the age of thirty? There was no family precedent. Love for wild things didn't seem to manifest itself in anyone's DNA in the family other than mine. My brothers had all married yuppie preppie homecoming queens and kept themselves busy reproducing similar progeny. I was cursed, cursed and marked.

Darn that Stanley Keefer! He was the one who awakened all this dormant confusion to begin with, I realized with a flash of intuition.

Stan the man was the one who was causing a serious disturbance on the emotional radar.

And not only that, but in the immediate moment, Skip was causing a flutter of electric activity in the pituitary gland. In fact, my entire endocrine system, which I thought was half dead, suddenly seemed fully alive. Darn! Hope I didn't drop dead from the sudden shock.

The song was over. I opened my eyes. Yup. I fully realized why all the girls had been mad about Skip. He was definitely a chick magnet and he still had the old engine purring like a Chevelle Super Sport. Oh, boy, get the fever reducer. I feel a hot flash coming on and this time it's the living hormones, not the dying ones, causing the problem.

"Mind if I join you and your friend?" asked Skip.

He had a boyish smile which was quite devastating. I tried not to feel anything, especially anything in the way of attraction. The man was still gorgeous and had an incredible magnetic force field. In fact, there was only one thing wrong with him. He was full of it.

"Please do," I said, planning to pump him for information.

It turned out I didn't have to work too hard. With a modicum of prodding on my part, Skip readily told Didi and me all about himself and his family. Then he added that he was out tonight because he didn't want to be alone.

"Why would you feel alone with that large family of yours?" asked Didi.

"I'm always alone in that house," said Skip with some bitterness. Then he added, "I'm always odd one out there. I just had to go somewhere and get away. You see, my best friend just died."

My sixth sense told me he meant Valerie, but I decided not to push it, and besides, how could Skip count Valerie as his best friend?

"Who was he?" asked Didi.

"She," said Skip. "Her name was Valerie Cooper. She was my high school sweetheart." A haunted, pained look came over him. Maybe he had forgotten to take his medication today.

"Valerie was your best friend?" asked Didi.

"We were very close," said Skip and drained his beer. I noticed he was drinking Special Export beer, my dad's favorite. "Like soul

75

mates ever since the day I first saw her in junior high," he said. "Even though we didn't end up together, we should have." How interesting. Had he and Valerie communicated by telepathy?

I looked at Skip's handsome haunted face and thought of Oscar Wilde's novel, *The Portrait of Dorian Gray*. Had Skip, like Dorian, made a secret pact with the devil? He seemed virtually ageless. It was remarkable how good he looked, considering his life style. Was there a portrait of an evil aging Skip under a velvet cover in a locked room somewhere? A shiver ran through me. Was all this heartbroken soul mate stuff a huge fake? This man was either a consummate actor or a master of deception, or perhaps a murderer.

And then it hit me. Something had been niggling at my brain since the second I saw Skip, and now I knew whom he reminded me of. Hold the phone! Jackie Jamison! I hadn't thought of Jackie in years. That's who Skip reminded me of; Mr. Charm, Jackie Jamison, or JJ as we used to call him.

JJ! I hadn't thought of him in a long, long time. JJ was my secret Waterloo. I hadn't succumbed to despair through all the husbands and boyfriends of my past, but JJ was the charming rattlesnake who almost destroyed my heart forever. I had known liars, downers, rakes, rogues, ladies' men, deadbeats, drinkers, and cheats in my time, but JJ had taken the cake for sincere and deadly charm.

And Skip seemed to have the same personality type. Had Skip really turned back to the past? Was he still in love with Valerie Cooper? Had the errant playboy returned to her after all those long, lonely years?

Could it be that Skip, the aging Don Juan, had needed Valerie to reinforce his exhausted ego? Could it be that a lifetime of philandering and begetting generations of models made him tired and jaded, so he turned back to his original inspiration? He knew, as everyone knew, that Valerie still adored him against all reason. That was the attraction that drew him like a moth to the flame. Valerie needed to worship Skip and he needed to be adored. Did he kill Valerie?

But why would he kill the purest thing he ever had? Was there money involved? And how much? Was Skip really a killer? He didn't seem to fit the profile. There was one fact I didn't question, though. Skip Winters was an operator who could turn the charm on and off like a faucet.

Only a woman who has been fooled and duped by a JJ can recognize a master operator at work. And Skip Winters was a master heartbreaker. He probably even believed his own lies. I had no doubt that he was a consummate liar. But was he also a murderer? The funny thing was, the usual type H for heartbreaker did not go in for murder. Skip's type preferred to string a girl along on a pearl rope of charm, to bind her with the chains of flattery. Why kill a person when you can easily get her to do anything you want her to do without too much effort?

Type H people were not, in my experience, driven by the rage, envy, jealousy, or greed monster. They were more likely to be driven by the narcissist's cry; adore me! Be my willing slave, and when I have used you, it's on to the next conquest, because I'm a bottomless pit of need for attention and admiration.

Narcissists don't usually like the sight of another's blood. After all, you can't see your own reflection in blood. You need a mirror image to admire yourself, so they go looking for their psychic twin in everyone they meet. Had Skip found his twin in Valerie, abandoned her, lost her, and then gone looking for his youth again? I had to find out to put together another piece of this puzzle. I tried to draw Skip out on the subject of Valerie, with little luck.

He grew melancholy and restless and took his leave. Didi and I headed for home in the Ford. We sat in comfortable silence, pondering the enigmatic Skip.

Just before we reached my house, a big black truck veered into our lane, almost sideswiping the Ford. Didi screamed and I swerved just in time. But that wasn't all. To make my day complete, when we reached my front porch, there was a note. It said, "Slut!" in huge black magic marker and taped to the page was a package of diet pills. "Use these!" was scrawled underneath the pills.

"Well, how do you like that?" I asked Didi. "A comedian."

Chapter 10

My Guy

Small is the worth
Of beauty from the light retired;
Bid her come forth,
Suffer herself to be desired,
And not blush so to be admired.

--*Go, lovely rose!*, Edmund Waller

Dear Val,

There never was any girl as beautiful as you, beautiful both inside and out.

Your loving, Skip

"Now which one of my many Scandal Acres friends and admirers might want to insult me in such a manner? Could it be my great pal and buddy, librarian Phoebe Keith?"

"Or do you think it was the murderer?" asked Didi in her soft, low voice.

"Don't know, but to me it seems like something a woman would do. Ever since Buddy "Beau" Dillon blubbered something about seeing a man being bad, I thought we were looking for a male murderer, but now I'm confused."

"Who was driving that big black truck? Could it have been our comedian?" asked Didi. "Whom do we know who owns a big, black macho looking truck?" asked Didi.

"Are you kidding me?" I screeched. "Half the men in this county have a big black truck, a Harley, and a sports car in their garage. It would be totally impossible to develop a list of the suspects based on the truck theory." I was still sore about the diet pills. Humph!

We took the evidence to Sgt. LeCaptain and shoved it under his nose. After he finished chuckling about the diet pills and the note and disparaging our story of someone trying to sideswipe us, he started in on the threatening notes left for Tabby.

"After all, Tabby is a punk and that arouses the hatred of some of the other kids," he droned in his Eeyore-like voice. "And didn't she just go to a political protest in Madison? Such actions can arouse the ire of the more conservative students."

"Are you keeping tabs on my daughter?" I asked in a none too friendly manner. "This is a free country the last time I checked. If she wants to die her hair purple, chartreuse, or violet, and march for the rights of aliens to mate with caterpillars it's none of your business!"

"I'm telling you, these notes are from some nasty little teenage pranksters and don't mean anything!" Le Captain insisted. "Valerie Cooper was not murdered and James DeBrall the coroner says so! And no one is out to get you or your daughter! You are paranoid!"

"We'll see about that," I said menacingly. "We'll just see about that. And by the way, I have the right to bear arms and the right to defend myself and my child."

"Mrs. Nolan, don't you dare go around meddling in these affairs or I'll . . ."

"You'll what?" I said, my eyes narrowing. "Cut off my right to shop at Jane's Grocery? End my driving privileges? Take away my keys and credit cards? Throw me in the pokey for having a backbone? I don't think so!" I stomped away, furious.

And when I'm furious I do serious therapy. I clean, therefore I am.

I was at home on my hands and knees scrubbing out the coat closet and praying that what I was looking at wasn't bat guano when Didi walked in.

"Baking homemade pie and cookies?" asked Didi, sniffing the air like a bloodhound.

"Not homemade," I said, my voice muffled from having my face buried in closet detritus. "Just cut and bake from the freezer section."

"Thank God! For a minute there I thought you were getting senile. I couldn't imagine you actually baking from scratch."

She watched me scrubbing.

"Would you stop it? You are an obsessive compulsive cleaner!" she said.

Tabby walked by.

"No kidding!"

"Speaking of baking," I said, "Tabby, aren't you supposed to bake something for Home Ec class?"

"We don't get any homework in Home Ec, Mom. Weaver replaced Miss Cooper with a cute little blond who never does anything but give us a study hall and make eyes at Weaver."

"Oh, really? How interesting," I said.

"Yeah, he drools whenever she walks by. I mean, he literally salivates. It is so, like, disgusting. Mom, I need some black ribbon and black candles for a goth project I'm doing for art class. Do we have any?"

"No."

"Can I put my Fancy Femmes bumper sticker on the Ford?"

"No!"

"Can you put on some longer shorts? Your legs are all veiny and it's making me sick."

"These are my long shorts," I said through clenched teeth.

"Then could you put on those weird pedal pusher things you wear?"

"No! Go away! Go shave your legs!"

"Mother, you are so immature! I will not give in to the patriarchal dominant male culture! I am a feminist! I do not shave!"

"O.K. you hairy little feminist, then go fold the laundry and muck out Sugar's stall," I said.

"She's obsessed. Do you see that she is obsessed?" said Tabby to Didi. "Didi, can you take the bakery out of the oven before Mom burns it like she burns everything?"

I ignored both of them and continued scrubbing. I felt an M&M attack coming on. Without looking up, I also felt Didi and Tabby shrugging and eye rolling at each other. They trooped off, presumably to rescue the baked goods, find longer shorts, black ribbon, and black candles. Why me, God, why me?

I finished the closet, cleaned the kitchen floor, raided the candy drawer, and immediately felt better. I popped a handful of M&M candies into my mouth and crunched absentmindedly while I decided to do some more prying into Valerie Cooper's affairs.

I ran upstairs and changed into my super sleuth outfit; black on black. And then I applied the final touch; my red lipstick. When I wore my red lipstick, I felt I could conquer the world. Five minutes later, I roared out of the drive in the Ford, destined for Ethel Saunders' office at the high school.

At the corner of Red Oak Lane, I almost collided with Mr. P in the ancient red rusted Chevy he called Chuck. How could anyone who only drove ten miles an hour be such a hazard? He rolled down the window of the truck and motioned for me to do the same.

"Hey! Where you off to in such a hurry?" he asked.

"Going to visit Ethel Saunders at the high school and ask her a few questions," I called.

"Glad it's you and not me," croaked Mr. P and guffawed. "That woman is an old bag. Real old, real old!"

"She's younger than you," I retorted.

"Hey! I'm still young and sexy. Remember, I had an Italian grandmother straight from the old country. When she married into the Belgian farming family I sprung from, I'm telling you, there was a ruckus so loud you could hear it clear to Shelbyville. Real exotic, she was. The ancestors were shocked. That's where I get my sexy, dark side, just like in them romance novels. Are you sure you don't want me? For you I could walk the line."

He gave me his chimp grin, showing his aged, yellow teeth.

I laughed, and then frowned.

"Speaking of romance novels, why did you tell everyone that I had an affair with Francis LeCaptain?"

"Do you wanna get a man or not?" he asked.

I shrugged.

"Dunno."

He shook his head in disgust.

"You'll never get a man if you don't set up a little competition. I'm just trying to help you out."

"Gee, thanks," I said. "Does this mean you'll be sending me roses with a card signed Dark Handsome Stranger?"

"Not likely. I'm too cheap. Right now I'm going to look at the floor boards in your house," he called out. "May need work."

"That's news to me," I said.

Mr. P shook his head.

"That's why you need me," he said. "See, you don't even know when somethin' needs fixin'. That whole darn house could fall down around you and you wouldn't have a clue what went wrong."

I clucked at him, waved him on, rolled up my window, and drove on through the countryside bright with the first signs of autumn. Pumpkin patches and roadside stands held nature's early autumn bounty. The leaves had started to turn, and the air took on a crisp, new feel. It was my favorite time of year.

I meandered on through gently rolling hills down into town, thinking of Valerie. Maybe if I could find out more about her past, I could solve the present puzzle. Ethel was not only one of Tabby's teachers; she was also the third member of the teacher triumvirate that had been Valerie's social network and mainstay for many long, lonely years.

In a few minutes, I arrived at the high school, parked the car, and jogged through the door. If I hurried, I could still find Miss Saunders in her classroom.

Chapter 11

Searching

Her air had a meaning, her movements a grace;
You turned from the fairest to gaze on her face.

-- *My Kate*, Elizabeth Barrett Browning

Dear Val,

    I'm so sorry I left you alone all those years. May God forgive me for being so selfish to the one I love. I'll love you forever.

Yours, Skip

In her later years, Valerie Cooper's appearance had become a bit of an outdated joke, but Val was a Vogue fashion plate compared to Miss Saunders. Miss Saunders, or Ethel Hell, as the kids called her, had stiff cotton candy blue hair, lined bifocal glasses on a chain around her neck, no makeup, and an unrelieved, colorless, grim slash of a mouth. Her thick legs were encased in support hose tougher than steel. Her platypus like feet ended in thick soled, sensible, black lace-up shoes like my grandmother favored back in the old days. Ethel wore a plain button down black shirtwaist dress which fell well below the knee. At her throat sat a brooch which looked like something the cat dragged out of grandmother's tomb.

I thought of Sister Martha as soon as I saw Miss Saunders, and my shoulders sagged. In my childhood spent in Catholic school, Sister Martha was one of those nuns who represented an elemental force of disapproval of everyone and everything. Nothing escaped her eagle eye. Ethel sat at her desk and motioned for me to take the chair in front of her.

I sat, swallowed hard, and extended my hand.

"How do you do? I'm Rhiannon Nolan, Tabitha's mother."

Miss Saunders said something that sounded like, "Humph!" She barely touched the tips of my fingers. Probably, she was one of those people who lived in deathly fear of germs and tried never to touch another human being. She lost no time in giving me what for, just as if I were some twelve year old caught skipping class.

"Oh, yes, you're that Mrs. Nolan, the lawyer. You're the one who fancies herself to be a crime stopper. Some people imagine crime behind every pillar and post, even when it doesn't exist. I don't hold with running all over the countryside searching for murderers. That's a task better left to our very competent Sgt. LeCaptain," said Miss Saunders with a gleam in her steely eyes.

She somehow managed to convey that she too, had heard about my alleged mad but doomed affair with the policeman. At the same time, she intimated by her tone of voice that she considered me to be a bit of saucy contaminated goods. What a joke! What would these old bags do if they knew what was really going on in their pristine little village?

"Well, enough about me," I said and smiled at her through gritted teeth. "What about Valerie Cooper? Were you upset when she died? I heard you two used to be friends."

This took her somewhat by surprise. Miss Saunders straightened her already ramrod backbone a little straighter, if that was possible. She puffed out her cheeks and stared at the ceiling, searching for words which would suffice to convey her grief.

"Let me explain it to you this way. Valerie suffered from delusions. She did all her life. She was of a particularly romantic disposition."

Undoubtedly, Miss Saunders didn't hold with romance either.

"Valerie lived in the past," she continued. "She refused to move into the technological age. She refused to take the obligatory computer training classes for teachers. She just wouldn't move with the times."

"Miss Emily said you and Valerie had a falling out," I prodded.

Miss Saunders primmed her lips.

"Emily talks too much. Val wanted to live in a dream world," said Miss Saunders harshly. "Then she accused me of betraying her trust. Me, of all people! I was her friend!"

I raised my eyebrows.

"So she liked her little romantic dreams. I guess that isn't a crime. And she wouldn't take the computer classes. Maybe she was a bit eccentric. So what? So you two had a falling out. Was that when you and Miss Hussey and Mr. Weaver signed the papers that sent her to the loony bin?"

Miss Saunders' face flushed.

"It was not a loony bin! It was only the old county home. Myself and three other teachers signed the papers. She needed a rest!" Her eyes regarded me coldly.

"How considerate of you," I said with a merciless stare. No wonder Tabby hated this old cat. I had only known Miss Saunders five minutes and I hated her already.

"It was for her own good!" Miss Saunders spat out emphatically. "She went off the deep end with all that talk about Skip Winters. Skip Winters! He never loved her anyway. Actually, he was mad about . . . ."

Abruptly, she broke off. I wondered if she were going to say, "me." Maybe all these old spinsters were mad about Skip. He must have been one dead sexy article, that Skip. To stay in the dreams of three friends from girlhood to late middle age and cause jealousies which lasted forty some years was quite a feat.

"Well, be that as it may," I said, "I really came here to talk about Tabby."

Miss Saunders' eyes hardened into little black bee-bees.

"Yes, Tabitha," she said in a steely voice. "On Monday, Tabitha left class, simply got up and left! And all just because I made her retype her outline three times! Tabitha is an underachiever. Obviously, you exercise no discipline, not a whit! Her appearance is disgraceful, her attitude is poor, her effort is minimal, and she won't have any future at all until she changes her ways. She must conform in this society if she wants to succeed! Purple hair, indeed!"

She eyed my own crazed blue do with a curled lip.

"If Tabitha were my child . . ."

Apparently, Miss Saunders failed to realize that her own hair was blue, but in her case, it wasn't cool punk rock purple or midnight blue. It was more like old bat blue. My eyebrows rose higher with each insult until they disappeared into my hairline.

"But she isn't your child, is she?" I whispered. "Thank God for small favors. Maybe if Tabby tries real hard, someday she will be just like you; sexually repressed, emotionally stunted, and a bitter, mean as dirt old bat!" I got right into her face and yelled, "And I thank God in heaven you never had children!"

Miss Saunders' mouth fell open and went slack. She was about to say something but I stopped her. I pointed my finger in her face and said, "Shut up! And as for Tabby's attitude, where do you think she got the attitude from, babe? It wasn't the corner grocery store!"

I rose from my chair and stared her down with the look which my mother had always told me could send a chill through her bones even when I was just a little girl. Then I turned on my heel and left, slamming the door with a bang like a gunshot. Far be it from me to deny Ethel Hell the instant karma she deserved. I always try to give people what they need, and if they need to see that they are acting like a jerk, who am I to quash the fulfillment of their needs?

That old witch could go rot! She was the epitome of every spiteful old hag in the world. She belonged in a Brothers Grimm fairytale, not teaching a bunch of kids. I was willing to bet she had never been a child. She was born in support hose and raised on the bitter brew of disapproval. They should have drowned her at birth.

My indignation lasted until I got home, where I promptly unloaded and told Didi and Tabby the story.

"Oh, Mom! You didn't tell off another teacher, did you? You're not doing me any favors! I told you to do two things! Stay off of our Internet because you'll wreck the computer and stay out of school! Don't you listen?"

"Yes, dear," I sighed.

The question is, who is the mother and who is the child in this relationship? Didi went off to work in her garden and I went off to my room to spray up my hair and put a little more blue color in it. I thought a visit to the library was in order and I wanted to look right, as befits the mother of a punk rocker.

When I walked into the New Belgium Public Library, the librarian, Miss Phoebe Keith, gave me the evil eye. Phoebe Keith was only thirty years old. She was tall, thin, and beautiful. She had long blond hair and cellulite free thighs which were very much on display daily in the library, and she did not care for me.

Phoebe didn't like me much since in my last case, I had dragged her lover George Wainwright Smythe's name through the mud. The fact that George was lover to half the county, including Phoebe's half sister Kelly McGuire, and his name was mud already didn't seem to matter to Miss Keith. She had taken an irrational dislike to me ever since, even though I had helped put George's murderer behind bars.

I sidled into the classic fiction aisle and browsed the titles. There was an old favorite, Wilkie Collins' *The Moonstone.* This one must have been here for decades. Inside the catalog pocket with the old fashioned stamped due date card from pre-computer checkout days, I saw Valerie Cooper's signature with a stamped date of October 18, 1959. My mouth fell open.

It seemed that Val haunted the whole town. What good handwriting Val had back then. She must have been eighteen years old and a freshman in college.

That was the year it all fell apart for her. She was, no doubt, attending the local community college while Skip and Scooter played football for UW-Madison in the fall of 1959 and chased after girls like Melanie and Babs. I could picture Val sitting on the velour couch reading Wilkie Collins novels, romantic stories of sad ladies with broken dreams. And meanwhile, her real life romance drifted away from her, never to be reclaimed. Sad, so sad.

It all happened so many years ago. Valerie Cooper waited so long for her dreams to come true. Was she unbalanced, or was she just better than the rest of the greedy opportunists around her, intent on their own satisfaction and immediate gratification? Perhaps Valerie wasn't crazy at all. Perhaps she was the only truly sane one in the bunch, and certainly the best of the bunch.

How in the world did she keep the faith for Skip Winters in the face of so much betrayal? Was it innocence, stupidity, or insanity which helped her through all the long, lonely years?

Certainly she had friends over the years, like Miss Emily and Miss Saunders. They must have been a likely crew before betrayal and bitterness drove them apart. The triumvirate of spinsters with their parties, bowling, card club, and summer jaunts to England, Paris, and Montana had a lot of fun. Val's friends had no doubt helped to fill the gap caused by an aborted love life, but could they staunch the gaping wound of a broken, bleeding heart?

On my way out of the library, I smiled at Phoebe Keith. She stared at me and curled her lip at my hair. Some people have no taste.

Chapter 12

When a Man Loves a Woman

And fare thee weel, my only luve,
And fare thee weel awhile!
And I will come again, my luve,
Though it were ten thousand mile.

--A Red, Red Rose, Robert Burns

Dear Val,

My daughters should be on their own. My granddaughters too. No more responsibilities for me. It's time for me to stop playing Daddy and breadwinner to everyone now. Soon it will be just the two of us.

Love, Skip

I was taking a leisurely stroll down Red Oak Lane on the road adjacent to my property when I heard a motor being gunned. I looked up and squinted into the sunlight just in time to see a big black truck aimed right at me and gaining fast.

I ran down the lane hollering as loudly as I could with the truck in pursuit. I tried jumping into the ditch and the truck swerved, following me. In a panic, I leapt for the fence and threw myself on it. The big black truck veered away and roared off down Red Oak Lane at a high rate of speed.

I jumped off the fence, intending to sail like Earl "the Pearl" Monroe into the field. Instead, I came down like Shamu. You've heard that old adage, white men can't jump. Unfortunately, neither can I. I fell flat on my face in the mud and I knew that when I got up, I would be dirt encrusted and in pain.

I struggled to my feet. Right again.

Why couldn't I be like I was at thirteen when aerial acrobatics were my preferred mode of travel? Getting old sucks canal water. Tabby's horse Sugar saw me and trotted over to nuzzle my fingers for carrots. Somehow I managed to haul myself up on Sugar's back and cling to his mane. I decided to get back to the barn before the maniac in the black truck had another chance to kill me. There was no way I was walking down that lane again today.

I wrapped my legs and arms around Sugar, leaned close to his ear and whispered, "Barn! Carrots!"

Whoever said animals don't understand English is an idiot. Sugar took off like a blue streak for the barn while I clung onto his neck for dear life. I used to ride bareback as a kid but then I was fearless. Now I shut my eyes and prayed. Oh Lord, please get me back to the barn alive before, ouch, my organs are jarred right out of my body. And don't let me fly off this horse because, ouch, I'm in the middle of too much karmic entanglement to die now. Just give me a few more years or at least until all my kids turn thirty.

The Lord heard me and Sugar settled down into a smooth rocking horse canter. For the rest of the ride, I hovered somewhere between terror and exhilaration.

Sugar plowed his way through the field up to the corral fence, stopped on a dime, lowered his silky neck, and deposited me neatly head over heels on the other side of the fence. I stayed there for a minute in a pile of horse poop wondering whether to go on living. I experimented gingerly with moving my torso, my neck, and each extremity. Nothing seemed broken. I rose to my feet very slowly and sidled sideways into the barn like a horseshoe crab. People who have even a mild degree of rheumatoid arthritis should definitely not go cantering about the countryside on a horse without a saddle, bit, and bridle. They should probably not go cantering about at all.

I might be in pain, but a deal is a deal. I hobbled into the barn, got a halter and lead rope, took Sugar into his stall, and fed him some grain and carrots. He didn't mind that I was covered in panicky sweat, horse poop, mud, and dust. I was his human and I held the carrots.

That was all that mattered to him. Having fulfilled my. promise, I moved, oh so slowly and tentatively, from the barn into the house. Tabby sat in front of the television.

"Don't ask!" I said.

She never took her eyes off the television screen.

"Ask what? Mom, could you get me some cheese and crackers and freshly squeezed lemonade? I've had a hard day at school."

Your wish is my command.

People really are much the same everywhere. Kids rule. Around the world, royalty speaks and moms answer the clarion call of duty. Neither heat nor cold, nor pain nor sickness can keep us moms from doing our mom thing. Death is our only release from servitude; that and loudly running hot showers behind barricaded bathroom doors with the music cranked to deafening. Thank God for Motown. When we emerge, we can always look around innocently and say, "But I didn't hear you ask for anything, dear."

When I had met my daughter's every need and sufficiently recovered from my wild ride, I decided it was time to talk to Moustache Mary and her mother about Valerie Cooper. This time I decided to play it safe and travel in the Ford. Considering my driving record, perhaps I should say relatively safe.

It took me a few minutes to locate Mary's house. Then I had to navigate my way through the rusted metal sculptures and garden gnomes which blockaded the entrance. I could see that Mary was a fond fan of one of my personal favorite cheese head cultural quirks; hanging curtains in the garage windows. When I rang the doorbell, Mary answered the door.

"Yeah, what ya want?" she asked suspiciously.

I was sorely tempted to walk away but I decided to overlook Mary's distinct lack of charm.

"I'm here to ask you about Valerie Cooper. I'm looking into the circumstances surrounding Val's death."

Moustache Mary's mother, Charlotte, popped into view behind Mary. They both gave me a look of profound hatred.

"Mind your own business!" said Charlotte Chantelle.

"Valerie may have been murdered and I'm trying to find out who was responsible for her death, either directly or indirectly," I said. "Do you think I could get a little cooperation here?"

"Why should we give a rat's behind?" said Moustache Mary. "Why do you think we care? That Skip Winters treated Mom like dirt and me like less than dirt. And if that stupid old Valerie got herself killed because of her love for him, it's her own darn fault! Everybody knows you don't go around pining after a man who dumps you! Even the idiots in *Cosmopolitan* know that, for cripes sake! We just don't care!"

I got a sudden vision of Moustache Mary poring over *Cosmopolitan* magazine and I blinked.

"You might care because Valerie's dead," I said evenly. "She was a sweet person who didn't deserve what she got handed in life."

"Huh!" said Moustache Mary.

That was about the most sympathetic syllable she uttered. Mary was one of those lethally unsympathetic types commonly found in the far cheesey reaches of the northern United States.

We in New Belgium probably have one of the last totally tribal homogenous populations west of New Guinea or north of the equator. To us, pizza is ethnic food and wintering in Florida is the only alternative lifestyle we recognize. We should be studied by anthropologists looking for primitive tribes of cheese heads. The only thing is, no one would consent to be studied, especially during football season.

On Sundays, everyone rushes home from church and God help the cleric who drags out the sermon. We have to be home by twelve o'clock when the game starts and our second religion begins or we turn into bratwursts. We enjoy ritual sacrifice of animal flesh on the barbecue. Who cares if the wind chill is forty below zero? We can still grill out! Ya, hey! And then comes the moment we've waited for all week; the kickoff. The game begins. The women get to admire the Packers in their tights and the men can get an eyeful of beautiful vestal virgin cheerleaders. Well, maybe not virgins, but who cares?

Who said religion is dead? Saint Vince Lombardi told us that only God and family can come before the team. And we take him seriously up until the point of game time, when the team becomes more important than breathing. You get between a cheese head and his television during a Packer game and you might not live to see another day. During the games we wallow in the trinity of the three sacred B's; beer, brandy, and bratwurst, not in liberal guilt.

Guilt is for those cheese deprived nuts out on the coastlines. The only guilt we feel is a vague sense of uneasiness about anything pleasurable which doesn't include work. Generations of northern European poor immigrant workaholism combined with residue left over from private school indoctrination takes its toll, but we manage to suppress it long enough to watch the game.

In New Belgium, you're considered ethnic if you wear bangles and broomstick skirts, own Amish furniture, or drive a Volkswagen. Voting for the democratic ticket could mean you're on the highway to hell. And reading anything more serious than the fiction bestseller list could get you forever marked with the euphemistic "interesting," meaning one of those weird eggheads who might be persuaded to become a Communist or work for a liberal newspaper. Either way, you might as well leave the county. There isn't any room for you in frozen tundra land, bud. You probably don't even own a Packer jersey. What are you anyway, a sicko?

I sighed and stared at Charlotte Chantelle and Moustache Mary. Was it worth it? I handed Moustache Mary my card.

"I know it's painful for you, but if you could help out I'd be terrifically thankful until my dying day. If you think of anything, anything at all, that might be significant, call me at my law office or home. That's my cell phone number. You can call me on that, too."

I smiled my most charming smile.

"I know you'll do your best to help," I said.

"Huh!" said Mary and slammed the door in my face.

Ya gotta love these people.

I got back in the Ford and drove home to a very messy kitchen.

"Tabitha!" I called. She came down the stairs.

"What went on here?" I asked. "Preparing for a world punk rock conference? How many kids did you have over here today?"

"I am not like you mother, with your German hausfrau obsessively clean and detailed mentality. I am like my dead father, a beautiful rebel outlaw. And there isn't a thing you can do about it!"

Oh-oh, I'm in trouble now. How did we get from cleaning the kitchen to emulating her late rebel father in one quick jump?

A picture of my late husband flashed before my eyes. Drugs, sex, rock 'n' roll doesn't begin to describe his youth. I think I blacked out for a second as I contemplated Tabby emulating him.

"I'm a feminist rebel and we're taking this country back from the dominant white male culture. What do you have to say to that?"

"O.K., rebel with a cause," I said. "Before you go out and save the country from the dominant white idiot males, could you clean up the kitchen and pick up your dirty laundry from the bathroom floor?"

"That's right, be sure to belittle me, Mother. And ruin my self esteem while you're at it!"

This kid must have been reading her big sister's psychology books.

"I got another infraction from Principal Weaver for walking out of Ethel Hell's class," she said with gusto. "I consider it an honor."

"Why did you do that?" I asked.

"Mom! That class is idiotic. I hate it! I hate the teacher! It's useless and it's required. And furthermore, it's full of dummies. A good half of them will become teen parents and clog up our welfare rolls and court systems with another generation of self perpetuating idiots. There's a reason this nation does not have a balanced budget! We have idiots giving free money to idiots. I'm in revolt against all the stupidity I see around me every day."

I shook my head. Lord help me. She is so good at confusing the issue.

"Have you been reading Jennifer's psychology textbooks?" I asked.

"Mother! I am not like Jen. At heart, she is really a yuppie cheerleader masquerading as a baby pseudo-shrink. She is only a few years away from a yuppie house in the 'burbs with a football coach husband, three perfect children, a soccer mom mini-van, and a high paying job pushing prescription drugs to kids like me. And why? So we shut up and kill our rebel creative side which does not accept the violent, porno driven materialism of this racist, fascist, white male power, sex and money hungry sick society. I am an artist, a rebel, a zit on the normal business as usual face of the crap pile that is the modern world. Any questions?"

There was a brief silence.

"So what do you want for dinner?" I asked.

"That's it?" she screeched. "Food is your way of pretending I'm still a baby! Why are you always pushing food at me?" she yelled.

"Because you don't eat!" I screamed.

"I eat plenty! I just don't like meat! I refuse to eat dead animal flesh!"

"Look at you!" I said. "You are a bag of bones! You eat like a bird!"

"Birds eat six times their weight every day! I do too eat! I just don't support the rape of cows and the bloodthirsty meat and dairy assembly lines! You always wanted me to be different and now I am, and you can't stand it!"

I screamed, stamped my foot, and held my hands over my ears.

"I can't take it! I can't take any more!" I stomped up the steps. When I reached the top step I called down. "I'm going to my room to read Agatha Christie and eat chocolate and listen to Motown. Do not call me! Do not bother me until you turn thirty!"

Tabby glowered at me and curled her lip.

"Grow up, Mother!" she growled.

Chapter 13

And It Goes Like This

Search, seek, and know how this foul murder comes.

--William Shakespeare, *Romeo and Juliet*, Act V,
Scene iii

Dear Val:

If I had half a brain, Melanie, Babs, and Scooter would never have convinced me to drop you. I was young and hungry for cheap thrills. You know how boys are. I just hope someday you can forgive me.

Love, Skip

Some days start out badly. Zoro and I were in the middle of a lovely walk through a field of purple clover, bright asters, and wild phlox when we met Mrs. Drusilla Swinkle, resident gossip and supreme sour puss of New Belgium. Drusilla stumped along her slow, stolid way and blocked the path for ten minutes while she grumbled about her taxes, modern life, the state of the nation, and finally, my daughter Tabby and I.

"Emily tells me you've been married three times," she sniffed.

Miss Emily strikes again. A real charmer, that one was.

"So what?" I shrugged.

"I was married fifty years to the same man," Drusilla said proudly.

He must have been blind and deaf, not to mention asexual, if he put up with you for all those years, I thought.

"And how about Tabby? Do you want her to repeat your mistakes? Can't you control that child of yours?" she carped. She didn't know how close she came to getting punched in the nose.

"I heard from Ethel that Tabby's music is revolutionary, her politics are pro-anarchy, and her philosophy of life is pagan. You better stop that child before someone finds her burning little animals in the cemetery and worshiping the devil," she continued.

I looked up at the sky. God help us. Leave it to Ethel Hell to have a friend like Drusilla Swinkle. Then I looked down at Drusilla and her ugly little eyes filled with venom.

"Really? Well, don't let Tabby fool you," I crooned into her chronically disapproving face. She had an unswerving, unblinking gaze. It was unnerving, like staring into the eyes of a gorgon. But my motto was, never let 'em see you sweat. I smiled at her and pressed on.

"Tabby's politics are actually Republican and her primary philosophy is that there should be no free lunch for anybody. She's simply an artistic free spirit, and quite a brilliant one at that. And she doesn't believe in the devil, let alone worship him. Surprised?" I asked.

I couldn't help smirking with glee as I turned away with a spring in my step and a swing in my hip. But my triumph was premature.

Mrs. Drusilla Swinkle played her ace in the hole, which was what she had been pining to do since the second she saw me meandering over the meadow.

"If Tabby is so conservative and Republican then why are she and Krystal checking out *Our Bodies, Ourselves* from the library? Don't you think you should do something about that?" she asked in a voice that made me want to strangle her. She grinned. She had the smile of a cobra and the personality to match.

I stopped dead in my tracks. Phoebe Keith strikes again. I turned and sauntered back to Mrs. Drusilla Swinkle, Zoro in tow. He gave a brief growl, as if to say he had already had enough of Drusilla and wasn't interested in hanging around.

"Let's get one thing straight," I said. "Phoebe Keith shouldn't be telling anyone what anyone checks out of the library. Secondly, if Tabby wants to check out *Our Bodies, Ourselves*, the *Koran*, the

Bahagavad Gita, the *Kama Sutra*, or anything else, it's her business, not yours. Got it? It's a free country the last time I checked."

Drusilla stuck out her gorgon chin, shook her long, pointed nose at me, quivered with indignation, and walked away. I was sure she and Ethel Hell and all the other old crones would have a good time running my name through the mud. Well, let them.

That would fix her wagon, I thought with barely controlled rage. I decided I needed a library book. The minute I got home, I ran for the car and drove myself to the library in about three seconds. I squealed into the lot, parked the Ford, and barged through the double doors like I was walking into the saloon in the old west. Too bad I didn't have my six shooters along with me. I felt in the mood for a little shootin'.

I walked directly up to Phoebe Keith and announced loudly, "Phoebe, I want to check out *The Joy Of Sex*. Got a copy?"

Phoebe blushed.

"Well, no," she admitted.

"Then you can get it for me on interlibrary loan, right?" I asked in a booming voice. "I really need it quickly. I haven't had any sex since the death of my husband three years ago and I've decided it's time to come out of my shell. I need a brushup though, since the last sex I had was the long married, boring, routine variety and I feel the urge for something unique and different."

I looked around, satisfied that Mrs. Thorpe and Mrs. Dillon, two elderly ladies from Shelbyville, had heard me. They were sisters. Both were short on brains and long on wind. Right now, they both looked pregnant with gossipy purpose. Mrs. Dillon headed for the exit. She probably wanted to be the first to make the announcement.

"Set it up for me, will you?" I queried in a booming voice. "And make it snappy, O.K.?" I asked enthusiastically. "I can't wait to get started! After all, use it or lose it! They say it actually gets better after menopause and I can't wait to find out!"

Phoebe's bulging eyes looked like she belonged in a cubist painting. Mission accomplished. Considering the fact that she looked like a Victoria's Secret model, she probably thought no woman over the age of forty remembered what sex was. She pulled out the paperwork. I leaned over the counter and gave her my best toothy crocodile grin while she took down the information.

Mrs. Thorpe set down her book with a bang and tottered quickly for the exit. I sauntered out behind her, whistling a catchy little Ramones song. It's a wonderful world.

I did a few errands on the way home. When I stopped in for some bread, I thought that a few people at Jane's Grocery looked at me strangely. Kelly McGuire, who owned the Gilded Lily Arts, was there stocking up on tofu and organic lettuce. She refused to speak to me, but that wasn't unusual since she, like her half sister Phoebe Keith, hated me anyway. But a few other people seemed rather uncharacteristically mum. Could it be that fifteen minutes was enough to start the gossip wheel turning? I breezed into Mike's Hardware for a few things and thought I registered more quizzical stares. I stopped and bought a coffee from Joni Devlin at the Coffee Buzz.

"Don't worry, Rhi," Joni said when I paid. "You're still a woman. Just do what comes naturally," she said in her musical voice which ran up and down the scale.

"Oh, I always do," I answered brightly.

I hadn't a clue what she was talking about.

By the time I arrived at home, the telephone message light was blinking madly. I pushed the message button.

"This is Didi! What is this *Joy of Sex* stuff? Can I be in this book club? Call me!" Click.

The second message was an anonymous male giggler. The third message was from Betty Bogens, the owner of Tarnished Tack Antiques.

"This is Betty Bogens, doll," she said in her coarse voice. "Just talked to Phoebe Keith. I can set you up with a date if you need one. Chucky and I know a lot of men. Call me!"

That was an understatement. Betty knew them all right, in the biblical sense anyway. There was another beep and another message.

"This is Stan. I, uh, just heard. I'm sorry I accused you of having an affair with LeCaptain. I don't think you should be reading *The*

Joy of Sex, though. It might be too shocking for you. If you need help just call me. Uh, with your car, I mean."

Click. Interesting. Another beep and a message, this time from Eunice.

"Hi, Rhi. I just got a call through the grapevine. Mary Alice Medina told Alice Schuttle who called Maida who called me. Skip was spotted at Mr. Tibbs Bar in Porcupine Junction flashing an awful lot of cash around, and he seemed inebriated. But it was the kind of inebriated which stems from a profound emotional upset, not happy drunk.

"Also, I have learned that Maida's sources have informed her that Babs O'Reilly is going to the county seat and checking ordinance maps. Babs was asking a lot of questions about Valerie Cooper's house. We thought that seemed significant because why would she want to buy that old thing? We heard her daughter may get a divorce and come home. Perhaps Babs thinks she can get the Cooper place for a song and set her daughter up there.

"And dear, let me tell you about the time I checked out *Creole Firebrand* from the library. It was a hot romance. Boy, did I hear about it! Anyway, dear, don't let it bother you. If you want to read filth, it's nobody's business but yours. Fayne has some novels under her bed that would knock your socks off. I'll borrow them from her if you want me to. See you at the office, dear."

There was a click and another beep.

"Yup, this is Paul Pavalik here. If you need sex, I'm your man. Remember, I'm good with my hands. And I think other parts still work, too. At least I'm willing to try to make 'em work. I always knew you were hot!"

He gave a croak and there was a click. God save us.

Chapter 14

Stranger in Town

Could I revive within me
Her symphony and song,
To such a deep delight 'twould win me,
That with music loud and long,
I would build that dome in air,
That sunny dome! Those caves of ice!
And all who heard should see them there
And all should cry, Beware! Beware!

--*Kubla Khan*, Samuel Taylor Coleridge

Dear Val,

This town was never kind to either one of us. We should run away together.

Luv U Always, Skip

I went to church on Sunday and marched myself straight up the center aisle to the first pew. Was it my imagination, or were people whispering as I passed? The sermon, delivered most boringly by Father Ryan, the younger priest, was about the evils of pornography. You would think such a spicy subject would have an intense interest quotient, but no such luck. As usual, it was a real snoozer.

I wondered why Father Ryan looked pointedly at me the entire time he talked. Just because my eyes were closing was no reason to glare at me. After all, I could be in a state of Zen, or I could be thinking about *The Joy of Sex*. Or maybe he, too, had read *Our Bodies, Ourselves*. Ha!

I guess no one suffered any longer under the delusion that I had ever had an affair with Sgt. Francis LeCaptain. The only bad part about that was that he would now start feeling less afraid of me and my need for male commitment and start hounding me again with his little ticket book. Perhaps the rumors about my man hungry nature would keep him away.

Guess Phoebe Keith was good for something after all, and her running off at the mouth had been a nice diversion from my real problem, which was finding Valerie's killer. Tabby was in danger and I needed to find a murderer before anyone else got killed. Where should I go for some advice?

Father Dunn was a good candidate. He came highly recommended. First of all, he was Eunice's youngest brother, which spoke well for him. Not only the Catholics but also the Lutherans were known to seek solace at Father Dunn's door. He was probably the most well liked and trusted man in town. Dollars to donuts, he wouldn't accuse me of checking out pornography at the library, nor would he blab my private business all over town.

Luckily, he was in when I rang the bell on Sunday afternoon. He was a balding little man, small in stature and big of heart. He always carried a pipe with him. Usually the pungent smell of cherry tobacco encircled his bald pate in a wreath. And best of all, you never needed an appointment to see Father Dunn. He was on call for God and man twenty-four hours a day, free of charge.

"Hi!" I said when he answered the door. "Got a minute to chat?"

"Always," he said and led me into a masculine looking office. His little dog Mickey trotted at our heels. The only place Mickey didn't go with Father Ray was the sacristy.

"I had a husband named Mick once," I said wistfully as I sat down.

"So I hear from Phoebe Keith," he said and smiled a delighted smile. "What do you need?" he asked, getting right to the point. My kind of guy.

"I don't know what to do with Tabby," I blurted out. That and a few other things, but she was as good a place as any to start out.

"Just do what you are doing," he said. "You're doing a great job. Tabby is a wonderful girl, a real keeper."

"Think so?" I asked, surprised. "That's not what I hear from all the old crones in town."

"I know so," he said with assurance. "Ignore them! They don't have anything better to do than be miserable. But what about you? You don't always have to go it alone and be the strong one, you know."

"Yes, I do have to. There is no one else to lean on."

"You are forgetting Someone who can shoulder any burden and all the troubles of the world," he said. "Give it to God. He'll help."

"Like you do?" I asked gently. Father Dunn smiled a rueful smile.

"Like I should," he said and drew on his pipe. There was a moment of peaceful silence into which came the ticking of the clock which bore the legend, *Tempus fugit.*

I glanced around at the deep, well worn leather armchairs and the book lined walls. Mickey the schnauzer sighed and closed his eyes, and into the room came a calm which only hovers near people infused with a spiritual light. Father Dunn was one of those people. He had the settled air of a man who has found his true calling. He was of the world, immersed in the world, and yet apart from it. He had that rare ability to be both highly spiritual and ideally human. How does one get to be so great? *If only I could do that*, I thought ruefully.

"And by the way," he said, suddenly sharp, "Continue on with that quest of yours."

"Which one?" I said.

"All of them, but especially the Valerie Cooper thing. There is a lingering evil revolving around her death, and I wish someone would get to the bottom of the muck and bring light and goodness where darkness and evil hold sway."

"Think I can do all that?" I asked and smiled at him.

"I think you're quite capable," he said, his ginger snap brown eyes penetrating. This guy was nobody's fool. "God gave you much strength and many talents. There's nothing wrong with following your heart to what God gave you, especially if you can use it for the common good. You must accept your destiny. You're a mover and a shaker, and I think you have quelled that part of yourself for way too long. It's time to let your true nature come forth. The gospel specifically tells us not to hide our talents under a bushel basket."

If he knew my true nature I'm not so sure he would want it brought forth. I gulped.

"So be it, then," I said, and rose.

"Good. I'm glad that's settled," he said. "God bless you. May God be with you." Coming from him, it didn't even sound corny. Then he smiled and added, "And luckily for us, you're fighting on the right side. I would hate to have you fighting for the devil. I think you could be hard to beat." We both gave a conspiratorial giggle.

At the door I turned and said, "But about Tabby, everyone says . . ."

"Don't listen to what everyone says. Follow your own heart," said Father Ray. "Tabitha is a thinker, not a sheep, and in my experience, thinkers usually at some point, turn to spirituality. Just be glad she isn't a sheep." I smiled and stepped out onto the porch. My shoulders felt about a hundred pounds lighter.

"She's definitely not a sheep," I said and turned to go.

"And neither are you, so get out there and kick some ass!" said Father Ray and closed the door. My eyes opened wide. Well! I guess I'll take that as a directive from the highest authorities. If Father Ray thinks I was put here to kick some criminal butt, then that's what God must intend for me. And who am I to question the will of God?

Chapter 15

A Crazy Little Thing Called Love

she laughed his joy she cried his grief
bird by snow and stir by still
anyone's any was all to her

> *--anyone lived in a pretty how town*, E. E.
> Cummings

Dear Valerie,

The thing about it is, you and I are so much alike. No matter what the world hands us, we're both winners.

Love U Always, Skip

I was sitting in a tree in the woods in back of Valerie Cooper's house watching Scooter O'Reilly lurking about. I had decided to scout out Val's house ever since I drove by and noticed Scooter's big black truck parked down the block.

The question was, could it be the big black truck I was looking for? Could Scooter be the murderer I was looking for?

There was a noise below. I looked down. Little Kaleigh Merriott, rascal, urchin, and delinquent in training, the unholiest terror this side of Lake Michigan, came up and planted her size five tennies squarely in front of the tree.

"Hey! Old lady!" she called up to me. I pressed my finger to my lips and said, "Shh!"

"What the sam hill are ya doin' now, old lady?" she lisped.

Her face was filthy, her clothes dirty, and her eyes wise beyond her years. I put my finger to my lips and shushed her again.

"I'm doing research on wayward children for the FBI, so you better get your little butt out of here fast, before you get put in a foster home somewhere in Canada, where you'll have to do laundry all night and work in a paper mill all day," I told her. "You'll never get to come home until you're grown up."

"Bull! Yer spyin' all over town ta see who offed Miss Cooper. Do ya think I don't know what's goin' on in this town? Think I was born yesterday? Gimme some candy an' I'll go away an' not tell on ya. If ya don't have no candy, I'll take money, ya kook! Everybody and their brother knows yer nuts!"

I gave her a steely glare. She folded her arms over her thin bony chest and glared back.

"You should join the mafia," I hissed. "Where is your mother?"

"Sleepin' it off with her boyfriend. I'm spose ta get lost."

She held out a grubby paw.

"Oh, all right," I said. "You made me cave in." I dug deep in my pocket, produced a five dollar bill and a chocolate candy. "Is that the price of silence? Do you know that this is blackmail?" I asked.

"No it ain't," she said. "It's extortion, just like on TV."

Out of the mouths of babes! I threw down the candy and the money.

"Go to Diane's Diner and get yourself a sandwich off the kiddie menu. And that's an order!" I said sharply.

"Stick it, old lady!" she lisped. She grinned, grabbed the candy and the money and ran off, her clothes flapping around her like rags on a scarecrow.

"And get milk to drink, not soda!" I called after her.

"You suck rotten eggs!" she called back and scampered away. At least she took off in the direction of Diane's Diner. I would be seeing her in court in the not too distant future. I shook my head and concentrated on watching Scooter break and enter Miss Valerie's house. His hearing must not be too acute because he didn't seem to have heard my conversation with Kaleigh. If he did, he wasn't paying any attention to it. He probably thought it was a domestic squabble between grandmother and child.

One thing I had found that tipped the scales of justice to my side was that people tended to ignore middle aged ladies like myself. Not only were we judged harmless; we were practically invisible. And no one cared enough about kids like Kaleigh to pay much attention to what they were doing. I might as well have worn a big sign around my neck which said, "Scooter, ignore me."

Scooter wrenched off a small basement window, set it carefully on the side of the house, and disappeared through the hole. Well, wasn't he special? Ten minutes later, he reappeared, replaced the window, and looked around furtively. When he glanced in my direction and squinted, I pulled down a branch with a clump of orange and gold leaves and hid myself. I peered through the leaves.

Scooter took out a cigarette, lit it, and took a deep drag. Then he strolled off in the direction of his pickup truck at the curb, just as pretty as you please, and all in broad daylight.

Well, I'll be dipped. If Scooter can do it, so can I. I waited until he started the engine and chugged off. Then I slipped down the tree, which was a lot easier than climbing up had been, except when I hit certain vulnerable spots. This tree climbing thing had been a lot easier when I was twelve.

All of a sudden, there was a loud crunch. I looked down at a broken glass. Next to it, there was another unbroken replica of the first. Gingerly I picked up the first glass. It smelled faintly of beer. The second glass still held traces of a cola drink and had partly rainwashed bright red lipstick stains. How interesting.

Did these glasses belong to Valerie Cooper? The one with the lipstick stain could be hers, but who drank from the other? I placed the glasses neatly up against the tree.

Then I strolled nonchalantly through the woods until I reached Valerie's back yard, glanced around, and bent down to wrench off the window just as I had seen Scooter do. I broke at least two fingernails in the process of prying off the window.

"Ouch!" I said. I placed the window against the house exactly as Scooter had and slipped in the window head first.

For a fearful moment, I thought I was stuck like Pooh Bear in the rabbit hole. Oh dear, this was embarrassing. *I do hope no one wanders by and sees my rear end caught in this window,* I thought. I vowed to go to Shapely Lady five times a week and eat forty percent fewer calories. That should help matters.

With a few tugs, some scraping, and quite a bit of mental cussing, I finally managed to drag myself through the hole and fall onto the cement with a painful thud. Maybe four times a week at Shapely Lady and thirty percent fewer calories would be enough after all.

Who in their right mind would want to be a cat burglar? There is no future in it, no benefits, no retirement plan, and plus that, you have to be young to do this type of thing, not to mention starved to the point of gaunt. I pulled myself up with a groan and looked around the dark basement for traces of Scooter. What had he been searching for? I examined the entire house. Nothing looked out of place.

There was the neat laundry room, the furnace, the dirt floor, the cupboard at the back of the stairs. Nothing interesting here. I climbed up the stairs to Valerie's old fashioned kitchen, the drab living room straight out of 1959, the shrine to Skip, the rose arbor. Nothing had changed. I went back to the kitchen and opened the dishes cupboard. Sure enough. There were glasses which exactly matched the two in the woods through the back yard.

Had Miss Cooper been entertaining Skip at the time of her death? Was there a late night tryst beneath the old oak tree? Or was it another man? Or had the murderer taken those two glasses out of the house and placed them in the back yard away from prying eyes? Or had he planted them there with Skip's prints on them to incriminate Skip? How long had they been there?

I climbed the stairs to the two tidy bedrooms and bath beneath the slanting roof. Neat, clean, and unremarkable. In Valerie's room was a rolltop desk with numerous cubbyholes which proved irresistible. I applied gentle pressure here and there, looking for a secret drawer, but I couldn't find anything. The bottom right door was stuck. I wrenched it open and voila! There was Valerie's diary, or pile of diaries.

I stared in wonder. Each diary was clearly marked through the years. I began reading eagerly, turning the yellowed, fragile pages. I speed read my way through Val's childhood and all American girlhood. I read about her parents, her friends, school, parties, clubs, college, and her job as a Home Ec teacher at New Belgium High School.

The diaries were exhaustive in their scope, describing each major event in Val's ordered life. The only thing which was conspicuous in its absence was any mention of Skip Winters. I realized that everything about Skip was no doubt in a separate diary which was well hidden somewhere in her room. And I would be lucky if I ever found that Delphic oracle. Val had probably squirreled it away somewhere well hidden from her mother's prying eyes. What I wouldn't give to get my hands on those entries.

The only thing in the diaries which yielded some food for thought was Valerie's perception of why she was put in the loony bin and what directly preceded it.

It seems that Valerie found our dear Principal Weaver, corporate CEO material and modern scion of technology and newspeak that he was, engaged in some extracurricular activity behind the stage door in the auditorium with young Ashleigh Kane. Ashleigh was Tabby's age, for Pete's sake. I always knew there was something seriously wrong with Weaver. Val wrote that she was so concerned about Ashleigh's scandalous behavior that after agonizing for days, she decided to speak to Principal Weaver about it.

He won't get away with this licentious behavior. I spoke with Ashleigh about the incident and told her that boys don't marry tarts. I had to explain to her what a tart was. Ashleigh laughed and asked if that was why I wasn't married. I'm afraid our Ashleigh is getting to be a little strumpet. I truly think Principal W has some explaining to do. I spoke to the principal. He became incensed and threatened to sue me for libel. He said he was comforting Ashleigh on the loss of her pet parrot. It didn't look like comforting to me. It looked like something far more serious. I wonder if I should have a talk with Mrs. Weaver.

Perhaps Val threatened to tell Mr. Weaver's perfect wife that their perfect marriage was a sham. Perhaps Val demanded that he go to counseling. Perhaps that was when Weaver tried to force Valerie to retire and she warned him that she would go public with her knowledge if he tried to force her to retire. In any case, Weaver retaliated by signing his name to have Valerie put in the old county home for a rest.

They're putting me in the rest home. They say it's because I'm exhausted and need a rest. They say I'm in a state of hysteria and nervous exhaustion. I think they're putting me in there to retaliate because I demanded that the principal stop his scandalous behavior and grow up.

I should have ignored his behavior like everyone else does. And I knew I should have agreed to learn how to use the school computer. I just gave them more ammunition for their lies about me. I can't believe

Ethel would do this to me, Ethel of all people.

She referred, of course, to Ethel Hell. So Valerie spent some time in the county home. She hadn't been treated badly there. It sounded like their mental health program consisted mostly of feeding her sedatives and letting her sleep her time away. When she got out and returned to her home and job, there was no more mention of Principal Weaver or Ashleigh Kane. I read on through each diary until the end. A lot of them were about movies, favorite recipes, memories of trips taken, or treasured childhood pastimes and playmates. Valerie retreated more firmly into the happy past.

Skip Winters was nowhere to be found, yet I was sure that he lurked in the background somewhere. There must be some paean to their love somewhere in Val's letters or diaries. I just had to dig deeper to find it. Or could it be hiding in plain sight somewhere? I remembered the story of the purloined letter and how my dad had said that the best way to hide something was to leave it where everyone would see it and overlook its importance.

I closed the last diary and sadly put it back with the others. Poor Val had endured so much treachery, so much betrayal. Was there no loyalty anymore? Why should someone so sweet and innocent have to suffer?

I looked around the room and my eyes came to rest on Valerie's closet. I couldn't resist a little wardrobe analysis. Valerie had everything stowed away ship shape. There were six pairs of flats, three pairs of heels, ten twinsets, two suits, ten A-line skirts, three slacks, two shorts, and twelve white blouses. I found one pink poodle skirt and a lot of surprisingly sexy silk underwear; probably the only indulgence which Valerie had allowed herself.

And everything was a disgustingly well preserved size six. Valerie must have been in possession of a small appetite, a good metabolism, and a firm will. I sighed and put everything away carefully. Oh, that Valerie and her little figure unspoiled by the passage of time! It was just no darn fair!

I retraced my steps downstairs, through the basement window, and back to the Ford which was parked not far from the spying tree through the back yard. Just as I reached the Ford, I felt a tap on my shoulder and almost jumped out of my skin.

"Yipes!" It was Sgt. LeCaptain.

"Mrs. Nolan," he breathed down at me through his moustaches, "I shouldn't have to tell you that trespassing is illegal, and breaking and entering a crime."

"So who is trespassing?" I asked. I folded my arms over my chest and glared at him. "Did you see me break and enter?"

"No, but I'm sure you were thinking about it."

"The last time I checked the Constitution, thinking wasn't a crime."

"But doing is a crime, isn't it?"

"Doing what?"

"You know."

"Don't worry, you won't catch me doing you know." I smiled at him serenely.

"I hope I won't!" he said, a look of self righteous indignation on his face. "And now I have better things to do than stand here arguing with you." Yes, like sleeping in the park and hanging out at Diane's

Diner. I watched him waddle back to his police car on his little tiny feet in their shiny little black shoes. I wanted to steal his shoe polish. I wanted him to suffer shoe polish deprivation. He turned around.

"Do you lie awake at night thinking up ways to drive me insane?" he asked.

"What do you think I am, a teenager?" I countered.

Chapter 16

Little Town Flirt

Thou'rt gone, the abyss of heaven
Hath swallowed up thy form; yet, on my heart
Deeply hath sunk the lesson thou hast given,
And shall not soon depart.

--*To A Waterfowl*, William Cullen Bryant

Dear Val,

Of all the women I have ever known, you are the kindest. You are the epitome of everything I hold dear, everything I admire, everything I love.

Love U, Skip

When I arrived at home, the girls announced that they were readying themselves for the date of the year. I heard much giggling and laughing from the bedroom while Tabby and Krystal tried on innumerable color combinations. When the masterpiece was finished, I could not believe my eyes.

Tabby came out wearing a leather mini skirt, midriff showing halter top, and what could only be described as hooker shoes. She had on lots of unpunk makeup, and her hair had been dyed blond and done up in curls instead of spikes. Her nails were painted pink to match her lips and her exposed flesh. She wore gold hoop earrings and a necklace of blue beads. And not only that; she had actually shaved her legs and her armpits.

My jaw dropped. This could only mean one thing. Had hell frozen over? Was she about to kowtow to the dominant patriarchal culture? Suddenly, I badly wanted my little rebel punk rocker back again.

"What's wrong?" I asked. "Why are you dressed like that?"

"Like what?" said Tabby.

"What happened? Is it Halloween? Did the body snatchers replace my daughter with a skinny version of Britney Spears?" I asked.

"Mother, you are so immature! I'm going out with Todd tonight," said Tabby. She flipped her hair over her shoulder and gave me a look which clearly told me what she thought of my fashion sense. "And Krystal, Brandon, and Trevor are going too. We're going to Shelbyville to hear Dog Eat Dog at the Black Bart Cafe."

"Oh, you are, are you?" I asked. "And is this what we wear on a date? Junior playboy bunny attire?" I crossed my arms over my chest.

"She wants to be a sex object like me," said Krystal, suddenly materializing at Tabby's side.

Krystal had taken out her tongue stud, dyed her hair blond, and dressed in hip hugger bell bottom jeans, crop top, and platform heels. She wore a ring on each finger and an earring in her belly button. The gap between the jeans and the crop top exposed rolls of flesh which would have been far better covered.

"What happened to you, Krystal?" I screeched.

"I want you to call me Petula. I'm changing my name again," said Krystal.

"You've already changed it from Constance to Krystal. I can't keep up with all these changes," I said. "Let's go back to punk rock. I liked it better."

"Punk rockers don't get the prep men," said Krystal firmly. "And we really want to start going out with cool guys."

"Sounds divine," I said. "I know you would love me to tag along but I have to beg off this time. I'll take a rain check."

"And Todd is driving. He just got his license. Isn't that cool?" crowed Krystal.

I could feel my blood pressure rise along with my cholesterol.

"What kind of driver is he?" I asked.

"Real good," said Krystal as she preened in the hall mirror. "He hasn't run into anything yet."

The doorbell rang. Todd was here. Oh, goody. Tabby swayed to the door and smiled coyly at Todd. Why must that boy look so full of testosterone? He oozed sex, with that shock of surfer dude blond hair and all those muscles. He gave me a perfect smile full of whitened male model teeth.

"Hi, Mrs. Nolan," said Todd. "How are you today?"

"Oh, just fine, Todd."

I gave him my best motherly smile and tried to think of thirty ways I could kill him if he seduced my daughter and broke her heart.

This kid was too socially skilled. It was unnatural in a sixteen year old. Was it my imagination or did Todd look like a wolf? He flexed his biceps. He must pump iron in front of the mirror every day. Wasn't he supposed to be a lanky, skinny kid covered with zits and the shadowy precursor of his first moustache?

I decided I liked Tabby's last boyfriend better. He had been a punk rock musician who barely spoke and sported a four inch blue Mohawk. He shopped at the flea market and covered his clothes with patches, safety pins, and duct tape. He was devoted to his art and didn't have time for socializing. He despised drugs and alcohol because they "would like, interfere with the purity of my music thing." His favorite pastime when he wasn't playing his guitar was watching the catfish races and the cow chip throw contest. Now that boy was normal and wholesome! What was Tabby doing with this androgen infested surfer dude?

The doorbell rang. Tabby opened the door again and two other boys walked in. This must be Brandon and Trevor. They looked almost as androgen soaked as Todd. Krystal simpered at Brandon and Trevor. I gagged. Oh, for the good old days of punk rock rebellion.

"Later, Mom!" called Tabby, and they all trooped out the door. One evening of fun for her, five hours of agony for me.

Later? That's the recognition I get for fifteen years of worry, work, sacrifice, and prayer? Bring in the chocolate.

I walked out to the porch and sat down in the swing. Zoro came and curled up on the rug beside me. I ran my hand through his thick fur coat and his soft ears. He lolled his tongue out and gave me his great doggy smile. What a comfort he was to me. If only humans could be so loyal.

Oh, the trials of life. Was I doing the right thing? *If only Dad were here,* I thought. *He would advise me. Dad always knew what to do, but what would he make of this modern world?*

My Dad always taught me to put my money into education and land. With an eighty acre farm in La Follette County, a law degree, and my two older teens enrolled in the University at Madison, it would seem that I had done just that. I ran true to family type.

In my family, we held firm beliefs in God and the clan. Banks fail, Wall Street crashes, nations declare war, cars rust, and houses blow down, Dad told me. Material things decay, but learning and the land will never fail you. He believed in my mother, God, his family, his clan, and his country, in that order, and nothing could persuade him to think any differently.

I cocked my head and listened. Did I hear Dad's voice telling me to trust my instincts, or was that the wind sighing through the trees?

The next day was Saturday.

"Mom," said Tabby that morning as I stacked the dishwasher. "You won't believe what I heard just a little while ago."

"Try me," I said.

"You know, Babs O'Reilly asked me to come and wash her windows today and said she would pay me twenty bucks, right?"

"Yeah, I'm aware of that."

"Well, get this. I walked down Red Oak Lane and just as I was walking up to the O'Reilly house, I heard Babs having a huge, screaming meemie fight with Scooter."

"Oh, really?" I asked, my interest piqued.

"Yeah, and it was like, freaky the way she was screaming so the whole neighborhood could hear her. She was calling him all kinds of names and accusing him of having an affair and telling him to get out."

"You're kidding. What time was this?" I asked.

"I looked at my watch and I think it was about ten after ten," she said. "And what was really weird was, she screamed something about Valerie Cooper the cuckoo."

"I wonder what in the world that was about," I said.

"It was almost like she was accusing him of having an affair with Valerie," said Tabby and grabbed a chocolate chip cookie out of the jar.

"Valerie Cooper and Scooter? Please!" I said. "That is totally absurd. Valerie Cooper had no interest in any man but Skip Winters her entire life."

"That's what I thought," said Tabby and munched on her cookie. "And I never saw Scooter the whole time I was there. It was like he was having a time out or something. So I just took the window washing stuff and went outside and did all the windows. It didn't take me too long and Babs paid me and then I left. And I didn't hear them fighting anymore. And she was real fakey nice to me, too. You know the way she is."

"Oh, yeah," I said.

"And do you know what else I heard from Krystal and the girls at school?" asked Tabby.

"What?" I asked and started to stack up the clean dishes.

"I heard there's a cat thief going around town stealing poor, defenseless cats."

"That's crazy," I said. "Who would steal cats?"

"Somebody who is real, real creepy," said Tabby and reached for another cookie. "Who could harm a poor innocent animal?"

Lots of awful people, I thought, and opened up the cupboard.

"Don't listen to those rumors," I said. "It's probably just coincidence. Cats do like to wander. They will all turn up."

"Let's hope so," said Tabby. "I don't want to live in a town where some nut case is going around stealing all the cats."

I started to put away the clean dishes in the cupboard.

"I'm going upstairs to work on an art project," said Tabby. "Let me know if Todd calls, will you?"

"Sure," I said. *But not willingly,* I added to myself.

I finished my cleaning and decided to take Zoro for a long walk. The afternoon was golden, with a mellow sun bathing the September day in light, and a benevolent breeze stirring the leaves of the trees.

The wind took my spirits and sent them rushing upward to the highest clouds. I closed my eyes and felt a soaring rapture. Lately, I had been having moments like this. For no reason at all, a profound joy filled my heart and I seemed to fly on the wings of bliss to a higher state of being. If there is a heaven, then this is what it must be like. Such moments one feels in the first rapture of falling in love or upon the birth of a beloved child, or gazing at a great natural wonder. But was it normal to feel this way while walking in a sunlit meadow, contemplating the flight path of a sparrow, or upon seeing a bluebird or hearing a cardinal sing? The mundane world seemed to give me the highest, most spiritual joys. Maybe I was getting nuttier. Better not tell anyone or I'll end up in the loony bin. It doesn't pay to look too happy or people start to suspect you're not right in the head.

Was this a religious experience? It felt pretty darn close. Maybe I was about to become one of those super goody-goody two shoes. Oh Lord, can't I just be a regular half fallen Irish Catholic? I'm comfortable with that. This was just like when I was in eighth grade and God kept giving me the call to join the nunnery and I kept praying for the call to go away. Thank God it finally did!

Even the appearance of a humble spotted garden toad, or a lowly fuzzy caterpillar, or the buzz of the hardworking bumble bee in the lavender of the garden could take me by surprise and there I was, high as a kite with absolutely no chemical aid. What was happening to me? It was unsettling. It was scary. Was this a sign that I was about to die? I had, after all, recently revised my will and given Didi my instructions for my last earthly appearance. I told her to have me cremated and show an old movie of me when I was very young and very skinny. Vanity, thy name is me! What can I say?

Oh boy! In my clan we went fast; no lingering for us. Was this the sign that I was about to enter heaven, or at least plead my way past hell? Was I about to enter into eternal joy in the outer realms of the cosmos? That seemed too much to deal with. I didn't want to get overly happy. I wouldn't know how to act, and besides, people don't like you if you are too happy. They think you are uppity or on drugs.

After a long ramble, Zoro and I returned to the house and sat in the living room resting our joints and enjoying the peace and quiet. I popped a peanut M&M and pondered the possibility of staring eternal life in the face. Maybe I better just take a shot of whiskey and paint the porch. I looked out the window at the porch. Yes, it definitely needed paint.

Oh, no, who is that on the porch? Geez, can't I have a moment's peace?

It was Babs. There she was, nearly six feet tall in her high heels, tight jeans, and a low cut black tee showing way too much age spotted cleavage.

But wait a minute. Whoa! Where was the big eighties hair? Where were the sticking straight up bangs gooed with gel? Where were the pots of makeup? Babs looked bleached, whitened, and nearly her age. Something was very, very wrong.

I walked out the door before she had the chance to knock.

"Hi, Babs! What's up?" I said. The smile pasted on her face didn't reach her eyes, but then, her eyes always looked immobile, like doll's eyes.

"Hi, Rhi. Can I talk to you?" I hate it when people ask me that question. It always precedes something unpleasant.

"Sure thing." I sat in the rocker and gestured for her to sit on the bench.

"It's about something very serious," she said. "I've never told this to a living soul."

Oh, boy. Why do I always have to be the one they confide in? Is there something about me which begs to be told all the awful things you're only supposed to tell your priest or the shrink? I tried to look serious and encouraging.

"It's about Scooter," she said and looked down at the porch floor. "He was having an affair with Valerie."

"What?" I said. "No way! Valerie was in love with Skip Winters."

"That's what she wanted everyone to believe," said Babs evenly. "She went on and on about Skip so everybody would think she was crazy, but she was messing around with Scooter the whole time. Ever since forever, Scooter had a thing for Valerie and the feeling was mutual."

"I find that hard to believe," I said.

Babs' eyes grew wide.

"It's true!" she vowed and held up right hand. Her nails were unnaturally long and painted red with little lightning bolts of silver. Who could possibly do such art on such little canvases? I was so mesmerized by her nails I almost didn't hear her say, "Scooter loved Valerie."

"C'mon!" I said.

Babs grabbed me by the arm and looked into my eyes. I had a hard time not recoiling from her touch. She had a grip like an octopus.

"I'm telling you, Scooter had a thing for Valerie Cooper since he was sixteen years old!" she said. Now that she had my attention, she dropped my arm and stared intently into my eyes. "The only reason he never pursued her was because she was Skip's girlfriend. Skip and Scooter were best friends but there was competition too. You know how men are. They compete with everyone, even their best friend."

"Yeah," I said grudgingly. "I guess I can see that."

"After Skip dumped Val and took up with Melanie Barker, Valerie was hurt, and who do you think she turned to?" asked Babs, her eyes darkening. "Scooter, that's who, because she knew Scooter had a flame burning for her. She wasn't stupid, you know. She was very intelligent. She knew the score, and don't let that little innocent act of hers fool you. That was all for show. Even after Scooter met me and we got married, he and Val still had it for each other. Over the years our marriage fizzled but we stayed together for the sake of our kids, while his thing for Valerie stayed sizzling hot. My kids were off and gone long ago, and thank God they never knew their father was running around with Valerie Cooper the cuckoo."

I couldn't believe what I was hearing. I could not imagine Valerie falling for "that rotten Scooter O'Reilly" as she had called him.

"So what are you saying?" I said. "Are you insinuating that Scooter had something to do with Valerie's death?"

"I'm telling you that I think Valerie and Scooter had a lover's spat over Skip. Skip was coming for her. Don't you get it? Skip was really coming for Valerie. After all those years and all those women, he decided Valerie was the one and he had blown it. He was really going to leave Melanie and run away with Valerie. I know it!" she shrieked. "Skip was still in love with her, just the way she said! And she told Scooter, too. She told everyone, even Scooter, and expected all of us to be glad for her, glad that Skip was ready to leave Melanie for her. I mean, come on!

"I think Scooter went over to confront Val that night; either to run away with her or end it right then and there. I think that when Val told him about Skip, Scooter got mad and maybe he gave her a push. Maybe he didn't mean to hurt her, but she fell. Or maybe she was upset and accidentally tripped on her own and fell down the steps, but whatever happened, Valerie's dead and Scooter's gone."

I felt my jaw go slack.

"You mean Scooter has run away?" I asked in disbelief.

"We had a huge fight! He left me! He's gone to Florida! He always wanted to move there. I know that's where he went," said Babs and wiped a tear from her eye. Her voice broke up and she turned away to compose herself. She pulled a tissue out of her pocket and put it over her face. In a few seconds, she continued in a choked voice.

"Our daughter Gina is there and I think Scooter is going to stay with her for a while. He's had enough of me, of this place, of everything! And now, with Valerie dead, there is nothing to hold him here!"

She put her face in her hands and sobbed.

Well, ain't this a fine kettle of fish! Scooter was always in the background. Maybe Scooter got tired of playing second fiddle to Skip all his life. Maybe he was involved in Valerie's death after all. And Scooter likes to hunt. He owns guns and he owns a big black Chevy truck. Maybe Scooter was the one who was trying to scare the devil out of me so I would quit nosing around. Maybe Scooter got sick of always being the fall guy, the guy the girls overlooked and the coaches ignored. And maybe he decided to do something about it. Could he have murdered Valerie and stolen the money?

"Are you listening to me?" I dimly heard Babs say.

"Oh, yes, fascinating," I said, "but you know, I have a brief to write for a case I'm working on, so I have to run to the office."

"What do you think I should do about Scooter?" she asked and sniffed.

"I guess you should report him missing," I said. "Sgt. LeCaptain might have spotted him somewhere. Maybe you should tell him about it."

Babs pursed her lips.

"Oh, yeah, like he's gonna do anything," she said. "That idiot couldn't find his way home with a map."

I shrugged.

"Just a suggestion," I said as she stood to go. "I'll bet you anything Scooter will come back home soon. I think you shouldn't worry. He'll find his way home again."

I gave her my best comforting smile. Then I watched her walk down the drive and stomp onto the road in her high heels. She never would have made Hollywood with that clodhopper walk of hers.

Two minutes later, I was out the door, into the Ford, and on my way to Valerie's house. That story about having to do a brief at the office was bunk. I needed to do some investigating.

Chapter 17

Breathless

For some we loved, the loveliest and the best
That from his Vintage rolling time hath pressed,
Have drunk their Cup a Round or two before,
And one by one crept silently to rest.

--*The Ruba'iyat of Omar Khayyam*, trans. by
Edward Fitzgerald

Dear Valerie,

Only the best of people can truly forgive.
I believe you are one of those people. Please
keep loving me,

Yours, Skip

Over the hills and through the woods to Valerie's house we go. I had seen something that niggled at the corner of my mind. Now what was it? I drove to Viola Street, parked the Ford, and walked nonchalantly down the block, trying to look inconspicuous. It wasn't too difficult because Valerie only had two near neighbors, and neither of them cared much about watching Valerie's house.

Across the street there was fat Kenny *Blubber* King. He was only twenty-five, but already Kenny was set in his ways. The only thing he cared about was washing his truck, leaving work at the Diamond Packing plant, and going home to his Polish sausage and his beer. In fact, right now he was sitting on his stoop stuffing his face and swilling down a cold one.

I smiled at him and gave him a friendly wave. He frowned, squinted, and gave me a blank, brainless stare. Then he scratched his fat gut, belched, and spit into the weeds. I was quite sure he was completely uninterested in me, Valerie's death, or the state of the world. As long as there was Polish sausage and beer, who cared? Yup, Blubber was a prime example of a modern Falstaff. I'll bet he had no idea he could have played Shakespeare to a packed house, nor did he care.

"Hey, Kenny!" I called. "You want to meet a nice girl? I know someone who's looking for a guy."

I didn't know someone who was looking for a guy but I just wanted to see if he could show a spark of interest in anything beyond his immediate needs.

He looked puzzled.

"I don't wanna date nobody," he said indignantly. "Wimmin are trouble anyways."

You got that right, Blubber, I thought. *Women are indeed trouble, a trouble you'll never have to worry about.* I smiled and shrugged.

"Oh, Kenny! You're such a kidder!" I called out. He raised the beer bottle to his lips, drained the bottle, wiped his mouth on his hand, and said, "I ain't kiddin'!"

God save us.

To the left of Valerie's house sat a white shingled falling down shack with a worn dirt yard full of half dressed grubby children, discarded toys, and tiny bicycles. The Cranes and their many children lived there in squalid splendor. Jim Crane drank and caroused while Jeannie Crane tried to keep the wolf from the door.

She cleaned houses and took in laundry to keep the kids fed and half clothed while Jim held up the bar at the Pickle Jar. Nights and weekends Jim drank and Jeannie babysat, so the house was bursting with even more kids than usual. Jeanne was a saint who never complained or blamed her husband for their plight. Jeannie claimed she was just happy Jim wasn't a violent man. He was a good family man even if he did drink, and God had given them many blessings in their children, she said. A few too many, I would say. I guess attitude really is everything, and if cockeyed optimism makes for a long life, Jeanne should live to be two hundred years old.

At this moment, Jim's car, a battered Chevy, was gone and the myriad little darlings were engaged in an intense race on their trikes.

Confident that no one was interested in my comings and goings, I traipsed around the back of Valerie's house to enter through the basement window. But to my surprise, the window was gone, and where it had been was a cement block.

"Well, I'll be dipped," I whispered. "Looks like I'm not getting in this way."

Whose bright idea was it to block up that window? The nerve!

I strolled around the house to the front door and tried it. It was open, so I walked in. Our dear Sgt. LeCaptain must have been here and left things unlocked as usual. I peered around the first floor. Everything seemed unchanged, so I climbed the stairs to Valerie's cozy bedroom under the slanting roof and went immediately to her desk.

There, at the bottom of a pile of her ungraded papers, notebooks, and teacher's activity books was a cardboard box tied up with a red ribbon. I untied the ribbon with trembling fingers. Aha! Dad was right! Treasures are best hidden in plain sight.

I hit the jackpot. It was full of love letters. And every one was signed with love from the sex god himself, Skip Winters. Oh, boy! Am I good or what, hey, as we say up here in the north country.

I took out each aged piece of paper and gently unwrapped it from its envelope, read it, and carefully replaced it again. It appeared that the letters were grouped by year, with each bundle tied up with a different color ribbon; pink for 1956, blue for 1957, yellow for 1958, and red for 1959. Yes, Skip the sex god had indeed been in love with Val, and here was the proof in black and white. He may have flirted around a lot but clearly, Val was the chosen one. And these letters brimmed, boiled, and burst with hot adolescent emotion.

Oh, Skip! Now where did you learn to write like this? Lord Byron himself couldn't have wooed his lady love more artfully; the passion, the drama, the lover's spats and the glorious reunions, not to mention the oblique references to what was, no doubt, going on in the 1957 Chev parked in Lover's Lane. No wonder Val's heart was taken hostage. This guy was one smooth operator, just as I thought.

I guess heartbreakers are born, not made. It would appear that Skip never needed lessons.

I sat mesmerized through every juicy paragraph, every term of endearment, every phrase figuratively chock full of male hormones spewing over the page. Guess I had forgotten how adolescent love feels. I'm not sure I want to remember. For every glorious moment there had been at least five of frustration, anger, misunderstanding, jealousy, and some of the finer passions, not to mention raging rivers of adolescent lust. Thank God I never have to go through that again.

Wait! What am I saying? I've been through it with Matt and Jennifer, and it would appear that Tabby is just about to put me through the cuisinart of love again. Oh, Lord! And then there is Stanley waiting in the wings of my consciousness. What am I going to do about Stan? I don't think I can stand any more love trauma.

And yet, the heart has its stealthy ways, and no one knows better than I do how insidious a thing love can be. Just when you think it's a disease you have developed immunity from, it sneaks up behind you and clobbers you over the head and there you are, down for the count and drooling, as laughable as the king's own fool. It was enough to make me cry, if I ever cried that is. I sighed and returned to Val's letters.

High school for Val had been one long glorious victory; cheerleader, homecoming queen, most popular girl, yearbook club, band, straight A student, and Skip's own darling girl. But the end of 1959 was the end of the dream. That was the year Valerie graduated high school and went on to teacher's college at the local community college in the fall. The letters continued red hot through the summer after graduation and the first few months of the new college year when Skip went off to university at Madison. Then abruptly, they ceased altogether with no explanation.

The explanation was sex bomb Melanie, no doubt. Poor Valerie. I put everything away exactly as I had found it. I glanced around the room. There at the foot of the bed was a wooden cedar chest. Now how had I overlooked a hope chest ripe with snoop possibility? I walked over to it and lifted the lid. It opened slowly, with a creak which sent a shiver down my spine, and rendered up its treasure;

Valerie's hopes for the honeymoon that never was. I put my hand on the silks and satins, the beads and the frills, all the soft, feminine finery which Valerie's modest salary could afford.

A tear fell onto the satin and smudged it. Tears I never wept nor admitted to, except perhaps in secret, fell from my eyes. Oh, Valerie, you are breaking my heart. I kneeled down beside the chest, leaned my head into the crook of my elbow, closed my eyes, and let my right hand dangle down into the chest.

And entirely by accident, I struck pay dirt. Tucked down into the corner of the satin was something hard and square. I opened my eyes and brought it up. It was a box wrapped in white satin and tied with a red ribbon. Again, with trembling fingers I untied the ribbon, opened the box, and discovered the stash of recent love letters from Skip.

There was the familiar handwriting; not an illegible scrawl, but a beautifully scripted and sculpted hand. And here was the proof that Skip had indeed, again courted Valerie with all his considerable charm, and from the looks of things, he was dead on serious.

I sat for a long time reading through every letter, and my final analysis of the situation was that Skip was telling the truth. He did love Valerie. He had always loved Valerie, and he fully intended to prove it. He, like Valerie, lived in the past, in a dream world, in the world he and Valerie came from way back in 1959. It would appear that Valerie Cooper was not the only fool in love.

I finished the last of the letters, tied them up exactly as I had found them, and lowered the cover of the hope chest.

After making sure that everything in the room was just as I had found it, I descended the stairs and headed for the front door, but just as I passed by the kitchen, I heard something.

I jumped. What was that? I froze and listened intently. It sounded like a meow. A cat in Val's house? How could that be? There it was again, more distinct this time, and perhaps there was more than one cat. I followed the sound to the basement door.

This time the thick metal door was closed, latched, and locked with a skeleton key. Beyond the door I heard a distinct meow. I unlocked the door and opened it slightly. Out squeezed a fat Persian cat; an unhappy cat who opened his mouth and meowed long and hard at me.

From down in the basement I heard more meowing. Was this where all the disappearing cats had gotten to? If so, how had they gotten in the house? Had they come in through the basement window before it had been cemented up? Had they wandered in through the front door which may have been left ajar? Or had they been kidnapped and stuffed into the basement for a cruel joke?

Slowly I crept down the stairs, following the sound of the steadily meowing cats. At the bottom step I turned and looked around. I don't know how many cats there were, but even though I am an animal lover, it gave me the creeps. Way too many hungry, scared, and angry cats inhabited this basement.

And there in the corner was something much worse than that. There was a lump of human flesh which was definitely not alive. It was Scooter, looking very still and very white, and he had an anguished, tortured look on his face, as if he had died in a great deal of pain. Oh, dear. This is too terrible for words.

Behind me there was a noise. I turned and almost jumped out of my skin. I looked up at Skip Winters, and he didn't look happy.

Chapter 18

He's a Rebel

I am a lady young in beauty waiting
Until my true love comes, and then we kiss.

--*Piazza Piece*, John Crowe Ransom

Dear Valerie,

You are the only person in this world I know
I could trust with my life.

Love, Skip

I almost fainted with fear. Skip looked big, taller than I remembered him to be, and again I realized how amazingly well preserved he was in the muscle department. His arms looked like the proverbial iron bands of Longfellow's blacksmith. The cats meowed and rubbed against my legs. Had Skip come to get the money that was still hidden somewhere in this house? Had he killed Valerie? Had he killed Scooter? Was he about to kill me? He looked wild-eyed and crazy.

"Is it you?" he whispered. "Are you the one who killed Valerie?"

"No!" I cried, my eyes tight with fear.

He came closer, towering over me, his eyes dark and scary. I remembered how Tabby had described Skip as a gothic beach boy. There was something beautiful and menacing about him. Why hadn't I seen it before? Why hadn't I noticed the crazed look in his eye? His breath smelled like hundred proof booze. Had this man never heard of personal space?

I felt the world fall away from me. I almost blacked out.

"I just came from putting roses on Valerie's grave," Skip whispered. He loomed over me.

"A nice gesture," I managed to croak out. About forty years too late, but nice. His eyes flicked to Scooter's dead body.

"I think that whoever killed Valerie has also killed Scooter," he said and stared into my eyes. In the semi-darkness, his gaze seemed hypnotic. I nearly forgot where I was. Snap out of it! Think, I told myself.

"Did you kill Scooter?" he asked and frowned at me.

"No!" I screamed up at him. "I didn't kill anyone! I didn't kill Valerie! I didn't kill Scooter! I don't want anyone's money! I think you did it!"

His face contorted. He raised his hands and covered his face. Had I sparked him into a fit of rage? Was he about to kill me with one well aimed blow? I calculated how hard it would be to push past him and run for the door. He was so big it appeared hopeless.

Suddenly, he crumpled, folded, and went down on his knees. His body was racked with great sobs.

"Valerie!" he cried. He grabbed my legs and put his head on my left hip bone, just where it used to stick out before it got covered with unwanted flesh. Oh, God, I need help. I need some serious help here. I'm in the basement with forty cats, one dead body, and one crazed maniac who may or may not be a murderer. I do not like crazy semi-strangers invading my space, let alone my formerly svelte hipbones, even if I did dance one dance with him in a smoky bar.

I forced myself to remain calm.

"Well, maybe you didn't do it," I said to the top of his blond head. My lips trembled with fear. The sobbing stopped and there was a great heaving of breath in and out. "No, I don't think you did," I continued desperately. "I think you loved Valerie too much to do anything like that. You wouldn't do anything to Scooter. He was your best friend. I don't think you could murder anyone."

Especially not me. Tell me you wouldn't even think of committing murder.

"I didn't do it! I didn't do it!" he blurted out between gulping great lungfuls of air. Was he trying to convince me or himself?

"That's good," I said in as soothing a voice as I could conjure up. "Perhaps you would like to help me find the one who did do it." The sobbing stopped. That's right. Give him a plan of action. He looked up. Then he grabbed my arms and hauled himself up to a standing position. He towered over me again and looked down.

"I don't think I can do that," he said slowly, like a man who has had a stroke and has to weigh and measure every syllable. "I'm not clever enough. But you, you can do it. You are strong enough and smart enough to find out who did this awful thing."

Was he serious or was this a bad acting job?

He grabbed my shoulders and squeezed. His hypnotic blue eyes looked dark gray and cloudy in the dim light, and they stared straight through me. I was just about to cry out in pain when suddenly, he let go and blindly turned and ran.

I stood frozen in fear, afraid to run after Skip and afraid to turn and look at Scooter's corpse. My mother said there would be bad days, but hell's bells! I put my left hand on the wall and felt my way to the steps like a blind man. Then I prayed my slow and trembling way up the basement steps, hoping against hope that Skip had not locked me in the basement with the cats and the corpse.

I emerged thankfully into the bright light of the kitchen, pulled my cell phone from my pocket, and dialed nine one one with shaking fingers. There was a fine film of fear and perspiration over my entire body. I felt pale and sick.

LeCaptain's voice, maddeningly slow and deliberate, came on the line.

"Good evening. This is the New Belgium Police Department. Sgt. LeCaptain speaking. Can I help you?"

"O.K. skip the greeting," I said. "Rhi Nolan here."

"This is not Mrs. Nolan's voice," said LeCaptain. "It sounds too shaky."

The man was too exasperating for words.

"Perhaps you would like to examine the chip embedded in my fingernail to make sure that I am whom I say I am," I said.

"On second thought, that must be you," said Le Captain and sighed.

"Once again, this is Rhiannon Nolan. I've solved the mystery of all those missing cats. I'm at Valerie Cooper's house and I've got lots of starved stray cats and another dead body here in the basement."

"Oh, no. Who is it this time, Mrs. Nolan?" sighed the cheese head's Poirot.

"Scooter O'Reilly, and he doesn't look pretty. You better send out the whole team."

"Have you made a positive I.D.?" asked LeCaptain.

That old song from childhood ran unbidden through my brain. The worms crawl in, the worms crawl out.

"Positive I.D.? No, it might be Winnie the Pooh! Yes, I'm positive!" I screamed.

"Are you sure he's dead?" he asked.

"What do you mean, am I sure he's dead?" I screamed into the phone. "Do I have to see maggots crawling in his skull? Is the Pope Catholic?"

"Well, yes, why?" asked LeCaptain.

"Because Sheila's a punk rocker now! Get your butt over here!" I ordered in a voice which was beyond hysteria and hung up the phone. Why, oh why, Lord, do you always require me to deal with this idiot? I could cry from sheer frustration. I would like to go utterly and completely mad but I won't. I concentrated on breathing. Calm, I told myself. I am calm. I am the ocean. I could cry but I won't cry. No, I won't cry. Do anything, but just don't cry, I told myself. I grabbed onto the kitchen counter and forced myself not to run.

Eventually, the usual suspects showed up. Mr. James DeBrall, the coroner, arrived accompanied by an ambulance, an officious assistant, and Sgt. Francis LeCaptain. After much weighing, deliberating, and officiating, death was determined to be caused by a severe allergic reaction.

Doctor Sidney Jones was called. He was just about to tee off at the golf course but he breezed in within minutes in his knit shirt and khaki golf slacks. Doctor Jones always seemed to appear and disappear like Mercury. He darted about swiftly and silently with efficient, deft movements. He was a small, balding man with pale, thinning hair and freckles.

He descended into the basement and a few minutes later, reappeared and confirmed that Scooter O'Reilly had a severe allergy to cats. Scooter also had no inhalers on his person. The basement window had been closed up with cement block and the upstairs door, which was metal, had been latched and locked. Scooter had accidentally gotten trapped inside Valerie Cooper's basement with a blessedly suspicious lot of stray cats. He had no phone, no inhalers, and no way out. How convenient that had turned out to be for someone, but not for Scooter.

On top of it all, they called Babs to come down to the scene and claim Scooter's body. Then they wrapped him in a body bag and threw him in the ambulance while Babs looked on. Big mistake as far as I was concerned. Babs came in weeping and wailing and gnashing her teeth like she was doing Broadway. She went out wringing her hands and sobbing. Very touching. Just about enough to gag me, it was.

"He must have come to steal some of the money that was rumored to be in Valerie's basement and got caught and trapped down there with all the cats," wailed Babs. She sobbed pathetically into her masterpiece of a manicure. "I begged him to take his inhalers everywhere but he never would listen! If only he would have carried the cell phone I bought him for Christmas! He might be alive right now!"

The great ones agreed that it was all a horrendous accident. The stray cats must have wandered into the house and down the basement to find shelter, they said. Scooter had undoubtedly been nosing around Val's house. He was a known snoop, not above doing a little poaching, or stealing, for that matter.

Perhaps he believed the money rumors to be true and came to see if he could score a little cash in Val's basement. He must have been searching for the money ever since Val's death. After all, many of the townspeople had believed for years that Val's parents had hidden a fortune somewhere in the house and Val had never bothered to excavate it.

The latch to the basement door had fallen closed and the more Scooter struggled the tighter it had become. He couldn't kick the door in because it was steel, though he had obviously tried. He didn't always carry his inhalers. There were no windows to break since the one window we had all used to get into the basement had been discovered and cemented up. The rest of the basement was cement block with no way out Poor Scooter had died of a severe allergic reaction. But was it by accident or by design?

Sgt. LeCaptain took a statement from me. I said nothing about Skip Winters. I had to think things through. I confessed that I had been in the house looking through Valerie's love letters in the hope of finding some evidence.

"Mrs. Nolan," sighed LeCaptain. "How many times do we have to warn you to mind your own business? Valerie Cooper's death was an accident. Scooter O'Reilly's death was an accident. You are a lawyer with no knowledge of police procedure. You have to keep out of police business!"

I stared at him.

"Are you aware that you could be arrested for trespassing?" he asked. I looked noncommittal.

After several minutes of the go and sin no more lecture and dismissal, I was free to go. When I left, I saw Tiffany Winters strolling Emma past Val's house.

"What happened?" she called to me. "Why is LeCaptain here? I just saw Grandpa a while ago and he was crying and wouldn't talk to me."

"Scooter is dead," I said. "You better go home and take care of your grandfather. He is in a bad state."

Tiffany put her hands to her mouth. The tears welled up in her eyes. She turned abruptly and wheeled the stroller off at an amazing rate of speed. Emma banged her teddy bear's head on the bars of her stroller and screamed, "Go! Go!"

So I took Emma's advice and drove to Didi's house, where I consulted with my dear Watson into the wee hours of the morning. The consultation centered on why cats were found locked in the basement with Scooter. Those cats were not strays. I believed that I had seen some of them before, chasing little Emma and Olivia around Melanie Winters' house. And others of the cats had looked familiar too. I think a lot of people in town were missing their beloved pets. I hoped LeCaptain found their owners because I didn't feel like starting a kitty delivery service.

There was no funeral for Scooter. On Tuesday, Babs held a small memorial service at the grave site instead. We all stood by uneasily while a non-denominational prayer was said. Babs and her daughters threw white roses on the casket and sobbed as Scooter was lowered into the ground.

The daughters were tall, blond Nordic types like Babs. There was Gina from Florida with her husband and two kids, and the other daughter Sabrina, who had flown in from Detroit with her daughter. Behind Babs and her daughters and their families stood Skip, Melanie, and the whole family, looking pale and chastened.

Skip looked like he had given up the ghost. First Valerie, and now Scooter. To lose two such important people in so short a time must surely be taking its toll on him. But was it grief or guilt that I saw registered on his face?

Chapter 19

Harbor Lights

Lay your sleeping head, my love
Human on my faithless arm.

--Lay your sleeping head, my love, W. H. Auden

Dear Valerie,

*One of my favorite memories is of you
and me out on the lake in the Lund with
the Mercury cranked, or even just the times I
fished while you read your poetry books. We
had some good times. The best times I ever
had were with you.*

I Love You, Skip

The week went by in a whirl of activity at the law office. On
Sunday I thought I deserved a treat. I suggested to Didi that we take
her little fishing boat out on Loon Lake and make a day of it. We
packed a picnic lunch and a cooler full of soda and set out. The sun
was high and warm in a bright blue sky, and the air fresh with the
promise of a halcyon autumn. The water was clear and soft. The
boat slid through the water swiftly and silently. A few fluffy clouds
were reflected in the mirror of the lake, with nary a ripple to mar
the image. It was a day designed to make me forget murder and
mayhem, the kind of day one treasures.

What I know about a boat can be confined to a few words; put on
life jacket, turn key, steer, hope for the best. If anything goes wrong,
get a man to fix it. That's why God gave men mechanical ability,
to fix things so I don't have to worry about it. I never think about

things like getting up in the morning and checking the gas gauge right before we set out and before I get to the middle of the lake. Who would think of something like that?

Suddenly the motor sputtered and went silent.

"Oh, dear," said Didi. "What's wrong?" I looked at the gas gauge.

"Oops. Houston, we have a problem here. No gas."

Didi started to swear at me.

"Idiot! Why didn't you check the gas gauge before we set out?"

"Hey! I'm your friend!" I said. "Don't treat me like a husband! I swear I looked at that gauge last night and it was full! I must have read it wrong. Besides, it's your boat so you should have checked the gas gauge yourself this morning!"

A shot rang out and a bullet whizzed past our heads, effectively ending our argument. It would appear that someone was shooting at us with a shotgun.

"Lie down!" I said. We ducked. More shots rang out and sang through the air.

Geez! Why was everyone always trying to kill me? Mopin' Moses in a mosh pit! Jumpin' Joseph on a pogo stick! Nobody ever tried to kill Miss Marple!

Dear God, I prayed, I never really thought I would die in a little fishing boat in the middle of Loon Lake, La Follette County. I had something a little more cozy and peaceful in mind, like dying in my sleep at age eighty-five, with my children and grandchildren keeping watch and praying for my soul, having had plenty of lead time to make their perpetual peace with me for the way they treated me when they were teenagers.

So you see, dear God, I really can't get my head shot off in this stupid boat. It just wouldn't look good in the obituary. So if You would please strike that wanna be murderer out there dead with one well aimed lightning bolt from a blue sky, I would really appreciate it. Thank You, and by the way, could You consider throwing that big Stoegbauer case my way so I can manage to pay the rent this month? You see, I really am grateful for all You have given me, and I would be even more eternally grateful if pot-shot Pete out there ran out of bullets or shot himself in the foot.

As if on cue, the shooting ceased. I knew God wouldn't let me down. Had the phantom run out of bullets? It would seem so. After all, there must be a limit to how much ammunition one could tote through the woods and not look suspect.

Didi and I slowly brought up our heads and peered cautiously over the side of the boat. Didi was beside herself with indignation.

"With the way news travels at the speed of light in this town, you would think a posse and a search and rescue team would have appeared twenty minutes ago. Are they all hearing impaired? Where is LeCaptain when you need him? Did no one hear the report of that gun echoing through the woods and across Loon Lake?"

"Oh-oh, I think we're in the twilight zone, Didi. It's you, me, and one really poor shot who just happens to be a crazed homicidal maniac."

Didi put her head over the side of the boat and threw up.

"What are you doing?" I yelled. "Do you want to make me sick? Stop it!"

She flipped me the bird and went on barfing. I turned away and swallowed hard. Oh, Lord, please stop me from throwing up. I really hate it. I just don't do vomiting well. I waited until the gagging sounds stopped. Then I said without looking at Didi, "Are you finished?"

She made a sound like a wounded bear.

"That was very inconsiderate of you," I said. "You know how I hate barf."

"I'm scared!" Didi screamed, the sound of her voice echoing around the lake. "Do something!"

"O.K. No gas, no oars, no one in sight. Let's see, here. Looks like we paddle," I said.

"With what, Dick Tracy?" she yelled.

"You are in a really bad mood," I said in an accusatory way.

"Well, I wonder why!" was the snarly answer.

"With our hands, princess, we paddle with our hands," I said, and tried to hand paddle us to shore.

"This isn't working too well," I said after five minutes.

"No kidding, dummy," sniffed Didi.

Good thing for us we were on shallow Loon Lake. I ditched it for the water and waded through the weeds and the muck, pushing the boat while Didi sat slumped and sobbing. Poor princess, she just wasn't used to being shot at in the middle of a lake. I thought maybe talking would soothe her.

"I guess by now it's pretty obvious that someone nearly emptied the gas tank for us before we ever set out this morning. To do that he would have to have gone stumbling around your back yard in the middle of the night, which is highly unlikely. It's more likely that he saw us fooling around with the boat stuff today and when we went in to pack the picnic lunch and get ready, he fooled with the gas. He was bold enough to spy on us and steal gas right in your yard in broad daylight."

"Bastard!" cried Didi.

"And the way he shot that gun tells me he isn't familiar with firearms," I said. "In fact, he has to be a rank amateur if he couldn't knock us out of the lake with a gun like that. Who could it be?"

Didi sniffed in a conversational way and stopped sobbing.

"Unless he is a very good shot indeed and aimed each careful miss close enough to us to scare the daylights out of us, he sucks at firearms," said Didi, her voice growing stronger.

"Maybe whomever it was meant the shots as a warning to us to stop investigating Miss Cooper's death. Maybe we should mind our own business and give up this investigation," I suggested.

I didn't really mean it but I wanted to find out if Didi thought we should quit.

"And maybe the moon is made of purple earwax," said Didi. I smiled.

"I was hoping you would say that."

We hauled our bedraggled carcasses into town and went straight to LeCaptain with our story.

"Now you can't tell me that someone emptied your gas tank while you were preparing your picnic lunch. That is impossible. You said yourself you didn't check the gauge again just before you set out. Maybe you didn't read it right last night. And I highly doubt that someone was shooting at you with a shotgun. You know how impressionable you are, Mrs. Nolan. It must have been someone bird hunting in the woods," he said. "Possibly a shot went wild. No cause for alarm."

"Do you think six shots could have gone wild?" I asked sarcastically.

"Sometimes the report of a gun can seem awfully near when the bullets are quite far away," said LeCaptain, giving me a level look. I dripped lake water onto his polished police office floor and mentally cursed him.

"And sometimes people might be putting hallucinatory drugs in your coffee. Are you dropping acid? Does your secretary Gillian sprinkle powdered sugar denial on your donuts in the morning?" I asked sarcastically.

I stomped out, followed by a bedraggled and indignant Didi. I slammed the door on the passenger side of Didi's Peugeot in a huff.

"We need to report him to the proper authorities," she said as we drove away. "Who are his superiors?"

"I don't think he has any," I said. "I don't think he is a real police officer at all. He is a reject from central casting, some fool off the back lot of some long defunct cops and robbers television show masquerading as the village copper. This is all a bad dream and when I wake up, I'll be back in Madison, safe in the big city, far away from Scandal Acres."

But I wasn't safe, and when I did reach home, I found that the tires on my car had been slashed, apparently in broad daylight, and there was a note on my car which read, "You are dead!" in letters cut out of magazine print.

First I called LeCaptain and told him to come out and see the evidence for himself this time if he didn't believe me. He appeared with his little police notebook, looked at the tires, and said nothing. I didn't trust myself to say anything to him so I left him with Didi and went into the house.

I called Stan to come and haul away the car for a set of new tires. Then I went outside and sat on the porch waiting for Stan. He appeared with his wrecker within ten minutes.

"I think you should leave it alone," was his advice. "You're going to get hurt." He looked worried. I glared at him.

"They should leave me alone!"

He shook his head. LeCaptain shook his head too.

"I just don't understand why nobody likes you," he said. I raised my eyebrows at Didi.

"Maybe I just rub people the wrong way," I said.

"Well, we know that for a fact," said LeCaptain and started to write out the police report.

Chapter 20

Never, Never, Never Let Me Go

Splendours of the sun grow dim.
Stars are darkened by that light.
Thoughts that burn like seraphim
Throng thine inner world tonight.
Set thy heel on Death and find
Love, newborn, within thy mind.

--*Journey's End*, Alfred Noyes

Dear Val:

You don't know what a rotten time it's been without you. My mother told me I'd be sorry I didn't marry a nice girl like you. She was right.

Love, Skip

The day dawned clear and dry, with a brisk west wind. It was perfect walking weather. There was enough air tumbling about to clear the cobwebs from the brain. Zoro and I took a long stroll up the cliff road past the golf course. We walked down to Piney Point and stood on an outcropping overlooking Lake Michigan. The whitecaps rolled in to pound the limestone cliffs with a soothing, ceaseless rhythmic swell.

From the cliff I looked out on a blue sky. Below me, pine trees clung desperately for a foothold in the worn crevices of the crumbling, pitted limestone. The ground around me was damp from a recent shower. Zoro sat beside me, eyelids drooping, dozing in his half asleep, half awake, Zen contemplation of the universe; his happy dog nirvana state.

The pounding of the waves against the limestone of the cliff was so loud I could hear nothing, and both Zoro and I were in a trance like state, which accounted for what happened next.

Someone gave me an almighty shove in the back and I went sailing over the cliff. Before I had time to be scared, I had fallen to a small outcropping below the cliff, where I clung with all my might to a scrubby little tree growing sideways out of the cliff.

Above me I heard Zoro bark and attack. I knew he had his teeth in something, and I sincerely hoped it was someone's backside. There was a muffled human yelp of pain. I couldn't hear much because of the pounding of the waves, but it sounded faintly like a scuffle and then there was nothing.

Eventually, Zoro's face appeared at the edge of the cliff. He looked down at me lying on the rocky outcropping of limestone as if he were wondering why I was down and he was up. Even though I was in trouble and in pain, I almost laughed at his quizzical look and his cocked, furry face. It looked like he was saying, "What am I supposed to do now, you human idiot?"

"Why can't you be like Lassie and go get help? Are collies the only ones who do that?" I yelled to him.

Zoro barked and whined. Then he sat down and waited patiently for me to crawl up the cliff. I tried to scramble up the steep limestone and succeeded only in wearing myself out. It was a long way down to the roaring thunder of the water below which hit the cliff with such force I could hardly hear myself think. I put my hand to my temple and it came away with blood. I looked down at the worn away rock and the water thundering under the hollowed out cave of the cliff. It made me dizzy with fear and dread to think I was trapped. I thought the wound on my temple was just a superficial abrasion but what did I know? I had visions of slowly bleeding to death. I started to have that sick, panicked feeling. My breathing grew ragged and my entire body felt cold and rigid with fear. My palms started to sweat. I wiped them on my jeans and felt my cell phone, which by some miracle, had not fallen out of my pocket.

Oh, thank you God for modern technology! I'll never complain about it again, at least not until I'm well and safe and sitting in my living room drinking diet ice tea and eating dark chocolate, the richer the better. The thought of my cozy home brought tears to my eyes. I punched in the numbers with dirtied, trembling fingers and listened to the phone ring at Didi's house. I prayed she wasn't out playing tennis at the country club with Prima Donna Peaselee of the mean backhand.

"Hello?" I could barely hear but I was sure it was Didi's low voice. Thank God!

"Hi! It's me!" I yelled. "I'm on the cliff by Piney Point and I was pushed off and I'm down on the cliff wall. Can you get a rope and pull me up? Like now?"

"Are you O.K.?" she screeched.

"Well, there's some blood on my temple but I think it's just a little abrasion."

"I'm coming!" she screamed into the phone. I hope I didn't alarm her unduly. Yet, this was a bit of a sticky emergency.

Minutes later, I saw Didi's Peugeot race up the cliff road. For a second I was afraid she would do a Thelma and Louise on me and just keep going over the cliff, but she screeched to a stop about two inches from the edge, jumped out, leaned over, and screamed, "What the hell are you doing?"

At least, that's what I thought she said. The roar of the waves beneath my feet was so loud I had to read her lips.

"I'm waiting for you to rescue me!" I screamed up at her in a strangled voice.

"God help us!" she screamed back.

She grabbed the rope out of the back seat and tied it securely around the steering column. She dangled the rope down to me and I grabbed it, trying to ignore the pounding rhythm of the water beneath me. I faced the cliff, wrapped the rope around my waist and tied it in a slipknot. I noted with almost clinical objectivity that my arms were shaking.

I always knew those Girl Scout knots would come in handy someday, and I had tied the best slipknot in the neighborhood when I was a kid. Didi jumped in the car and slowly backed up while Zoro barked like Lassie and I tried to simultaneously scramble up the cliff and hang on for dear life.

No slightly chubby fifty year old woman with arthritis and a fear of heights should ever be forced to climb a cliff wall on a rope with the pounding spray beating just beneath her terrified body.

God, just let me live through this, I prayed. I'll give my entire fortune to charity after I pay off what I owe which could be a few years. Well, O.K., decades. I'll never swear again. I'll never lose my temper again. Well, O.K., we both know that's a lie. I'll give up chocolate for Lent. Seriously, I really will. I'll be a better mother. I'll never complain about having teenagers again. Really, I will. Just help me, God!

By some miracle I gained the top of the cliff. I paused, prone and thankful for the damp mud in my face. Didi turned off the ignition and ran over to me. Zoro came and licked my hair while Didi dragged me up from the dirt to which I clung with superhuman strength.

I sidled away from the cliff's edge and tried to block out the sound of the pounding spray beneath the earth. Didi got the rope off of me and forced me into the car as I tried hard to prevent my feet from leaving good old mother earth.

Once we were home, it took me an hour to stop shaking. After a shower and a good belt of whiskey, I sat wrapped in an afghan in the rocker in my living room, with Zoro at my feet and a box of dark chocolates at arm's reach.

Didi sat in the armchair next to me. I rocked mechanically back and forth, thinking of everything and nothing. Didi slept on the couch that night, her blond locks adrift over her triangular face. Poor thing; rescuing me had left her completely exhausted. I tucked an afghan around her before I went upstairs to bed and read Agatha Christie.

I must have drawn some inspiration from my idol, Miss Marple, for I was up before the dawn. I left Didi snoozing on the couch with Zoro beside her on the floor and tiptoed past them out the door.

By six o'clock, I was out on Piney Point with my nose to the ground, looking for footprints in the soft earth which had been washed by a rain shower the day before. I didn't find any footprints. All I found was some indentations, as if someone had poked the ground with a stick. I found one print I got all excited about until

I realized it was mine. There was a dog's print right beside it. Ah, well.

Suddenly, it struck me that the person who pushed me off of Piney Point had been attacked by Zoro. And where do you go to report stray dogs and dog bites? Why, you go to the police station, of course. If I were really lucky, there might be a hospital report from someone who had a large chunk of their back end taken off by a Siberian husky.

But I was not to be so lucky. Sgt. LeCaptain was not in the mood to cooperate.

"I need to know who filed that report!" I told him for the fifth time. "The person Zoro bit is the person who pushed me off Piney Point Cliff! He almost killed me! Don't you get it? If he went to the hospital injured from a dog bite he was the one who attacked me!"

"Mrs. Nolan, Mrs. Nolan," LeCaptain said in a voice oilier than his greasy black hair. "We all know how excitable you are. You probably slipped and thought someone pushed you. The wind can feel almost like a push when it starts howling up on Piney Point. And anyway, the citizen who filed the report, who must and shall remain nameless, was nowhere near Piney Point when the dog attack happened. It occurred down on the beach and it was a stray German shepherd, not your dog which did the biting."

"Well, duh! Of course he is going to deny where it happened and falsify the report! That's what criminals do! They lie, cheat, steal, and commit murder!" I felt like committing murder myself, murder of one idiotic policeman. "Is the citizen a man or a woman?" I asked.

Sgt. LeCaptain closed his eyes as if to block out the pain of my existence in his field of vision.

"Mrs. Nolan," he said with exaggerated patience, "I am not at liberty to disclose the sex of the citizen nor anything else."

I opened my mouth to protest but just as I started to complain, an idea hit me and I shut my lips and smiled my Cheshire cat smile at Poirot.

"You're right, Sergeant, and I'm glad you protect the privacy of our citizens so valiantly. It was my egregious error to expect anything short of excellence from you."

His eyes clouded with confusion.

"Yes, well, now that it's settled . . ."

"I'll be off," I said with a breezy smile.

I walked away whistling. Fat chance, ducky.

Chapter 21

Follow the Sun

Tis true, 'tis day; what though it be?
O wilt thou therefore rise from me?

--Break of Day, John Donne

Dear Valerie,

I curse the day I let you go. I was blind to let you go.

Love, Skip

The wee hours of the morning found me burglarizing the New Belgium Police Department.

Boy, am I getting good at this, I thought as I walked on silent rubber soled orthopedic shoes over the graveled drive to the back door of the municipal building, plastic in hand. I stole a glance around at the post office and the volunteer fire department where one red gleaming fire truck sat like a giant Tonka toy. My Ford was parked in back of the swimming pool near Katie's Kurly-Q. I twirled my plastic in the air. Hurray for me! Such a sleuth.

It turned out I didn't even have to use the credit card to try to unlock the door, and a bit of good fortune that was, because it would have taken a blowtorch to break in. There was a pretty hefty Yale lock backed up by a deadbolt. However, lady luck smiled on me tonight. LeCaptain had forgotten to lock the place up. *Leave it to that moron,* I thought gleefully as I slipped in like a shadow in the night. *Mission Impossible ain't got nothin' on me, babe.* I moved swiftly through the office, my trusty pen torch in hand, my black clad bod moving like a thin shadow through the stillness. Well, O.K., maybe not thin. Let's say formerly thin.

LeCaptain's desk was a pile of old rubble, fast food bags, candy wrappers, and safety directives. Unfiled reports from the last six months were piled here and there. They consisted mostly of stories in LeCaptain's illegible scrawl about stray dogs and cats, suspicious vehicles reported by nosy little old ladies, loud teenage parties, burning violations, and illegal fireworks. We were a peaceful lot in New Belgium, except for the stray incidental death which LeCaptain steadfastly refused to admit was homicide.

I found a scrap of paper with a note on it to LeCaptain from Principal Weaver.

> *Rumor has it that Tabitha Nolan is on drugs. She was the one to find Valerie Cooper's body. Perhaps she pushed Valerie Cooper down the stairs. Have you considered the possibility?*

I growled and gritted my teeth. Boy, that made me mad! Here we go with the drug accusations again. I think Weaver was the one on drugs. All that this note proves is that our dear principal is a lying passive aggressive type with definite issues, or is he something worse than that?

I rolled up the scrap of paper into a little ball and sent it on a perfect arc into the wastepaper basket.

I pawed through three piles of junk before I came to the dog bite report incident. To my great dismay, there was no name on the report. The complaint caller was listed simply as citizen. I could not believe it! All these Catwoman shenanigans and highly professional sleuthing techniques for naught? Sugar!

The door rattled. I dropped everything and ditched it for the one jail cell in New Belgium, which happened to be conveniently ajar. Someone flipped a switch and the place flooded with light. I dove onto the floor, rolled under the cot, and clung to the cement block wall.

The cheese head's Poirot was here. I could tell by the shuffle of his little porcine feet.

"Now listen," said his Eeyore-like voice, "I'm going to put you in the cell overnight for your own good. You're a menace to yourself and others."

"No, I'll be good! I won't drink no more tonight," begged some poor drunken sod.

"You'll thank me for this in the morning," said LeCaptain. To my horror, he dragged the drunken sod over to the cell, walked him in, sat him on the bed, left the cell, and locked the door. I clung desperately to the cement block wall through the whole process, sending up a fervent prayer that LeCaptain wouldn't notice me. LeCaptain threw the keys on his desk and retreated, once again leaving the police station unlocked. Was he always this lackadaisical about security?

Did it really matter? The only lock that mattered was the lock to the cell. I was left alone in a locked jail cell with a moaning, weeping mass of stinking humanity. I mouthed a silent, "Oh, hell!" when I figured out that the drunk was none other than smelly Arden Wasserschmidt, a.k.a., Skunk the Drunk.

"Oh, Mama!" moaned Arden. "Don't leave Arden! Don't leave Arden!" This was too painful to bear. I tried to cover my nose and ears at the same time.

Now, I'm just not a bodily functions sort of person. To me, labor and childbirth did not add up to a spiritual experience. It had been more like being trapped in the body of a Sumo wrestler straining to lift a five hundred pound weight; an athletic event of gargantuan proportions, but not pretty.

You might say that having children and dealing with poop, pee, spit-up, and vomit on a daily basis, not to mention the dirt and sticky grime and occasional scraped knee or bloody toe or cut finger, was almost more than I could bear. But at least it was my own offspring's bodily functions I was dealing with.

Arden "Skunk the Drunk" Wasserschmidt was bad enough to smell coming at you in the open air, but when confined in close quarters with him and his various bodily functions, noises, and smells, it was enough to make one sick. Getting the full effect of the Arden aura, the ambiance, if you will, accompanied by a cacophony of Arden sounds and olfactory overload of Arden smells was just too darn much. I buried my face in my sweatshirt and tried to drown out the smells and sounds of Arden emanating in disgusting rhythmic waves from his person. God loves everyone and so should I, I told myself as I gagged into my fleecy black Catwoman sweatshirt cuffs and prayed.

Oh, God, why can't I just be a normal soccer mom? God, if You get me out of here alive, I'll never do anything bad again. I'll give up sex forever. I'll never take another lover. O.K., that's easy because I'm not having sex now or in the foreseeable future and why would I want to show anyone, let alone a man I was attracted to, this middle aged lumpy body anyway?

All right then, let's say I'll give up chocolate forever if You just work a miracle and transport me out of here on angels' wings. That's right, forever; a lifetime of Lenten sacrifice in exchange for one small miracle. Seriously, that is not too much to ask. I mean, the Blessed Virgin has appeared all over the place. I'm not asking for a vision or for the stigmata or anything too complicated. I just want out of here. Like, levitate me beyond here or something, will You? Hey, You supposedly did it for Saint Peter when he was in chains, and he was just a sinner like everybody else. So I'm sure You can do it for me, too. I have complete faith in You.

I waited.

And then a miracle occurred, a miracle of sorts, anyway. Arden fell asleep, or shall I say, passed out. After a few snores and snorts, he went completely quiet. Perhaps he died in the bunk right over my head, in which case things would soon smell even worse. And to top it all off, my cell phone rang to the tune of Beethoven's Fifth.

I had completely forgotten that I had it in my pocket. I carry my cell phone around with me all day willing it to ring so I can take it out and look important, and will it ring? No, but it rings in the middle of the night in a Stygian jail cell under a dead stinking drunk when I'm supposed to be committing the perfect burglary of the ultimate evidence. Oh, yeah.

My heart just about collapsed in upon itself with fear at the sound. I fumbled madly for the phone and managed to drag it out of my pocket and press the answer key.

Above me, Arden snorted loud enough to wake himself up. He mumbled something in a coarse drunken stupor, his voice raspy with years of cigarettes and alcohol. Then he belched and started to snore again. I stopped holding my breath.

"What?" I whispered into the phone.

"It's Didi. Where are you? I woke up and had a terrible feeling that you were in trouble and needed me."

"Oh, thank you, God! I do believe in miracles! And I do need you!" I hissed into the phone. "I'm locked in the jail cell in the police station with Arden Wasserschmidt snoring in the bunk above me. Come and get me out!"

"Are you serious?" asked Didi incredulously.

"I've never been more dead serious in my life. And bring a respirator. I may need CPR by the time you get here. I'll explain later." I clicked the phone off and waited.

Within a few minutes, I heard the quiet purr of Didi's Peugeot outside. In another few minutes, the unlocked door clicked open and Didi, resplendent in powder blue silk pajamas with matching robe and slippers, appeared before my eyes. She stared at me through the bars.

"Did you comb your hair and put on lipstick before you came here?" I asked suspiciously. I rolled out from under the cot and crept silently to the cell door, where I stood impatiently waiting for Didi to open the door.

"You know I like to look presentable," she said. I groaned and Arden stirred uneasily and mumbled in his sleep.

"Why is it that in all those westerns it is so easy to break out of jail? I have no metal file, no bars to saw through, no escape horse waiting, and no broom to lift the keys from the desk. Geez! I'm feeling claustrophobic! Hurry up and get me out of here!" I commanded in a strained whisper.

"Oh, shut up!" hissed Didi as she fumbled with the keys, her violet eyes wide in the semi-darkness. "These stupid keys don't work and my hands are shaking. I'll just have to use the credit card." She pulled the card from her purse and went to work.

"I think it's time to retire from motherhood and detective work," I said.

"Shhh!" said Didi.

"Time to crawl to the top of a mountain, become a Zen Bhuddist, and recite my mantra all day," I said in a stage whisper.

"You won't be going anywhere if this thing doesn't crack open soon," she said. "And why didn't you use your own plastic? You have it with you, don't you?"

"Duh, I forgot it was in my pocket I got so upset," I said loudly.

"Just be quiet before Arden wakes up!"

"Whatever! Just hurry up!" I whispered.

"Why the heck do you have to go around investigating murder?" she asked through clenched teeth. "Can't you just sit at home and write witty, urbane novels or something?"

"I think Gore Vidal has that one cornered and besides, you have such poise that it's not often I get the chance to watch you go ballistic." I giggled.

"Then take up a hobby," she growled softly as she wrestled with the lock. "Now I know the truth. Those husbands of yours weren't disturbed to begin with, after all. It was you who drove them there!" There was a loud click and the lock gave way.

"How come your credit card works and mine never does?" I asked.

"You've got to get the gold card!" Didi said as she wrenched open the door to the jail cell.

"Oh, yeah, that makes sense. Why didn't I think of that?"

Suddenly, Arden snored so loudly he woke himself up. His bleared eyes stared at us. We froze. His mouth, with its three day growth of scraggly whiskers, fell open in stunned terror.

"Oh, I got the D.T.'s again!" Arden cried. He hid his face in his grubby hands and wept like a baby. Didi and I clanged the door to the cell shut, locked it, vamoosed out the door, and sprinted to Didi's Peugeot. We were laughing so hard we could barely get ourselves in the car. I told her my story and entertained her with an Arden imitation until she dropped me at the Ford a few minutes later.

Ten minutes after that I was home in my rocking chair, chocolate in hand. The spirit is willing but the flesh is so, so weak.

Tell you what, God, I prayed. What I really meant was that I would give up s'mores. Yes, I'll give up those marshmallow chocolate graham cracker snacks we made in Girl Scouts. That's what I really meant I would give up. And I will. I really will, especially since s'mores aren't my very favorite food. How's that for a compromise?

Chapter 22

And We'll Have Fun, Fun, Fun

So we'll go no more a roving
So late into the night,
Though the heart be still as loving,
And the moon be still as bright.

--We'll go no more a roving, Lord Byron

Dear Val,

I'm going to make it up to you, baby. I
never spent any of that second box of money
I stole from your old lady. I've got it all in a
safe place in Paget Nature Preserve and you're
going to get it all. Plus I've made a lot more
money that Melanie doesn't even know exists.
I'll buy you a trip around the world, a fur
coat, a new house, anything you ever wanted.
You're the rightful heir anyway.

Love, Skip

Everyone wanted me to believe that Valerie's murder was a
fantasy just like her life had been, but I knew better. The bodies
were piling up in that basement and all LeCaptain could say was
it was all an accident. Please! Talk about being in denial! But with
Scooter, my prime suspect, dead, and Skip not fitting the personality
profile of a murderer, I was in a quandary. Who was writing Tabby
the threatening notes? Who was chasing me around the countryside
in a big black truck and taking potshots at me? Who had pushed me

off Piney Point? I was beginning to wonder if there were more than one person after me.

I got into the Ford and sailed up Main Street, unconcerned about the present day, thinking of Valerie and her lonely life waiting for Skip to come to his senses, thinking of her sad and totally unnecessary death.

I was unconcerned, that is, until I heard a siren at my back. There was my porcine pal, Sgt. LeCaptain, with that gleam in his eye. I could see it from here. Oh, goody. What in the world is his problem now? I haven't done one single thing wrong. I didn't even run over anyone's hydrangeas. I pulled over and waited.

As usual, the cheese head's Poirot took his good old time getting to my window. He leaned over and looked at me with his big brown morose eyes. His black pomaded hair shone in the sun. His moustaches twitched with the pleasure of arresting me once again. Then came the Eeyore-like voice.

"Mrs. Nolan, I clocked you going twenty-eight miles per hour in a twenty-five zone. Are you aware that you were speeding?"

"You call that speeding?" I shrieked. "You should have seen me on the highway last night cruising at seventy-five!"

"I call it speeding and so does the law."

"That is not speeding! It's a temporary lapse of foot rigidity caused by wearing orthopedic shoes. Can't you let me off for pseudo-geriatric muscle control?"

"No, I cannot."

"Didn't think so, since you have the heart of a jackal."

"Mrs. Nolan, insults will not improve the situation," he said in an overly patient voice. "But yes, if you want to know the truth, I am implacable in the pursuit of justice."

I burst out laughing. A real carnival, this one was. I wonder who taught him his social skills. I'll bet he was one of those kids everyone in the neighborhood avoided. Sure mom, I'll go play with Francis, maybe tomorrow. Maybe over Easter vacation. Maybe if you hold the potato peeler to my head and threaten me with the cod liver oil treatment. Maybe if Father Reilly assigns play with Francis as penance in the confessional. Maybe if I'm in imminent danger of dying and going straight to hell. Yeah, right.

"Do you doubt it?" he asked me. I focused on his luxurious moustaches. Was he talking to me again?

"Absolutely not!" I stated. "I know you to be a resolute martyr to the cause of justice. Can I go now?"

"No! I haven't given you the ticket yet."

"Oh, by all means, write it out. I'll add it to my collection."

He stumped away on his little tiny shiny hooves encased in their little tiny shiny regulation police shoes. Oh, Lord, I hated those shoes. Those shoes would haunt my nightmares. Here come the shoes. Here come the shoes. And here comes LeCaptain with the little ticket book.

I smiled my disturbed feral child smile at him. He gave me the ticket and smiled back. I had never seen his teeth before. They were unnaturally white and even. Donuts to dollars they were dentures. He ran his hand over his well oiled hair and stroked his luxurious moustaches. I stared with a mixture of fascination and disgust as he wiped his hand on his blue serge police uniform, leaving a greasy fingerprint. I caught a whiff of his cologne, a cheap knockoff of Polo. Gag.

"And by the way," he said, "Arden Wasserschmidt insists that there were two women in the police station last night. One of them fits your description and the other fits Miss Spencer's description. Was that you?"

"How did he describe these women?" I asked, just out of curiosity.

"One was middle aged, auburn hair, fair skin, an Irish type, dressed in black. The other was tall, thin, blond, beautiful, and dressed in blue silk like an angel."

"Well, there you have it," I said. "It couldn't have been us. I never wear all black. It's too aging and my mom said I don't look good in black, anyway. And I don't hang out with angels dressed in blue silk." LeCaptain glared at me.

"You better look out, Mrs. Nolan," he said in his deep voice. "I'm watching you!"

"And I'm watching you, sergeant, and so is God, so don't do anything bad!" I said through gritted teeth as I grabbed the ticket and slammed my foot down on the accelerator with one fluid movement.

"Bye-bye!" I waved my arm at him out the window as I put down some rubber. Can't wait to see you again on the mean streets. Oh, yeah.

Since driving seemed to be so risky for me, later that day I decided to take a walk in the Piney woods. I left Zoro sleeping on the front porch. He would be upset if he knew I had gone for a walk in the woods without him, but he was sound asleep and I needed to get away and think.

It was a beautiful early autumn day, a perfect day for a walk. The sun was strong and the breeze lively enough to blow away the bugs.

Ah! The cry of the blue jay, the chirr of the red squirrel, the rustle of the chipmunk, the heavy breathing of the . . . . Oh, boy. There was Todd with Ashleigh Kane and they were engaged in a hot and heavy makeout session which looked about to get even hotter.

I stopped, backed up, turned and quietly walked away. My first thought was outrage that Todd was two timing my daughter. But wait, wasn't that good, in a way? Then Tabby would dump him. But not if she didn't know about Ashleigh. And was I going to be the one to tell her? What would I say? Oh, by the way, Tabby, I just saw your pseudo boyfriend Todd making out with Ashleigh in the woods today. Not the right spin to put on it.

Oh, that Todd. He really was just one big stupid adolescent hormone factory. Poor Tabby. No, lucky Tabby. She could have fallen in love with this oaf and pined away all her life waiting for him like Valerie Cooper waited for Skip Winters. I walked away quietly, hoping that Tabby would soon discover that Todd the testosterone factory was not worth her time.

When I arrived home, I debated whether to tell Tabby about Todd and Ashleigh.

"Mom, I just thought of something funny," said Tabby. "Tiffany Winters was strolling her baby right past Miss Cooper's house when we came running out after we found Valerie dead."

"So?"

"She was also there again when we left the house after we gave our statement to LeCaptain."

"So?"

"She was there when you left the house after you found Scooter dead. Isn't that right?"

"So?"

"Don't you think it's a coincidence that she always seems to be around when people turn up dead? Don't you think it's unusual that she seems to hang out on the sidewalk by Miss Cooper's house a lot?"

"Tiffany? You must be kidding. She is incapable of planning a trip to the mall without her mother and grandmother. I don't think she could manage to plan the murder of a squirrel, much less a human being."

"I think she's up to something," said Tabby.

"I'm up to something, too," I said. "In fact, I'm going to spy on someone right now, and it isn't Tiffany Winters."

"Then who is it?" asked Tabby.

"It's someone even goofier," I said. "It's Babs."

"Why Babs? She's just an old fruitcake," said Tabby.

"Because I think she knows something," I said.

I decided Pavalik's farm would be a good place to spy on Babs and I was in luck. She happened to be at her roadside stand this evening. I had parked the Ford down the road a bit and snuck through Mr. P's cornfield to a place directly across the road from Babs' long, narrow drive.

I knelt down and peered between two corn stalks across the road at Babs. She was sitting at her roadside stand, selling pumpkins for five dollars apiece. At that price, the only ones who would buy them were the tourists. She probably designed it that way so she wouldn't have to talk to any of us non-Hollywood bound local yokels.

Never could tell when Stephen Spielberg would vacation in New Belgium, decide to stop and buy a pumpkin, see Babs at the roadside, get out of a two hundred thousand dollar vehicle, and sign her up for his next big movie on the spot. Who cared if she was forty years too old for the part? Not Babs. That screen test she did in the last ice age was fresh in her mind, I was sure.

There she was in all her glory; nearly six feet of aged blond bombshell. She was decked out in spike heels, tight jeans, a low necked black sweater, a leather Packer coat, two inch painted nails, and big, bleached eighties hair. She was everybody's quintessential big blond bombshell. She must have had one heck of a lot of plastic surgery and liposuction done, because she looked like something out of Madame Tussaud's wax museum. It was almost creepy, the way her face never moved except for the lips. She had probably used up half the botox coming out of the South American rainforest. Were there no conservation laws where botox was concerned?

Who else but Babs would be so bleached, corsetted, made up, painted, waxed, and peeled at this time of day? And why? To sit at a roadside stand selling pumpkins? And for whom? The tourists? She didn't look to me like she was in any depth of mourning for old dead Scooter.

I looked at her and couldn't suppress a giggle. Oh-oh! She heard it! Leave it to Babs to have sharp hearing. She was probably the kind whose ears curled around corners. She raised her head, squinted, and sniffed the air like a bird dog. Dang! She had spotted me! She rose from her sacred pumpkin shrine and trotted across the road on her ridiculously high heels. I hopped up and skipped down a couple rows. Shoot! She was after me!

I just love being chased by evil cheese heads in leather Packer coats through cornfields at dusk. I threw myself down in the corn and stayed immobile, hoping against hope she wouldn't find me.

Oh, yes indeedy-do. All manner of wee buggy creatures hide in a farm field. The tall grass yields myriads of wee mousies and other creepy-crawlies. A mouse ran up my leg, stared me in the eye, squeaked, and jumped for the corn. Fortunately for me, my kids had trained me. Years of pet hamsters, gerbils, mice, and guinea pigs had made me relatively immune to the horrors of rodents. Little creepy-crawlies didn't bother me too much.

And speaking of creepies, I saw Babs' stiletto heels at my eye level. Ha! I dared not move or try to see more of her for fear of making noise, but I got a good look at her skinny ankles, skin tight jeans and shoes which looked liked instruments of torture. And to think I used to wear shoes just like that all the time and think nothing of it. Five minutes in those shoes today would have me begging for mercy.

"So! It's you! What the hell are you doing?" asked Babs in a nasty voice. Good thing she had never been discovered and made it to Hollywood. She never would have gotten into the talkies with that voice. She towered over me, looming like some artificially blond man-made female Frankenstein. From this angle, she was downright terrifying.

Think fast. I cast my eyes upon the ground and the Lord my Savior provided me with an answer; a big, juicy, yellow garden spider in a big old web between two corn stalks. Thank You, God! I wasn't afraid of spiders but I have to confess even I felt a bit squeamish as I scooped her up, web and all, jumped up, and shoved her under Babs' nose.

"I'm looking for Tabby's science project and here it is!" I crowed triumphantly. "She has to collect five different varieties of spiders by tomorrow. You know how kids are. Everything is last minute, right?"

I had never seen anyone with bigger, bugged out overly made up blue eyes. Babs turned stark white and backed up. Seeing her sheer terror, I pressed my advantage and followed her, keeping the garden spider under her nose in my outstretched palm. Babs tried to run, stumbled, and fell backward into the corn. Ha! *That's what she gets for wearing stiletto heels in a cornfield,* I thought. Sometimes I'm not a very nice person, God forgive me, especially when I suspect people of being downright mean and nasty.

"It's only a little spider, for Pete's sake!" I said as she managed to right herself on her stiletto stilts which made her almost six feet tall. "No need to get so scared. See? She's cute!" I insisted and held her under Babs' face.

"Get that freaking thing away from me!" she screamed. "I hate spiders! Get the hell out of here before I call Mr. Pavalik and tell him you're trespassing in his cornfield!"

"I have his permission to be here," I lied smoothly. I would have it if I had asked, anyway. "So maybe you're the one who should take a hike!"

I eyed her with distaste. She flung me an evil look, turned, and stomped back onto the blacktopped road.

"You're a freaking weirdo!" she pronounced.

Sticks and stones. I puttered about in the cornfield for fifteen more minutes, pretending to catch spiders and keeping my eye on Babs. My watch was uneventful except for one visitor to her stand. A prosperous looking old guy got out of a silver Porsche and bought a few pumpkins. The way our Babs fawned over him and gave him her best face lifted botox grin and stuck her silicone breasts out at him, you would have thought he was the angel Gabriel.

The way she looked at him reminded me of a certain girl in my graduating class who looked up at all the boys with big bug eyed adoring wonder, as if she were their slave and they had just sprung her from the leg irons. Babs was a gal guaranteed to make me gag. I stopped and stared openmouthed as she gave the old goat her card.

"Here's my card if you ever need anything else," she purred and glowed at him.

He murmured something appreciative and slipped the card into his jacket pocket. I thought I was going to toss my cookies right into Pavalik's corn. Her card? What did it say? Former wannabe Hollywood actress? Happy antique hooker for sale? I do photos, films, and anything else a well preserved wax museum figure can do?

Everything I had was lower and wider than it had once been, but at least I knew it was mine and I had never stooped to selling it. I was so disgusted I marched out onto the road, gave Babs and the rich old guy a look of sheer revulsion, walked back down the road to the Ford, and went home. The evening had not been a total failure after all. I had found out one thing for a certainty. Babs was capable of doing anything for money.

Chapter 23

Always Something There to Remind Me

Blow, blow thou winter wind,
Thou art not so unkind
As man's ingratitude;
Thy tooth is not so keen,
Because thou art not seen,
Although thy breath be rude.
Heigh-ho! Sing, heigh-ho! Unto the green holly;
Most friendship is feigning, most loving mere folly:
Then, heigh-ho, the holly!
This life is most jolly.

--William Shakespeare

Dear Val,

Remember that night we parked on the cliff road and made Scooter walk around in the cold for an hour while we made out? I laugh every time I think about it.

Love, Skip

Krystal, Tabby, and I were on our way to a night performance of the drama club at New Belgium High School. As I drove the Ford, I hummed along with the Four Tops as we crested the cliff road and began the long descent into town.

"Mother, can we have one night off from Motown, please?" pleaded Tabby from the back seat. "And when we get to the drama club performance at the high school, please don't speak, and above all, don't hum. I would like to have one night without being embarrassed by you."

I gave her a salute in the rearview mirror.

"As you wish, it shall be, your highness! I shall remain mute. I am your robot. Just program me and walk away and forsake me. You'll probably be the first of my children to vote to have me put into the old folks' home."

I looked in the rearview mirror. She curled her lip at me while Krystal giggled.

"Your mom is so much fun," she said. Tabby gave her an open mouthed, bug-eyed stare.

We arrived in plenty of time to say hello to everyone and find our way up to our seats in the second row of the auditorium. The play was *Grease*.

"At least it's something I can relate to," I murmured to Tabby just before the intermission. "I think they're doing a wonderful job." She groaned.

"Bunch of disgusting no talent preps," she said.

"Oh, don't be mean. I notice Ashleigh Kane is playing the part of the tough girl. She's doing quite well."

"She doesn't have to act to play the part. That's why she's so good at it," said Tabby.

At the intermission we picked up a cola at the drinks table and mingled. A balding old man in a dramatic black suit with a claret ascot hurried up to us.

"Tabitha!" he commanded. "Introduce me to your darling mother! I have two minutes before I must run."

Tabby looked away and rolled her eyes, while Krystal pulled a face and looked up at the ceiling.

"Mom, this is the drama teacher, Mr. Perringbone," said Tabby reluctantly. "He's in charge of the whole production."

"Oh, how nice," I said. I smiled and held out my hand. "What a great job these kids are doing."

"Very strictly amateur but they're trying," he said. Then he grabbed my hand and kissed it. "Charmed."

He made a little bow and smiled at me, his mouth chock a block with yellow fangs.

"I only have a minute," he said into my ear, "so let me get right to the point. I heard you're looking into the death of our lovely Valerie. I want you to know I'm with you one hundred percent, and if there is anything I can do to help you out, please let me know. Valerie was so, so dear to me. Such a divine creature! So very special!" He clutched my hand.

Tabby and Krystal gave him the teenage look, turned away, and pretended he wasn't there. I smiled up at him.

"As a member of the legal profession, I feel it is my civic duty to help out in any way I can," I said and withdrew my hand.

I wasn't about to come right out and say that I thought Valerie had been murdered. In law school, I had a reputation for being the biggest schmoozer in the class. When the moment called for some blarney, I could rise to the occasion with the best of them.

Mr. Perringbone's eyes misted.

"My Lord! She was such a saint!" he cried. He wiped a tear from the corner of eye. Not given much to histrionics myself, I could only murmur my assent.

"Valerie was too good for this world!" continued Mr. Perringbone. "That Skip Winters should be shot! I wanted to marry Valerie for years but all she could talk about was Skip. Skip! Who is he, anyway? He is just some tiresome has-been, some little salesman! I'm the one who should have won her heart!"

Mr. Perringbone opened up his suit jacket. On the inside lapel, he had pinned a yearbook picture of Valerie. I stared at it with my mouth open. Tabby and Krystal couldn't take any more. They hightailed it over to the dessert table, leaving me to deal with the phantom of the opera alone.

"Do you see?" he asked imperiously. "Do you understand that I loved her? That I still love her? That I will always love her?"

I stared up at him.

"I think I comprehend," I said.

Oh, boy, he should win an Oscar for this performance. I watched his face, with its bloodhound jowls, quiver with emotion. Whether it was real or feigned was hard to tell. I reminded myself that actors act all the time, not just when they are on the stage.

"I hope you do! I hope everyone knows how much I loved Valerie!" he said loudly. "I can't stand it without her! I've loved her so deeply for so many years!"

He burst into tears. My eyes grew wide. I glanced to the left and the right, searching for a diversion, a little help, anything. In typical cheese head fashion, everyone deserted the area where there was any intense emotion displayed which did not involve sporting competition. O.K., thanks a lot everyone.

Mr. Perringbone pulled a seemingly endless white silk handkerchief out of his breast pocket and wiped his eyes with a flourish. Then he stuffed it back into his pocket, raised his eyes, stuck out his noble chin, and pronounced, "But the show must go on! My students need me!"

He rushed off, trailing dramatic effect through the lobby and into the side door which led back to the stage. I breathed a sigh of relief. Whew! Talk about a drama queen!

The second half of the play was less dramatic than the intermission had been. We lingered in the lobby talking to some of the playgoers before going out to the parking lot. When Krystal, Tabby, and I walked to the Ford, I thought I saw Mr. Perringbone staring at us over the roof of his Volkswagen Passat. He ducked down as I craned my neck to see if it were him. Yes, I was sure that was him staring at me through the windows of his car, with his affected claret ascot and his bloodhound face quivering with emotion. Hmmm, strange character, that one was.

On the ride home, I thought I saw a Volkswagen Passat in my rearview mirror. Perhaps it was my imagination.

But the next day, I seemed to see that Volkswagen Passat everywhere I went. It surely wasn't just my imagination that I saw that same gray car scooting around the back roads as Zoro and I took our morning walk. It wasn't my imagination that I saw Mr. Perringbone's Volkswagen as I walked up to the house. Nor was it my imagination that Mr. Perringbone sat across Red Oak Lane watching my house with binoculars.

I was quite sure that he followed Didi and I as we made our rounds to Jane's Grocery, Mike's Hardware store, and Eddie's Fifties

Diner. I was absolutely sure that I saw his gray Volkswagen Passat follow us as we drove down Main Street.

When we stopped at the Coffee Buzz to buy a cappuccino and chat with Joni Devlin, Perringbone pulled in behind us. Did the man think he was invisible? He sat at the wheel of his car pretending to read the newspaper while he watched us come out of the store and get into the Ford. His signature tweed cap was pulled down tightly over his eyes, but I could see his furtive glances as Didi and I drove away.

"Don't look now but we're being stalked by the high school drama coach," I said.

Didi giggled.

"Are you talking about that strange looking man in the Volkswagen Passat? I thought he looked weird. Somebody's got a crush on you," she said. "Looks like you've attracted the attention of yet another strange one."

"Shut up! Don't scare me!" I said. We made our last stop at the Cliffhanger Bookstore so Didi could buy the latest thriller from Eunice's sisters, Fayne and Maida Dunn.

We parked the car outside the store. Mr. Perringbone parked across the street. He pulled his hat down, picked up his newspaper, and pretended to read. Didi waved at him.

"We're going in to buy a book!" she called out. "We'll be out in about twenty minutes!"

Mr. Perringbone buried his head in his paper and looked noncommittal.

"Stop it!" I ordered. "This is so embarrassing. I'm being stalked by an elderly drama coach. This is just too much."

We escaped into the security of the Cliffhanger, which looked the same as it had for the last three decades. The worn hardwood floor groaned and creaked under the weight of the massive bookcases loaded with a booklover's delight. The peace of the true bibliophile reigned in this quiet haven.

Fayne and Maida sat at their desks. Fayne did the accounting and the record keeping. Maida did the ordering, and there was Eunice, who could frequently be found here when she wasn't at the law firm keeping me in line.

Eunice leaned over the counter and said, "Hi! Maida has a new shipment of books in. Get out your wallets."

Didi plunged over to the new bookshelf with glee while I explained the situation with Mr. Perringbone. The sisters got quite a kick out of my plight. They laughed heartily when I told them about Perringbone following me around town.

"Contrary to what you fear, Mr. Perringbone does not have one of his obsessive crushes on you," said Eunice. "Don't worry. He won't be pinning your picture to his lapel. He is following you because he thinks you will lead him to Valerie's buried treasure chest."

"You're kidding!" I said.

Fayne and Maida looked up from their books. Eunice smiled at them and then at me.

"On the contrary, we are deadly serious," said Eunice. "That man is the biggest blow in town!"

"So you mean it isn't my charms Perringbone is after? And here, all this time I thought I was a femme fatale!"

"Please! Don't be so naive!" said Maida.

Fayne clicked her dentures at me.

"Boy, are you off your rocker, sister!" she said.

"Why do you think he had that mad crush on Valerie?" Maida asked. "It wasn't her twinsets, hon. It was cold, hard cash. Our dear thespian thought he should marry Valerie and retire on her rumored hidden stash of hundred dollar bills."

"And all this time I thought he was a romantic!" I said. "I'm crushed! I'm disillusioned! Do you mean to tell me Perringbone is just another mercenary? It would appear that a lot of people were counting on that cash," I mused.

"And a lot of people are going to be very disappointed," said Maida. "Hundred dollars bills, even by the boxful, don't go as far as they used to, you know. And even if that fortune amounts to hundreds of thousands, someone has to find it first. And good luck!"

Didi bounded over with an armful of new books.

"Ring up the cash register, Eunice!" she said. "I found some treasures here!"

"That's just what Perringbone hopes to find if he follows Rhiannon around enough," said Fayne. Eunice started to ring up the books.

"Don't worry, dear," she said to me. "Mr. Perringbone is completely harmless. He's just crazy. If he bothers you too much, just give him a good kick in the shins and tell him to get lost. That's what Maida finally had to do in 1952 and it worked like a charm! Didn't it, Maida?"

"Yeah, except I should have aimed higher," said Maida and went back to her book orders.

Chapter 24

A Whole Lotta Shakin' Goin' On

About the trees my arms I wound;
Like one gone mad I hugged the ground;
I raised my quivering arms on high;
I laughed and laughed into the sky,
Till at my throat a strangling sob
Caught fiercely, and a great heart-throb
Sent instant tears into my eyes;
Oh, God, I cried, no dark disguise
Can e'er hereafter hide from me
Thy radiant identity!

--Renascence, Edna St. Vincent Millay

Dear Val,

I'll be coming for you soon, I promise. We'll run away together. Wait for me.

Love, Skip

The summer lingered well into September. The milkweed pods were ripe with promise and the monarchs flitted about the fields. Beneath my feet, woolly caterpillars searched for a suitable place to build their cocoon. The honeybees, drunk on nectar, congregated beneath the pear tree and buzzed lazily through the mums. In the evenings, a harvest moon, like a huge gold doubloon, hung low on the autumn horizon. I rambled over my eighty acres lost in a symphony of careless joy, in tune with the music of the spheres.

Oh, yeah, I've got issues and a volcanic temper, but there are the balanced moments, too. Sometimes when the planets are aligned and the Holy Mother shines her white fire into my soul, I'm alright. This was one of those times.

The September wind tossed the burnished leaves about on their branches and they turned golden faces to a bright sky. Out on Lake Michigan, whitecaps rolled in a frenzy on the blue swell. I loved to feel the wind around me, singing in my ears, tearing at my hair, and pulling the tails of my coat. My mood always lifted with the wind.

One early morning, Zoro and I took a long ramble through the fields. We waded into the tall grass, which parted like the Red Sea over Zoro's black furry back and closed around our tracks as we passed. The grass hummed with the buzz and chirp and swish of little creatures. Around us, the late blooming wildflowers shone on, unaware that the summer was drawing to a close. A breeze freshened my brow and skipped over the nodding heads of the flowers so that they seemed to roll in a crested wave to the sun. I couldn't help smiling at glorious nature bathed in light.

And even though mother nature occasionally gave us a glimpse of her dark, destructive side even here in God's country, the darkness fled, at least for the moment, and I saw with new eyes the testament of the grand design all around me.

The crows set up a cacophony as I passed and I laughed. From the top of a pine tree, a cardinal sang with a call as pure as a flutist playing the aria from Carmen in a sunlit meadow. Over the field it resounded and made its way up to the cathedral of heaven.

A pair of yellow finches skimmed the tall grass. A little group of sparrows flitted ahead of us over the tall purple clover and Queen Anne's Lace, while all around us grasshoppers danced.

I paused and looked down at a fat little fuzzy black and orange caterpillar making his busy way across the path to his next milkweed plant. God speed, little fellow. The year is turning and you need to become a butterfly soon.

And I need to solve the problem of Valerie Cooper's murder.

When we got home, I flung myself into a chair and called Matt in Madison.

"Hey, Matt! It's Mom. I'm working on this latest puzzle and I need a pep talk. I've lost my nerve. I don't think I can do this. Someone is following me and trying to kill me. At least one person is stalking me all over God's country trying to scare me. This isn't fun. I'm rattled."

"Mom, that's just what they want you to be. Mom, it's like out there on the gridiron. If you're wounded, you just have to suck it up, shake it off, and get out there and kick some butt. Don't think about it. Just do it."

"Yes, oh wise one. Any other Bhudda like wisdom for me?"

"You don't want to let the team down, Mom. Tabby is depending on you to block for her. Come on, use your brain. You can outwit this moronic murderer. You're smart and you have backbone. Think of a new move, a new play, a new twist. We're all cheering for you, Mom. Now get out there and kick butt!"

"Sure thing, Coach!" I said.

"Dad would be proud of you, Mom," said Matt.

"Yeah, maybe," I said. I had a searing vision of Mick in his youth, his dark hair shining, his blue eyes twinkling with mirth, his commanding physical presence. Magnetic Mick, I used to call him. He knew the way to set me off. I could feel the old scars leap up in technicolor on my heart's surface and throb with emotional pain. A lightning bolt of grief came to rest in its home territory; the back of my neck. Ouch! Darn scars! Would they never leave me alone?

Matt and I enjoyed a moment of silent salute to the Mick. Then Matt said, "You need to win this one, Mom. You have to, for Tabby's sake."

"Will do," I said quietly and hung up.

I decided that I needed a respite from the world, somewhere far from the madding crowd. I needed somewhere I could think.

I had to go to my secret place, a little private retreat at the bend of the Red Tail River, where the river slowed to a brown peaty brook. There was a little board bridge down on the water where you could stick your toes in the cold creek and sigh with appreciation for the absolute peace. There was the wind in the oaks and beeches, the chirr of the squirrels, the call of the bluejay, and the rustle of the woodland creatures to calm you. And there was no one there to spoil it. Just what the doctor ordered.

The air was filled with the cinnamon and vinegar smell of fallen poplar leaves, fresh cut grass, and the crisp, clear sharp scent of autumn. The acrid odor of woodsmoke drifted from afar.

I let Zoro off his leash and he ran about happily searching for rabbits in the woods. I had just sat down on the bridge, stuck my feet in the icy cold brook, breathed a sigh of relief, and sunk into a profound reverie, when I heard a soft footfall.

Oh, heck! Who could that be? Quickly I calculated that the nearest house was a mile away. I hadn't seen any other people or cars. Was someone stalking me? Or perhaps the question should be, who was stalking me now?

I was alone and completely defenseless. The hair on the back of my neck rose, a sure sign that I was in danger. A low hanging branch swayed in the breeze and its leaves brushed my arm gently, almost tenderly, as if in sympathy. A minnow nibbled at my toe as my sixth sense remained on high alert.

Suddenly Zoro paused. His nose, ears, and tail went into track mode. He raised his left paw like a pointer. And then he rushed into battle. What followed was a lot of growling, flying brush, and vicious snapping sounds. It sounded like whomever or whatever was following me had quickly retreated. I called to Zoro and he came running to guard me. I debated whether to run down to the rapids over the dam and throw myself in like the kids did in the summertime, thus gaining about five hundred feet of escape time, but the water was like ice and I wasn't a very strong swimmer.

I waited quietly on the bridge for another fifteen minutes but I heard nothing. I felt like such a wimp. Darn! I knew I should have eaten the breakfast of champions this morning! Maybe I should carry a gun, giving new meaning to the words armed and dangerous. With my luck, I would probably shoot myself in the foot. No, I wasn't a weapon toting kind of person. And it was ridiculous to think that here in God's country, I had to contemplate carrying a lethal weapon around.

I forced myself to walk to the car. I headed for home and once there, I slipped into a blue funk. This was depressing. I had to find the person or persons who were after Tabby and me. I had to find Val's murderer and bring him to justice. I had to find Scooter's murderer too, and hopefully, they were one and the same, because it was hard enough to find one murderer, let alone two. I opened up the newspaper and tried to distract myself. The obituaries; that should make me feel better.

Now just think about it, I told myself. Things could be worse. I could be in the obit pages instead of reading them. Now look here. Here's poor old Auden W. Schmidt, died aged eighty-nine. He worked at the shipyards fifty years and ushered at St. Paul's church since age fifteen. He is survived by his wife of seventy years and about forty three hundred grandchildren and great grandchildren. A tear plopped on the page. But was I crying for old Auden or for myself? I must be cracking up. Oh, just get on with it, I told myself.

What I needed was a new identity. Who was I kidding? I was no sleuth. I had difficulty enough just being a single mom and a lawyer, much less a detective. Things never seemed this difficult for Miss Marple. She would have had this case solved by now. Of course, Miss Marple was much smarter than I, as evidenced by the fact that she never married or had children.

Chapter 25

She Wore Blue Velvet

They flee from me, that sometime did me seek.

--Thomas Wyatt

Dear Val,

Remember our secret, love. Don't tell anyone.

Love, Skip

The phone rang.

"Hello?"

"Hi, Rhi, this is Stan. I just had a talk with my mother. She said to be careful about you."

"Oh, why?"

"Because you're after me for sex and money."

I sighed.

"Tell your mother and her old bat friends that I'm not after you for money, sex, fortune, fame, or most of all, your sperm. I have already had all the kids and all the sex anyone should have in one lifetime, and I have plenty of money of my own. I'm in menopause, so I can't get pregnant accidentally or on purpose and make you marry me or pay child support for twenty years. I'm fifty years old, for Pete's sake. Do I look like a sex crazed gold-digger? I'm a widow, not a wild woman on the make. If you really want to get me excited, come over here and clean my house. That would really turn me on. I would love you forever!"

There was a click.

"Hello?" Must have hung up. How rude.

Ten minutes later my doorbell rang. There was Stan holding a mop and broom. He was dressed in his usual uniform of jeans, boots, and black tee shirt, but I thought he looked better than a Chippendale dancer. I smiled at him through the screen door and tried to keep the lusty thoughts from creeping into my grin.

"Darn you, Stan. I thought my pituitary gland had gone dormant but you might have nudged it back to life."

"Is that a good thing?" asked Stan through the screen.

"Depends," I answered. "The thing I want most from a man is something most men least want to give," I said.

"What?" asked Stan.

"Companionship."

"Oh, like watching movies, walking the dog together at sunset, talking and stuff?"

"Yeah, stuff."

"I can do that, plus I can clean house, repair appliances, and fix your car."

Did this man know what he was saying? I opened the door, grabbed him by the shirt, and hauled him through the door.

"What are you thinking?" he said.

"What I'm thinking would make your mother swallow her false teeth."

Suddenly, a movement outside caught my eye. Over Stan's shoulder I saw Todd walking up the driveway to pick up Tabby for a date. My thoughts of Stan went into interrupt mode. My glands turned to ice. Why must that boy look so sexually mature? He was only sixteen. Why does he have such a well developed musculature? He already had Ashleigh Kane. What did he want with my daughter?

Todd walked up onto the porch and smiled at us.

"Is Tabby here?" he asked.

I did not like the sound of that voice. It was too deep, too husky, too sexy. Whatever happened to beanie babies, marbles, and roller skates? When had Tabby started to play with boys? Shouldn't I have about five more years to warn her about the kind of pain a broken heart can inflict? She was a child, for Pete's sake!

I opened the door. Todd came in and Stan turned away and started to sweep the kitchen floor as if nothing had happened. Well, nothing had happened, really. Perhaps a seismic shift in my thought patterns, but nothing much in reality. I looked at Todd.

"Tabby will be right down. Have a seat, Todd." I ran upstairs, casting a vituperative glance at Todd as I went. I burst into Tabby's room. She was putting on her makeup.

"Have we talked about human reproduction?" I asked.

"Mother! Cripes!" She put down the mascara and picked up her hairbrush.

"I mean have we discussed sex?" I asked.

"Would you stop?"

"Birth control?"

"Don't even start. I'm not discussing any of that with you. You're my mother, for Pete's sake. Besides, I get nagged about it at school five times a day."

"Abstinence is in vogue these days."

"Stop!"

"Masturbation is not a sin."

Tabby screamed and put her hands over her ears.

"Mother! I'm not having sex! I'm not ready to have sex! Would you stop talking about sex?"

"Good! Because you're too young, so don't even think about it!" I said and went out, slamming the door as I left. I descended the staircase.

"She'll be right down," I said cheerfully. Todd smiled at me. I smiled at him. Stan swept the floor and made a point of not looking at me.

Suddenly, someone pounded on the door. It was Pavalik.

"Hey! Heard downtown that Sgt. LeCaptain is sitting at the counter at Diane's Diner going through the personals section of the big city newspaper looking for a girlfriend," he said through the screen. "Should I tell him that you're still interested?"

"Oh, didn't you hear?" I said. "I'm not after Sgt. LeCaptain. In fact, I never was. I'm interested in a real man now."

I looked at Stan with a goofy loving glazed donut stare. Stan stopped sweeping and blushed three consecutively beautiful shades of red. Pavalik's deep set brown chimp eyes opened wide and glowed with glee.

"Well," he said, "Gotta get down to the Pickle Jar and have a frosty one with the boys! They got the TV on. Gotta go catch Mel Greene on Channel three on the bass fishin' show. He's right in the middle of a life and death struggle with the biggest bass in Turtle Lake. See ya soon!"

"Sounds riveting! You do that," I called. "And make sure you tell everyone what I just said!"

I had never seen Pavalik shuffle his old carcass so fast as he did getting to his ancient pickup truck, Chuck the red Chevy.

Chapter 26

Bring It on Home to Me

O, here
Will I set up my everlasting rest
And shake the yoke of inauspicious stars
From this world-wearied flesh.

--Romeo and Juliet, Act V, William Shakespeare

Dear Val,

Sometimes dreams really do come true. I followed my heart around the world and back again in the Navy, but everywhere I went and everything I did, all I could think of was coming home to you. For so long it was enough to live in Maybelle knowing that you were close by, but now it's not enough. Life is short and for the last part of our lives, we should know the ultimate happiness.

Love, Skip

After work on Monday, Didi and I decided to take some flowers to Valerie's grave. St. Catherine's cemetery was set back beyond the railroad tracks at the edge of town. The autumnal sun slanted through the trees, lighting up the reds and yellows of the maples and making them look like soft parchment in the late afternoon light. The day was warm. Indian summer was upon us, bathing the land in glorious raiment. Could anything compare with the brilliant colors of a sunlit autumn day? Didi and I breathed in the crisp, clear air.

179

We drove the Ford back into the cemetery to Valerie's gravestone near the statue of Mary.

"Oh-oh! Look at that," said Didi. "What is that on Valerie's grave?"

"It looks like a big gray bundle," I said as we got out of the Ford and approached the grave. But as we drew near, I saw it wasn't a gray bundle. It was a body, and a dead one. Didi and I huddled together as we realized with a jolt of recognition that it was Skip Winters lying on Valerie's grave.

From the looks of it, he had blown his brains out with a pistol.

Oh, Lord, please don't let me throw up. My knees buckled but I grabbed on to Didi before I went down all the way. The sight of Skip's still handsome face with half his head blown off and blood and gore everywhere is not a sight I should ever have seen or should ever see again. I closed my eyes and eventually, my knees straightened and the spots in front of my eyes stopped dancing. When I opened my eyes again, I was careful to avoid looking at Skip, even in my peripheral vision.

Life went on oblivious to poor Skip. The birds chirped and the cicadas thrummed in the trees. The sun lit the turning leaves of the maples with gold halos, but no angels sang a requiem.

Didi leaned her head on my shoulder and sobbed. I felt as pale as she looked. Wasn't it Dorothy Parker who said of F. Scott Fitzgerald at his funeral that the dead look so very, very dead? Even in the strongest among us, life is so tenuous. I clung to Didi and prayed for Skip, for Valerie, for all of us.

Didi and I shepherded each other back into the Ford. I put the flowers on the back seat and took out my cell phone. I dialed nine one one. Within minutes, we heard LeCaptain's siren.

He came to a screeching halt beside the Ford, hopped out, and went to view the damage. Then he came back to the squad and called an ambulance. I watched him exit his police vehicle and waddle up to the Ford in his little tiny shiny police shoes.

"Apparently," he said to us through the window of the Ford in his ponderous Eeyore voice, "Skip couldn't take the death of his childhood friends so he cracked up and killed himself. I guess the deaths of his two best childhood friends were too much for him. Valerie, Scooter, and now Skip."

"You still think they were accidents?" I asked.

"I know so!" he insisted. "And why are you always discovering dead bodies? Would you mind your own business from now on?" he said indignantly.

"I didn't do anything but come to put flowers on Valerie Cooper's grave!" I yelled at him. I revved up the Ford and threw it into gear.

"You'll have to make a statement tomorrow!" LeCaptain called after me as I roared out of the cemetery.

The next day when I opened my mail at the office, there was a letter from Skip Winters.

I opened it with trembling hands. It said,
Dear Rhiannon,

You will get this letter after I'm gone. I hope you will understand and won't think too badly of me. I just wanted to explain a few things to you. The first thing I want you and everyone to know is that I loved Valerie Cooper and I have always loved her more than anyone or anything. The money I stole from Valerie's parents years ago was spent on wine, women, and song. At the time, I didn't care about Valerie's crazy old mother so I took the money and ran. Now I feel terrible about it.

The worst thing about it was that Valerie knew I had done it and never turned me in. She knew I had repented long ago and she never mentioned it again. I bought nice cars and a big boat with the money and spent the rest on my wife and daughters and granddaughters.

But there is a second chest buried somewhere, and I'm not telling you where. If you or anyone else ever finds it, the money is to go to the Valerie Cooper scholarship fund. That's what Val had planned for it. The third chest of money was stolen from the basement.

*That was to be Valerie's retirement money.
I know it's gone and the person who has it
killed Valerie and Scooter. I just hope it isn't
someone I know and love. Take care of things
for me. You'll have to sort out this mess. I think
you're a good person, just like Valerie was. She
was the best one of all of us. Tell everyone I'm
sorry for everything.*

Skip

What was this? The third chest of money was stolen by the
murderer of Val and Scooter, and the second chest of money is buried
somewhere. Shouldn't Skip at least have left me a treasure map or
a list of hints for this scavenger hunt? Perhaps he had pickled a few
too many brain cells. I wasn't about to go toting a shovel around in
my car making random digs for the buried treasure. And why in the
world hadn't he left me the names of his suspects? Was this person
too close to him, or was it someone he shouldn't have been dabbling
with?

I stuffed the letter into my purse and told Eunice I had to run an
errand.

I went to see my old friend, the handsome Doctor Winston Devlin.
I needed to ask him a few questions. I got the nurse to squeeze me
in between a check on a leg cast and a woman who looked ready
to deliver a very big baby. Feeling guilty and talking fast, I looked
into Doctor Winston's big, sad eyes behind their thick tortoise shell
glasses and begged for help.

"Rhiannon," he said, "I really cannot help you. I can't go running
around the countryside looking for murderers. I don't have time."

"And you think I do?" I said indignantly. "I'm a professional
woman! I'm supposed to be raising Tabitha, running a household,
and by the way, trying to remain financially solvent in my law
office. Is there any physical evidence I haven't been told about?
Come on, Doc. Can't you throw me a few crumbs? I did, after all,
help find George Wainwright Smythe's killer, which cleared you of
suspicion."

I didn't bring up the fact that his wife Joni had an affair with
George and half the town had been afraid that it was Doctor Winston

who had altered George's Lanoxicap pills and caused his death by digitalis poisoning. Of course, no one wanted to believe that their favorite doctor was capable of such a thing, but human nature being what it is, they had their suspicions.

"Oh, all right," he said, "but all I can tell you is that our coroner James DeBrall says he is absolutely positive that Skip's death is a suicide."

"Yeah, I figured that," I said. "But what about Val's death?"

"DeBrall says she fell down the stairs, and LeCaptain says she fell down the stairs, but I have my doubts."

"And?" I prodded.

"And I think she was pushed," he said.

"By whom?" I pried.

"By Scooter," he said. Now we were getting somewhere.

"But why is Scooter dead?" I asked.

"Scooter found the money and someone planned his death and took the money, is what I think," said Doctor Winston. "And if I were you, I would say, cherchez la femme. And that is all I'm saying and don't ask me why or whom I suspect because I don't really know."

"That's better than nothing," I said. "At least you and I are in agreement on Valerie's death and the motivation. Now all I have to do is find the mastermind behind the whole thing."

"Good luck," said Dr. Winston.

Later, I stood in my bedroom in front of my full length mirror and decided that mirrors, like scales, were deceiving. I could not possibly weigh as much as my scale said I did, nor look like my mirror said I looked. This must be some fun house mirror someone installed for a joke. Was this the body women had envied and men had lusted after? Life is just full of fun little surprises. Look on the good side, I told myself. Vanity is no longer a problem for you. You don't have to torture yourself with tight clothing and high heels anymore. Orthopedic shoes can be cool if accessorized correctly. Besides, Miss Marple never wore anything but sensible shoes.

Wasn't it only yesterday that I had lingered in front of the mirror admiring my reflection? Or was it thirty-five years ago? Time seemed liquid, like a Salvador Dali painting. Yesterday, today, tomorrow;

they were all meaningless. Who knew where my mind would take me next?

I frowned at my reflection. I had never had to work at looking good before. And now I was working really hard for very little return in the weight loss department. Too bad I couldn't hire someone younger with a rip roaring metabolism to do it for me, but it was all up to me.

And who is going to take care of this Valerie Cooper thing? I guess it's up to me to do the dirty work. Everyone wants justice but no one ever wants to get their hands dirty. It's just like being a mom. They all want a harmonious environment but no one wants to do the cleaning. They all want decent meals, but no one wants to cook. They all want clean clothes, but no one wants to do the laundry. Cripes!

LeCaptain is in denial about the whole business. Dr. Winston is too above it all. Father Ray is too busy and overworked already, not to mention too spiritual to go digging around in this earthly muck. And everybody else is too scared to get involved. It's going to take a woman to sort out this mess. I looked at myself in the mirror, squared my shoulders and lifted my chin. It's up to me then. And Jesus have mercy on the one who caused this unholy mess because I sure as heck won't.

That night I dreamed that I saw Skip and Valerie walking together through a field of wildflowers. They were in that place where love lasts and all loves are true. At last Skip was with the person he should have chosen to begin with, the one who could have made him live up to his potential. He could finally do the right thing; be true to the best in himself.

And there was my dead husband Mick, dear Mick. He was just like himself only even more handsome and a lot nicer than he had been in life. He held out his arms to me. This must be heaven. I walked through a sea of daffodils and held out my hands to touch him. Then I smiled and woke up. Oh, goody, reality again. Bring in the chocolate.

Eunice, Didi, and I went to Skip's funeral together. Didi looked terrific in a cloche knit hat and twenties style linen dress, black heels, black pearls, and matching bag. Eunice wore a navy blue suit and

I wore black jeans and a white poet's blouse. I even sprayed a blue streak into my hair in honor of Valerie and Skip.

It was closed casket, of course, but we all remembered Skip's handsome face with regret. Skip's women were all there; Melanie, Bobby, Amber, Candy, Brandy, Taffy, Tiffany, and the whole crowd. Even little Olivia and Emma were there. And what a vision they were, all dressed in their best funerary black; so dignified, so proper, so perfect. Hair was braided and controlled. Makeup remained on the subdued side. The crying was discreet, and not enough to make the waterproof mascara run or the powdered noses appear an unseemly red.

Mr. Perringbone warbled the hymns from the pew opposite mine. He tried to make eyes at me but I ignored him. He smiled at me, showing his yellow, tobacco stained fangs. I winced at the sight. I couldn't help wishing he would choke himself one day while tying that insufferably phony ascot of his.

Babs O'Reilly was there too, showing her support for the family and getting all touchy feely with Melanie for old times' sake. After all, they could be even closer now because Mel had just joined Babs in what I guessed was a not entirely unwelcome widowhood. And when they sang the hymns, Babs made sure that her golden honeyed voice rang out louder than anyone's voice. As far as I was concerned, she should have kept quiet. It must have been a long time since she won any talent contests.

There was an exotic looking woman in the sixth pew with a hair color which defied description. She gave a two thumbs up performance in the grieving mistress category. She wailed, sniffed, snorted, and sobbed until I thought I would go mad. Her grieving was on a par with the existentialist poetry I wrote in high school; self indulgent and poorly executed.

"She belongs on Broadway. Must be Skip's latest," I whispered to Didi. She nudged me in the ribs and shushed me.

"Oh, shush yourself!" I said aloud. After the ceremony, we repaired to St. Paul's basement for the funeral luncheon. I schmoozed about a little and then sidled up to Tiffany.

"Hey, Tiff, I'm really sorry about your grandpa," I said.

She sniffed.

"Poor Grandpa," she sighed. "What will we all do now?"

What indeed? Grandpa Skip didn't seem to have passed on his ambitious genes to anyone in the family. The females of the family seemed content to be merely decorative and willing to remain that way. Unless, of course, something like a big chest of money conveniently popped out of nowhere and sustained them for the rest of their days, they would all have to find work.

"Who was the old babe making a scene in pew six?" I inquired. Tiffany wrinkled her nose.

"That old scag is Grandpa's latest mistake," she said. "Have you ever heard of Mugs Malone of Mizzen?"

"No! Not Mugs Malone the stripper! I thought she was retired long ago! Or dead."

Everyone knew about Mugs. She was a famous, or shall I say infamous, traveling stripper who advertised herself as a modern Gypsy Rose Lee.

"Not quite!" sneered Tiffany. "She's still performing, if you can believe it. How could anyone show that ancient body and expect to get money for it? Grandpa met her at some bar and felt sorry for her and next thing you know, she's acting like she's a part of this family. He just sort of adopted her out of the kindness of his heart."

Oh, uh-huh, and I volunteered to adopt Brad Pitt out of the kindness of my heart but they told me I was too old to be an adoptive parent.

"Skip really was a great guy," I said, hoping I wouldn't choke on the words.

"The best," sobbed Tiff. Amber came up and gave me a disdainful glare. Too bad she didn't have a gun to polish so she could give me the scary lunatic look. I left Tiffany in Mama Amber's capable arms and trailed off to talk to Mugs Malone. She was sitting at a table alone.

"Hey! Not to draw attention to you or anything, but just between you and me, aren't you Mugs Malone of Mizzen?" I asked.

Why would someone so totally gauche and ostentatious want to draw attention to themselves?

Mugs drew on her cigarette and closed one eye. Fascinated, I watched as the cigarette hung in her plum colored mouth while she talked and the smoke rose and curled around her head.

"Just between you and me, hon, I am," she said. "Do you want my autograph or somethin'?" Her open eye examined me from head to toe.

Mugs set her cigarette in an ashtray, took out a mascara wand from her pocket, and plumped up her lashes with black goo without benefit of a mirror. Then she applied a liberal swipe of plum lipstick to her lips and the area around her mouth. It all blended in nicely with the streaks of black mascara which had run down her face in the service. I wanted to reach out and touch her hair to see if it really was pink cotton candy or some strange aberration of the same.

"Tell ya what, hon. I'll give you my autograph, but don't tell anyone who I am," she said. "I hate to draw attention to myself. Give me a napkin and I'll give you my John Hancock."

"I can see that you're very discreet," I said as I pushed a napkin and pen toward her so she could sign it. "Did you know the deceased well?" I tucked the autographed napkin into my pocket.

Mugs slapped the makeup into her handbag which was the size of Jupiter and sighed.

"As well as his own mother," she said. "And a nicer fellow you won't find this side of the Mississippi. A real pussycat, but let me tell you something. That wife of his is as cold as they come, doll."

Mugs' spiked lashes and large blue eyes strayed to where Melanie sat surrounded by her womenfolk across the room.

"Mercenary, absolutely mercenary," said Mugs. "I've known hookers more charitable than her." She drew a small silver revolver from the depths of her bag and flashed it in her palm. I gasped.

"Hey! You aren't going to use that thing, are you?" I gulped.

Mugs gave the gun a loving look.

"I guess not," she crooned. "It would be fun to put a hole in her, though, for the way she treated Skip all those years."

"Let's not do anything rash," I breathed. Mugs replaced the gun, reached deeper into her bag and drew out a silver flask. She opened it and took a few good belts before replacing it in her handbag.

"Besides, hon, I'm the one who should get the money after all the years I took care of old Skipper," said Mugs, her voice a raspy whisper. *Must be a two pack a day girl,* I thought.

"Took care of him?" I queried. "You mean financially?"

"That and other ways," said Mugs. "I was the big secret. Not even the family or the other women knew about me, so I decided it was time to show my face and to hell with it. Everyone can know I was the queen of the harem. And I mean for years, doll, for years."

My eyes opened wide in astonishment. She eyed me suspiciously.

"You weren't one of the sisterhood, were you?" she asked. "You know, you and old Skipper?"

"Me?" I asked incredulously. *God forbid. I would rather burn at the stake, stick pins in my eyes, and join the Mick Jagger fan club,* I thought. "No, I guess I wasn't so lucky."

"Luck had nothing to do with it, sister," said Mugs and winked at me. "Guess I'll blow this pop stand now that everyone has seen me." She drew out a card which read, "Mugs Malone, Exotic Dancer and Entertainer." There was a phone number and a silhouette of a nude woman beneath the gilt print.

"Nice," I said as she handed it to me.

"I like to do things classy," said Mugs. "Give me a call if you know anyone who needs my services. I plan to retire next year so they better hurry up and book me."

I restrained myself from telling her that sounded like an idea whose time was overripe. She stood up to her full five feet eleven inches and looked down at me.

"Better go before I get tempted and go over there and put a bullet in Melanie's head. Somewhere there's a big pot of money and Mel's gonna get rid of anyone in the way to get to it, so just you be careful. There's three people dead already. Don't be the next one!" And with that bit of advice and a wink, she was gone.

"What did that old hag want from you?" quizzed Didi when I returned to her.

"She wanted to warn me off," I said. But who should I beware of? Melanie? Or a gun toting Mugs Malone who thought she deserved the money? Or someone else entirely? There was Babs, fawning sympathetically over Melanie and doing a bad acting job. There was our very own drama king, Mr. Perringbone, sitting right over at table number four, leering at me. Was it lust or greed in his eyes? There was Principal Weaver looking suitably somber. Whatever the occasion called for, he delivered. He was the one who should be teaching the drama class. And beyond him, there was Melanie's entire sisterhood of freeloading offspring with gilt designs in their little hearts of gold.

Were there multiple guilty parties with a vested interest in Skip's financial affairs who wanted me dead? It wasn't just a question of whom. It was a question of how many people had pursued me, stalked me, and made numerous attempts on my life and health. Our little New Belgium had become a hotbed of greed.

Maybe Grandma was right when she told me that money was the root of all evil. Money and the rich bastards at the top of the food chain, she said, would be the ruination of this country. Right on, Grandma!

Chapter 27

You Send Me

This bud of love, by summer's ripening breath,
May prove a beauteous flow'r when next we meet.

--William Shakespeare, *Romeo and Juliet*, Act II,
Scene ii

Dear Val,

Look for me by moonlight. I'll be there
soon.

Love, Skip

I was on the ab machine at Shapely Lady thinking about switching to sugarless chocolate and calculating the degree of deprivation I would feel when the telephone rang. Kitty, the human praying mantis, walked over and said, "There's another phone call for you! What do they think this is? Your office?" I ignored her and ran gratefully to the phone.

"Hello?"

It was Moustache Mary.

"Hey, dummy!" she said. "Mom and I are watching Melanie Winters. She's gone nuts! She's diggin' up the ground in Valerie Cooper's back yard. It looks like a bunch of giant moles were makin' tunnels back there. Whaddaya think she's lookin' for?"

"Enlighten me," I prompted.

"Money, dummy! She's looking for the money Skip stole from Valerie's parents long ago and stashed somewhere. She knows Skip never cashed in all the money and she figures there has to be some around somewhere. She's looking in every place she thinks Skip might have buried it."

"Are you telling me you think Melanie is the murderess?" I asked.

"Well, ain't you the smart one!" groused Moustache Mary. "Why else would Valerie Cooper and Scooter O'Reilly be dead? Do ya think the fairies came and stole them away? Melanie Winters is a dirty rotten dog!"

"She may be digging to China but we still don't have any proof that she is the murderess," I pointed out.

"Melanie Winters is a greedy bloodsucker!" blurted out Mary. "And who else is going to go around shooting up the countryside with a shotgun?"

"How about Bobby?" I suggested. "Or Amber, Tiffany, Taffy, Candy, or Brandy? They all seem to have a gun or dangerous equipment fetish. Plus that, Brandy told me that Amber was a locksmith at one time. I heard she is very good at breaking and entering. They could all be in cahoots, you know. They all adore their mercurial Mama Mel. And none of them like to make money the old fashioned way, by working for it."

"What the heck is mercurial? Melanie done it. It's Melanie. That's all you need to know. Trust me, dummy," said Moustache Mary. "I'll prove it to you eventually. Me and Ma will be watching her. Stay by the phone." She hung up.

Oh, goody. Moustache Mary and Charlotte Chantelle Charpentier, known as Char-Char for short, were on the case. We can all rest easy in our beds now.

Dear New Belgium, La Follette County, Wisconsin; so full of nut cases and still such an endearing place. Sometimes grownup kids in their twenties and thirties who had been broken and battered in spirit returned from the outside world to the protective cocoon of New Belgium. Sometimes they decided to stay here and heal, here where life was better.

New Belgium was that kind of town where kids swung themselves into circles of enraptured dizziness on lush green lawns on summer nights filled with velvety blackness. It was a town where time had stopped in the fifties. It was a safe, quaint, and boring nature haven. Tourists loved it. Of course, they didn't have to survive the winters.

Kids could ride freely around town on their scooters and bikes without keeping one eye peeled for perverts, weirdos, and gangsters. Not to say that New Belgium was perfect, human nature being what it is. We had all the problems to be found in the wide world. We just had them on a much smaller scale. And they were cushioned by our firm belief in God, country, hard work, family, and our ability to rise above it all.

As long as there were cows, corn, beer, and cheese, we could make it. God and the tourists loved us. We were after all, the chosen cheese heads. Ya, hey! Life is good. You just have to ignore the fact that our little town is made up of about thirty percent nut cases.

I headed for home. I happened to glance into my driver's side rearview mirror. I saw St. Paul's clock tower reflected in the mirror and noted the time. It was ten minutes to two, but in the rearview mirror it looked like ten minutes after ten. Now wasn't that interesting? Mirrors certainly can distort things.

So many things are a matter of vantage point, not to mention interpretation. The same exact thing can be viewed so many different ways. It all depends on who is looking at it, the angle they are looking from, and what they see. Sometimes it comes down to the fact that we see what we expect to see and what we have been taught to see, when in actuality, a thing might be a whole different kettle of fish if one viewed it from a different perspective.

When I arrived home, I tried to apply my newfound observations in logical ways to the puzzle of Valerie's murder, but before I could get to the intuitive and logical conclusion which hovered just outside my mental reach, Tabby bounced into the living room.

She turned down her headphones which I could hear across the room were blasting the Ramones and said, "Have I told you recently that I love you, Mom?"

Oh, dear. This was going to be a big one.

"What do you want?" I asked with trepidation.

"I want to practice driving alone and take the Ford over to Krystal's house."

"No, absolutely not! You are only fifteen and you don't even have your practice license yet, and even then, you can only drive with me in the car. You can't drive alone over to Krystal's house. That is illegal and simply out of the question," I said firmly.

She got the exact look on her face that she used to get when she was two years old and I prevented her from applying the sidewalk chalk to the lampshades.

"I am taking the car to Krystal's house!" she yelled. *That corks it,* I thought.

"Don't question me! I'm a mom! Don't mess with me! I know what I'm doing! I'm your mother!"

"Don't be such a fascist!"

"What?"

"Don't be such a Nazi!"

"Watch your mouth young lady or you won't be driving until you're eighteen!"

"Oh, yeah?"

"Yeah!"

"Watch me!" she said, grabbed the car keys off the table, and stalked out the door. I ran after her, but before my rheumatic knees could bend, she was in the door of the Ford and down the drive. I trailed back into the house and stood swaying helplessly in the living room, my head in my hands.

I can see the headlines now.

Mother at the end of her rope tied up in knots over child abuse verdict. Sentenced to swing at high noon on Friday in town square. Judge, father of four teenagers, sympathizes with mom but his hands are tied. Mom's lawyer alleges elder abuse. Demands retrial and a new rope for mom to hang herself with.

I could feel my veins closing up with murderous teenage induced rage. Stop! Control yourself, I told myself. Breathe. Don't do anything crazy. Do you want social services to come and take her away? Well, sort of. Uh, no, I couldn't live without seeing her dear little purple head on the pillow, without hearing her dulcet tones of "Mother! Where is my hot chocolate?" in the morning.

O.K., I am a nice person. I am a good person. I see the waves on the ocean. I feel the calm. Visualize. Ah, that's better. I will live through this and fifty thousand more terrible moments. Bring it on! C'mon! I dare ya! I double dog dare ya! Ruff! Ruff! Oh, scared, huh? Well, huh! I am mother! I am stronger than Hercules. Atlas was a wimp compared to me! I am woman! Hear me scream! Help, God! Help!

God heard me, and at that moment, Stan banged on the screen door and walked in.

"Hi, anybody home?" he called and lumbered into the room. "I just saw Tabby driving away in the Ford. I didn't know she had her license."

He smiled his grizzly grin. Stan was dressed in his usual uniform of plaid shirt, jeans and boots.

"She doesn't," I said. "And she's in big trouble!"

Stan looked so concerned, so warm, so male, so alive, so sexy. This was a revelation. Had I ever realized just how sexy Stan was? A strange feeling came over me, a feeling of immeasurable abandon. I don't know how it happened and I don't know why. Who can explain these things? It could have been stress or intestinal upset, dementia, or a low grade fever, or maybe it was something in the air. I forgot that I was a cynic. I forgot that I was too old to feel wild, unrestrained passion, too old for love. Oh, heck, let's go for it, I told myself.

I had grown used to having almost no hormonal activity going on and now that the unwitting Stan had unleashed the sleeping Mata Hari in me, well, darn him. On his head be it.

"Take this," I growled, and, pulling Stan by the shirt collar, I drew him to me and gave him the ultimate forty carat diamond treatment; the all systems go that still have any juice at all left in them, four alarm fire smokin' pinball light 'em up kiss. Wow! And I was sailing, skimming over the water somewhere between the ocean and a deep blue sky.

Judging by Stan's response, I would say this old magician still has a trick or two left up her sleeve. We melted into a pool of butter, just like the tigers in Little Black Sambo. I think I sent my aging hormones into jet lag shock as they jumped back in time to raging river status. Crikey, mate! Mother nature really is a miracle worker!

Just at that moment, in my mind's eye, Tabby walked by.

"Eeeeeuw! Old people in love! Yuk!" I heard her mental image say. Leave it to Tabby to be there criticizing me even when she wasn't really there. *I'll show you, you little teenage punk rock rebel*, I thought.

I ignored her image and pulled Stan into another clinch. When we came out of it, Stan drew back, his eyes open wide. He put his giant grizzly bear paws gently on my shoulders and leaned into me. And I heard Jerry Lee Lewis sing *Great Balls of Fire*. I would say that Skip Winters, former sex god and ladies' man of La Follette County, ain't got nothin' on this guy.

Chapter 28

The Great Pretender

Most wounds can Time repair;
But some are mortal, these:
For a broken heart there is no balm,
No cure for a heart at ease---

--At Ease, Walter de la Mare

Dear Val,

My heart belongs to you. I'll be coming for you on Friday night.

Love, Skip

The next day, I decided that since I could be falling in love, it was only right to try to lose twenty pounds within the next two weeks. If I burned off three thousand calories a day, worked out sixteen hours a day, and ate nothing from now until Halloween, it could be done.

To prove it, I decided to limit myself to one tiny little square of baker's chocolate a day and take ten mile hikes. I was on the second ten mile hike of the day and taking my constitutional past New Belgium Park when I realized someone was dogging my tracks.

Oh, dear! My whole body ached from all the hiking and this time I had no Zoro to save me. He was at home ripping his squeaky toy porcupine to shreds.

It seemed that all of a sudden, the glorious golden autumn sank into murkiness. A fog descended. Cold fingers seemed to reach out and envelop everything in mist. Within ten minutes, I could hardly see five feet. I could hear nothing in the insulating fog.

Why in the world hadn't I checked the weather report before I started out? Love must be clogging my thought processes and ruining my synapses. Visibility quickly approached zero, and I felt, rather than saw, someone following me through the fog. I veered off into the park and headed for the empty swimming pool. Whomever it was followed me.

Necessity is the mother of invention. I looked around wildly, squinting in the fog and the murk, and spied an unlocked padlock on the swimming pool gate. Francis LeCaptain strikes again. He loves leaving things unlatched. I opened the gate and slipped in, but my stalker had seen me and followed.

Sniffing the heavy, damp air, I could smell her signature perfume; Halston. The perfume was mixed with the smell of cigarettes and hairspray. It was Melanie. I heard the click of her stack heels on the cement. She was very close now, and probably armed and dangerous.

As a former smoker, I knew her sense of smell was impaired from years of cigarettes, so she probably couldn't smell my perfume; Innisfree. I knew she couldn't run because of her smoking habit and her insufferably fashionable stack heels, and I also knew that she was terribly vain and would not wear her glasses. These two facts had probably saved my life on more than one occasion. *Luck be with me again,* I thought.

I made a run for the water slide, knowing it would be difficult for her to follow me up the high, winding staircase. Silently I crept up the ladder on my orthopedic soft soled shoes. I couldn't believe it when I heard Melanie behind me, breathlessly trying to follow me, her stack heels clicking on the steel steps of the slide.

How had she found me? Perhaps the mist had opened up for a minute and she had spied me. She was more tenacious than I had thought, and maybe not as nearsighted. I kept going. She kept going. Beneath me, I heard her panting from exertion.

The clicking heels stopped. A shot rang out somewhere to the left of my head and I heard Melanie swear. Grimly, I marched upward. I paused and listened. Melanie's nerve must have failed her. Maybe she was afraid of heights. Maybe she ran out of bullets. Either that or she stopped breathing. I heard nothing for a few seconds. Then the click of heels receded back down the slide and away. I found myself at the top of the slide. I knew I was high in the air, and fortunately for me, I couldn't see anything through the fog and the murk, because heights made me dizzy and sick.

But as an experienced mom, I had forced myself up so many water slides for so many years that I was completely unafraid to go down the slide the easy way, feet first in the dark. It also helped that I couldn't see a darn thing.

Actually, it was quite a giggle going down the slide, except when I hit the end, fell five feet through space, and landed on my left side on the cement of the empty pool with a resounding thump. Fortunately, I managed to cushion my fall with my shoulder, my elbow, and various other padded parts, but I knew that the next day my entire skeletal system would feel like I had just put myself through the blender.

Oh, dear. Miss Marple never had to endure such punishment. Of course, she never would have survived it, while I, on the other hand, was built to take the rough spots in stride. I was a mother. That meant I was used to hardship. I was physically and mentally tougher than a marine. Yeah, right.

I groaned and pulled myself to an upright position. Gingerly, I felt my way toward the side of the pool. Blindly, I found my way over to the railing and dragged myself up the cement steps and out of the empty enclosure. As soon as I gained the cement and felt my way through the fog over to the iron fence, a spotlight shown directly into my face.

Ouch! I thought. *That thing hurts my eyes! What is this, some kind of a joke? If so, it isn't funny.* I stood blinking in the white light, wondering if I had hit my head. Was this a near death experience? Had Melanie shot and wounded me without me feeling it? Gingerly I took stock and decided I wasn't dying. There was no blood anywhere.

This was totally ridiculous. The white light glared into my eyes. *It's like being a prisoner of war in a terrible cheese head war camp,* I thought. Then I saw a familiar looking bulky shadow through the glare. Oh, Lord! It's my nemesis, the great one again.

"Mrs. Nolan!" came the booming sound of LeCaptain's Eeyore-like voice through a police megaphone. "Freeze!"

"I am not freezing, you dumb cluck!" I screamed. "I am not a criminal!"

I was in pain from falling into the pool, and when I'm in pain, I get very uncooperative.

"What are you doing on the children's water slide in September when there is no water in the pool?" roared the voice through the megaphone. I squinted into the bright light.

"I'm playing!" I yelled. "What does it look like I'm doing, having a quilting bee?"

"You are trespassing in the swimming pool after swim season! And you have specifically disobeyed a park rule! You went down the water slide in the off season!"

"Well, golly gee! Better lock me up and throw away the key!" I screamed. "Even though you won't lock up Melanie Winters for shooting at me! She shot at me on the slide! She shot at me in the boat! Everyone is trying to kill me and no one cares!"

I threw up my hands and started moving in the direction of the police car.

"Should I throw down my weapon?" I called. The point was moot because the only weapon I had was my wit, and I wasn't about to sacrifice that.

"Mrs. Nolan, no one is trying to kill you! You are delusional! And your park privileges are suspended as of now!" was the answer. I slipped out the gate and banged the door shut behind me.

"No, they are not!" I yelled.

"Yes, they are!" LeCaptain insisted through the megaphone.

"That's unfair!" I pointed out loudly. I walked right up to him, grabbed the megaphone, and slammed it onto the hood of his squad car. He pointed a finger at my eyes.

"You may not enter this park or its environs for one year!"

"Environs? Was that a recent *Reader's Digest* vocabulary word?" I asked.

"Keep up your smart talk and it will be two years!" The man was getting red faced and bug eyed.

"Oh, have a stroke!" I said.

I stuck out my chin and marched off through the fog with my head held high, deliberately ignoring his histrionics. The sky is falling, Henny Penny. Fat chance you have of keeping me out of this park, Ducky Lucky.

When I got home, I marched directly to the candy drawer and reached for the chocolate, but before I could get the ambrosia to my lips, Tabby waltzed in.

"Can we talk?" she asked.

Must be momentous if she actually volunteers to talk to me, I thought. *What huge issue are we about to tackle?* Just thinking about it made me anxious, so I threw all the candies into my mouth at once and hoped for the best.

"Mom, remember when we all used to play Peter Pan? Jennifer and Matt said I had to be Wendy and I told them to stuff it because I wanted to be Tinkerbell. Remember?"

"Oh, I remember it well. At least you didn't get stuck playing Captain Hook like I always did," I said ruefully.

"It's the same thing now. I'm not playing surrogate mother and helpmate to Todd. I'm a Tinkerbell, not a Wendy. I'm not into this patriarchal chauvinist anti-feminist crap he keeps dishing out."

"Good! Tell Todd to take a hike!"

"Don't you think I'm right?" she asked.

"Yeah!"

"Then you don't mind if I become a lesbian, right?"

Chapter 29

And A Thing Called Love

Till a' the seas gang dry, my dear,
And the rocks melt wi' the sun;
O I will love thee still, my dear,
While the sands o' life shall run.

--*A Red, Red Rose*, Robert Burns

Dear Valerie,

I'd give anything to be young with you again. That was the best time I ever had.

Love, Skip

I dropped the candy drawer on my foot.

"Holy Mother!" I screamed. "Are you trying to kill me?"

"No, I'm not trying to kill you! Would you listen? I have decided that Todd has a major case of male machismo gone awry and I'm going to become a lesbian," she announced.

"No! Is this going to be like the year your sister declared she was going to be a missionary in the Congo? I'll have to go and see Doctor Winston and get in a good supply of valium."

"I've decided and that's it!" said Tabby.

"You are grounded!" I pronounced. "Yesterday you drove the car without me, a temporary license, or permission, and today you announce you want to be a lesbian."

"You can't ground me for wanting to become a lesbian!" Tabby protested.

"Oh, yes I can!"

"Oh, no you can't!"

"Can!"

"O.K. fine! I'll just be a bisexual and remain a virgin for now and practice abstinence! I hope you are happy! Have it your way! I'll probably be a geek virgin until I'm as old as you are. Are you happy now, Mother?"

Happy? I heard the Hallelujah Chorus. I smiled my Cheshire cat smile.

"Only if that is what you truly want," I said. "I don't want to force you into anything." Years of motherhood had made me craftier than old Reynard himself. But Tabby was having none of it.

"I can only remain a sex object for so long without being seduced, you know," she said with a calculated gleam in her eye. "It might be by a male. It might be by a female. But soon someone will see how devastatingly attractive I really am."

She really knew how to push my buttons. Seduced? And in the getup she had on, it wouldn't take long. I looked at her long legs in the black seamed nylons and black high heels, at the black leather mini-skirt and the midriff top, the blond curls and the makeup, and despaired of ever getting my Tabby back again.

"I reiterate, you are grounded! Go to your room!"

Tabby sneered at me, turned on her heel, and stomped away, making sure to make little black high heel marks on the hardwood floor.

I sighed and decided to go for a drive. Perhaps that would fend off the migraine which was already threatening to ruin my entire day, at least, that part of it which had not already been ruined by Melanie and Sgt. LeCaptain. As if getting shot at, chased up a slide, and treated like a criminal weren't enough, I also had to deal with teenage angst. *I hope the heavenly scorekeeper is watching*, I thought, *because this day is a big ten pointer for moi.*

I grabbed my purse and headed for the Ford. I peeled out onto Red Oak Lane and headed for the lake. Behind me, I saw Mr. Perringbone's Volkswagen Passat following me once again, so I put the pedal to the metal and gave him the slip on the back roads, turning and twisting my way through the woods and green hills as I sped my tortuous way to the lake.

The murk had lifted and I actually had a good view of the last rays of the setting sun over Lake Michigan. I practiced my deep breathing and tried some positive self talk while I listened to the teenager tape that my daughter Jennifer had sent me.

The tape explained in an exceedingly patient voice that parents must expect inconsistent behavior from teenagers. I listened with one part of my mind, while with another part of my mind I struggled desperately to reclaim my mental equilibrium.

I am a good person, I told myself. I am calm. I am serene. I am good at dealing with teenagers. I am a great friend, a great lawyer, a great amateur sleuth, and a great mother, and if the self fulfilling prophecy works, someday I might actually be all of those things when it's too late to matter.

Somewhere in the vicinity of the cliff road, I decided to throw the *How to Talk to Your Teenager* tape out the window. It wasn't doing any good, anyway. And I had been worried about childbirth? Ha! Labor is just the beginning. It's a cosmic conspiracy. I ripped the tape out of the cassette player.

Of course, people never act the way they are supposed to act in the self help books and tapes, or the way the psychologists presume they will. But then, I never talk the way the shrinks say I should talk. Instead of saying something like, "Your behavior is inappropriate and it's making me unhappy. Perhaps together we can plan some life goals for you to pursue which will result in mutually satisfactory results," I scream something like, "I'm going to freaking kill you if you don't knock it off!"

Just for good measure, I also threw the other tape out the window. It was called, *Parenting your Teenage Daughter, A Mother's Guide.*

Just as I threw the tape out the window, I spied LeCaptain's squad car in my rearview mirror, and at the same moment, he spied the tape leave my not so well manicured fingers. Too late, I made a Hail Mary effort to grab and retrieve the tape, but it was no good. The tape was gone. The wail of a siren pierced the air. He turned on his flashing lights. Oh, goody.

Words I had not been taught in Catholic school escaped my lips as I pulled the Ford to the side of the road and awaited the inevitable.

LeCaptain got out of his squad, leaned over, and picked up the tape off the ground. He rolled up to my window on his little black shod porcine trotters. A familiar egg shaped head loomed into view and bobbed just outside my window. LeCaptain smiled at me and said, "Good evening, Mrs. Nolan."

"Good evening, Sergeant," I said between clenched teeth. "What fine weather we're having."

"Did you throw something out your driver's side window, Mrs. Nolan?" LeCaptain asked. His moustache fairly quivered with delight. A gleam of rapture suffused his normally morose visage. *Sadist,* I thought.

"Possibly," I said.

He read the title to me.

"How to Talk to Your Teenager." He leaned in my window and smiled. "I don't think it's working. No wonder you threw it away. Mrs. Nolan, this is the second time in two hours you have gotten yourself in trouble. Do you think you should hang it up for today? Do you know what kind of a ticket I have to write you for littering God's country with this trash?"

He smiled his evil anticipatory ticket writing smile.

"A big red, white, and blue one with a flag on it?" I asked and looked at him adoringly. "You look so handsome today, Sgt. LeCaptain. Did you buy a new tube of Brylcreem? Have you had your teeth whitened?"

"Flattery will not work with me, Mrs. Nolan," he proclaimed and gave me a stern look which caused me to lose my temper.

"Nothing ever works!" I said. "That's another of God's little jokes! And I don't find it particularly funny so write the ticket or buzz off!"

"While I'm writing that ticket out, perhaps you will have the good grace to go and fetch the second article you tossed out of your vehicle."

"Fetch? I'm not a dog. And since you're going to charge me so much money for having the pleasure of tossing those audiotapes out of my window, why don't you fetch it yourself?" I smiled at him, showing my incisors and curling my lip.

His eyes narrowed. Without a word, he stepped away and plunged into the tall grass on the other side of the road. I gazed at his broad bent over backside and mentally gave it a good swift kick. After a few minutes of searching, he came up with the tape in hand and a triumphant look on his face.

"Exhibit A!" he cried gleefully. "I'll just keep this for evidence."

I guess when you are Sgt. Francis LeCaptain, it's the little things that bring you happiness. Tape in hand, he tripped off to the squad car on his tiny little porcine feet in their little shiny black police shoes. He wrote out the ticket and brought it up to the car. I glared at him, grabbed the ticket, and peeled out onto the road, laying rubber as I did so, unrepentant and in an ugly mood.

In the rearview mirror, I saw him scowl at me and knew I would live to see another ticket; maybe not today, maybe not tomorrow, but soon.

Help me God, I prayed. I need to escape New Belgium. I need to run away and become a beach bum. Maybe I could do it even though I don't like hot weather, won't wear a swimsuit, can't surf, burn easily, and don't fit in with laid back cool people who talk in code.

God help me! I just can't face any more loco legal clients, cheese heads, police harassment from Poirot, lunatic murderers, stalkers, and most of all, teenagers. Do You think You could give me a break here? I need to solve this case, make some money to keep my law firm afloat, and get on with my life. I didn't know it at the time, but God was listening. Within twelve hours, things were going to break wide open.

Chapter 30

It's In His Kiss

Time, wouldst thou hurt us? Never shall we grow old.
Break as thou wilt these bodies of blind clay,
Thou canst not touch us here, in our stronghold,
Where two, made one, laugh all thy powers away.

--*The Double Fortress*, Alfred Noyes

Dear Val,

We could have had beautiful children together. You were the prettiest, sweetest, nicest girl in school. I know that deep in your heart you're still the same girl and way down deep, I'm still the same boy. We're just a couple of kids. That's why we belong together.

Love, Skip

The next day, I was working the ab machine at Shapely Lady when my cell phone rang out to the sound of Beethoven's Fifth. Thank God I could stop my tortured midriff muscles from suffering any more! I ran over to my purse, grabbed the phone, and registered a nasty look from Kitty the human praying mantis, trainer, and anorexic stick girl.

"Hello?" I said.

"Hey, dummy! It's me, Mary!" Without any identification at all, I would have known it was Moustache Mary by the degree of antisocial fervor in her voice.

"Mary, you don't have to yell!" I yelled. "That's why Alexander Graham Bell invented the telephone! So we don't have to yell!"

"Ya, whatever, hey! I ain't used to these cell phones. Anyways, listen! You gotta come out here once! Melanie Winters is excavating under the love tree and you better get here right away. Mom and I always suspected Skip hid the money there and we've been following Mel around. She finally figured it out. She's got a pickaxe she can hardly raise off the ground and a sorry excuse for a shovel and she's digging away like there's no tomorrow. And there's a shotgun on the ground beside her purse, so be careful. The both of us is here in hiding. We're waiting until she brings up the money box and then we're gonna nab her. When you get here, the three of us will take her down, hey."

"What is the love tree?" I asked. "And exactly where are you?"

"You dunno much, do ya?" said Mary with her usual phlegmatic humor. "The love tree is the first oak tree to the left of the wood shed in Paget Nature Preserve. That's the tree Skip carved his and Valerie Cooper's initials on forty-five years ago. Then he burned 'em in by igniting lighter fluid. Naturally, he wrote his own name first because he was such a . . . ."

"I'm on my way!" I cried. I grabbed my keys and my purse and sailed through the door of Shapely Lady.

"You forgot to sign out!" called Kitty the stick girl to my fast disappearing back. What is this? Freshman year at the dorm?

Ford, don't fail me now, I thought. I jumped in the car, turned it over, and cranked it. As I peeled around the corner, I caught a glimpse of a Volkswagen Passat in my rearview mirror. Mr. Perringbone was hot on my tail again. Would the man never give up?

In three minutes flat I was inside Paget Nature Preserve. Turning to the left and careening over the grass, I aimed the Ford at the wooden shed and pushed the accelerator. *I didn't know a car could hop like this*, I thought as the Ford bumped its way over the tussocky grass. *Have to tell Stanley I need new shocks.*

Such gorgeous color, I thought as I took in the blur of the golden maples and red oaks of autumn. *What a shame we humans have to spoil everything.* I gunned the Ford and squeezed my eyes shut. In another few seconds, the wooden park shed was history and so was my right front fender. Oops!

I turned the wheel to the left again. I had Melanie in my sights now. She was under the big oak, lying flat on the ground next to what I presumed was the money box she had unearthed from beneath the love tree. And she had the shotgun aimed at my windshield. I gunned the Ford again, aimed at the tree, ducked down behind the dash, and hoped for the best.

A shotgun blast shattered the peace of the woods and blew out the glass of the windshield, spraying a blast of glass above my head. Jumpin' Jericho! Melanie finally hit something! My hearing would never be the same again, but I felt my blood pressure react marvelously. It went from zero to sixty in two seconds flat.

Now that made me mad! I peered over the dash through what had once been my windshield and accelerated straight at Mel. Her mouth opened in surprise as she let go of the shotgun and rolled to the right. It must have been a shock for her, me trying to kill her for once instead of the other way around. Melanie and the tree rushed past me in a blur. Darn, I missed. I turned the car in a circle, bumping and skidding on the grass, and aimed at her again. *I have really lost it this time,* I thought. *And what is even worse is, I just don't care.*

That's when I saw what appeared to be two hairy little dwarves scamper out from the trees and literally throw themselves on Melanie's prostrate form. I slammed on the brakes, shoved the car into park, and jumped out.

It seemed like some bizarre Disney feature film. Melanie, with her pale skin, dark hair, and blue eyes, looked like an aging Snow White being trounced by two of the dwarves. The tackling dwarves were, of course, Moustache Mary and her mother. Mel made a grab and got her hands on the shotgun. Again she aimed at me.

Moustache Mary kicked the gun out of Melanie's well manicured ringed fingers while Mama Chantelle sat on Mel and put her in a headlock. Mary pulled the silk scarf off Melanie's neck, rolled her over, and none too gently tied Mel's wrists and slender ankles together like you would tie up a roped calf.

I leaned my head on the hood of the Ford and willed my pulse to stop jumping around in my neck before I burst a blood vessel.

"Hey, dummy!" called Mary to me with satisfaction. "Are you gonna get your lazy butt over here and help us put her in the trunk or what, hey?"

Why me, God? Why me? I looked up and spotted Mr. Perringbone sitting in the parking lot watching the whole drama unfold before his eyes. I hoped the spineless swine was happy and comfòrtable, and well aware that I would make darn sure he never got his hands on one single penny of Valerie's fortune.

It wasn't easy getting Melanie into the trunk of the Ford. She was heavier than she looked, and even though she was trussed up like the Christmas goose, she kept kicking out and connecting with my chin. She also called Mary a bastard hairy dwarf, Chantelle a hairy hooker, and me a freak mental case punk rock idiot. Finally, I had enough. I pulled off one of Mel's heavy stack heels and tried to crack her head open.

"Brutality!" she screamed.

"So sue me!" I screamed back. We threw her into the trunk.

I slammed the trunk shut on her as she continued to scream. With any luck she would pass out. Moustache Mary and I picked up the filthy box full of money and threw it in the back seat. Mama Charlotte Chantelle Charpentier, or Char-Char, as they called her for short, sat beside the box and rubbed it lovingly. Mary took the front seat with me.

The road to the police station was a long one. My car was wrecked and barely driveable, what with the blown out windshield, dented right front fender, and the crushed passenger side. I had one screaming banshee in the trunk. There was one hairy, aged Skip mistress in the back seat counting out money and stuffing it into her bra by the handful. And there was one anti-social, smelly hairy Mary next to me saying, "Stuff some down your underwear too, Ma!" I gagged quietly at the odor of unwashed hairy flesh and tried to hold my breath.

I looked in the rearview mirror. Just as I figured, Mr. Perringbone turned on Willow Lane and disappeared from view. He finally gave up. I guess he figured that money was gone forever now, so what was the point in stalking me and pretending to be in love with me, or at least obsessed by me? My endearing young charms alone could not hold him.

Eventually, Char-Char, Moustache Mary, and I delivered Melanie and the stolen money to the police station, except for the portion of it which was tucked away in Mama Chantelle's underwear. And there was no way I was going in there to get it. I figured she and Mary deserved something for helping to make the capture.

Disposing of Melanie was a traumatic experience for all of us, especially Sgt. LeCaptain. He simply could not understand how someone so perfect could commit attempted murder and larceny, but eventually we got it into his head. It got a lot easier after Melanie started spitting on him and calling him all those names. Once she was in the jail cell, which I personally made sure was securely locked, the three of us gave our report to LeCaptain and I drove Mary and Charlotte Chantelle home.

After I dropped them off, for a minute I was relieved. Melanie was my stalker and now Melanie was in custody, but was she the only one? Mel was a nearsighted bad shot. My real problem was still on the loose, because I knew that Melanie did not kill Valerie. Neither did she orchestrate Scooter's death. Mel didn't have the brains or the finesse to be the master manipulator. I knew I was looking for someone much more clever than Melanie. And I knew I better work fast or it would be too late.

Chapter 31

Stop! In the Name of Love

Tears, idle tears, I know not what they mean,
Tears from the depth of some divine despair
Rise in the heart, and gather to the eyes,
In looking on the happy autumn-fields,
And thinking of the days that are no more.

--*Tears, Idle Tears*, Alfred, Lord Tennyson

Dear Val,

When I die I want to be buried next to you and not this old witch I'm married to. I don't know what I ever saw in her when I could have had you. I must have been crazy.

Love, Skip

My first task was to deliver the Ford to Stan for the latest in a series of innumerable fix-it jobs.

I dialed Stan's number at the garage on my cell phone.

"Stan here," came his dear grizzly bear growl.

"You won't believe what I just did to my car and how I did it," I said.

"Try me."

"Be there in ten," I said.

When Stan saw the car, his only comment was, "You never cease to amaze me."

"Whew!" I said to Didi an hour later. "Mel is sure to be put away for this. I guess the daughters and granddaughters will all have to get jobs and support themselves, now that Skip is dead and Val's fortune

211

is unavailable. I hear Katie is hiring at the Kurly-Q. Maybe they can get a discount on hair spray and nail polish. They'll have to learn how to do helmet hair, though."

We sat in my den sipping a diet soda. Didi shook her golden head in sympathy.

"It won't be easy for them without Grandpa and Grandma there to indulge their every whim," said Didi.

"Life is tough," I pronounced, and just as I said it, I felt a migraine coming on. It promised to be a doozy. I put my hands to my head. The agony had begun.

"Oh, Didi," I whispered. "This is one of those sudden ones; the really bad ones."

Her violet eyes fluttered in alarm. She rushed to draw the drapes and shut out the light from the room.

"Lie down on the couch," she said.

I stumbled to the couch and went down like a brick, my eyes shut against the blinding lights, the numbing buzz of the stabbing pain, my hands at my temples in a vain attempt to ward off what I knew was a certainty. Didi flew about like a ministering angel, gathering pills, water, and ice packs. I descended into my own private hell and for a time, everything was blackness.

When I awoke from the dark, I sat up with a rush.

"I know!" I said.

Didi put her hand on my head and checked for fever.

"Know what?" she asked in her soft low voice.

"I know who is responsible for the deaths of Valerie and Scooter, and by extension, Skip."

"Why, it must have been Melanie, wasn't it?"

"Wrong, my dear Watson. It was someone much more clever than Melanie, and a lot more deadly."

I ran to the phone. It was time to set a trap for one clever little murderess.

The phone rang and rang. I prayed she would be home. Finally, there came a desultory, "Hello?"

"I've got the money, sweetie," I said. "You know, the other box that you never did find? The box that Skip had buried beneath the love tree? Didn't know that, huh? You never did manage to find it, did you? Well, I have it now. Melanie is in custody and with any luck she can take the rap for everything. And I know all about you and your dirty little schemes. Meet me at Valerie's house in fifteen minutes with all the money and I'll bring mine. I've already counted it and it's over two hundred thousand. We'll split all of it half and half. That way, neither one of us can rat on the other one without getting caught herself."

"And if I don't?" she said.

"If you don't, sweetie, I'm going to the police and blow the whole thing sky high."

I hung up and counted on her greed and avarice. I wasn't disappointed.

Fifteen minutes later, Krystal, Didi, Tabby, and I jumped out of Didi's Peugeot, walked around the yellow police tape, entered the house through the unlocked front door, and stood waiting in Valerie Cooper's kitchen.

Within five minutes, the back door opened and in walked Babs, the stinking cow. No, I guess comparing Babs to a cow is an insult to cows. I should say stinking, crawling snake. Maybe I could arrange it so that she and her old friend Melanie could share a jail cell together until death do them part.

"Surprise, surprise!" I said. "The money is safely locked up with Sgt. LeCaptain. Wanna go down to the police station and confess to the murder of Valerie Cooper and Scooter?"

Babs sneered at me.

"Where's the proof? Who's gonna take me in? You and your little posse here?"

Her face contorted into an evil mask. She opened her fist and I saw what looked like a wicked Samurai knife flash in her hand. Obviously, she had expected to find me alone and planned to kill me and take the rest of the money too, nasty little piece of work that she was.

I looked at Didi. Her eyes looked glazed. She was going into her I'm not really here mode. I didn't want to involve the girls in anything physical. Sigh. It was going to be up to me once again.

"The police are on their way here now!" I lied. "Just give up, Babs! It's over!"

"You bitch!" Babs flung at me. "You've spoiled everything! If I'm going down then I'm taking you with me!"

Babs came at me like some aging wild Valkyrie. *She must be totally and completely mad,* I thought. She looked like an enraged Viking warrior woman; huge, blond, and deadly crazy. I gasped, and in that lucid split second I knew how my Irish ancestors felt under attack by the fearsome ax wielding Vikings. Holy Mother of God! St. Brigid defend me against this beast!

We clashed in an ear-splitting shriek. It was a hair pulling, punching, slashing, kicking melee, but Babs had an advantage. She had the Samurai knife in her right hand and it struck home twice; once on my left shoulder and once on my left hand.

I recoiled in pain and gave her the inroad she needed. Babs pushed me backward down the open basement staircase with a vicious shove. I somersaulted, tucked my head under, and prayed I wouldn't be the next one with a broken neck. It seemed to take forever to roll down the stairs. The last thing I saw before I hit the concrete was Babs' hand slip around Tabby's neck and the knife at Tabby's jugular. I hit the bottom step with a thud and collapsed. I looked up in time to see Babs' evil smiling face. At the same time I heard Tabby scream, "Mom! Help me!"

It would appear that Babs was about to use Tabby as a screen, or possibly a hostage to make her escape.

A flash of lightning ripped through my mind's eye; Tabby in her crib wrapped in a pink blanket. Tabby reading in the maple tree in the back yard. Tabby refusing to get on the pint size kindergarten school bus, standing firm in her little buckle shoes. I couldn't say these were distinct thoughts. They were more like visions which blazed through my mind, leaving me homicidally deranged at the thought that anyone would do her harm.

That was all I needed to turn into Superwoman. I moved into automatic pilot mode, totally unaware of age, pain, or of any injuries I might have sustained in battle with Babs. I rose like the Phoenix from the ashes, reborn and with one single burning purpose in my soul; to destroy Babs.

My normal play nice-nice drawing room mind set snapped. My mind went black like a fuzzy television screen after they play the national anthem. My hypothalamus took over and I don't remember what happened next, but Tabby tells me that I made the Hulk look like a pussycat. She said she never saw anything scarier in her life than me as I exploded up the steps and through the doorway.

I sprung on Babs like a lioness and went for her throat. The knife fell to the ground. When I got my hands sufficiently wrapped around Babs' neck I threw her down with a vengeance and started squeezing her windpipe and banging her head on the floor simultaneously. Apparently, I made a roaring guttural noise the entire time I tried to kill her.

Eventually, Babs stopped struggling and slipped into unconsciousness. Too bad. I wanted her to die thinking about how she was going to hell. When it was over, there was hair and blood everywhere. Didi and Tabby pried my bloody fingers off Babs' throat while Krystal called the police and an ambulance on her cell phone. Babs regained consciousness enough to choke out a few curses at me. If I didn't have arthritis and my hands were as strong as they used to be, she might not have lived to curse another day. It took all of them to hold me back from finishing the job before LeCaptain arrived to take Babs away to the county jail.

If we were real lucky she would get two consecutive life sentences without parole. I was so wound up I took a swing at the ambulance driver who came to take me to the hospital. Once we got into the emergency ward, Dr. Winston threatened to immobilize me if I didn't settle down so he could manage to stitch up my arm and hand.

"So go ahead and sedate me!" I roared. "Me and Joey Ramone, honey! We're two rockers! We wanna be sedated!"   ·

Dr. Winston looked puzzled.

"Who the devil is Joey Ramone?" he asked.

"Are you kidding me?" I screeched. "You don't even know who the father of punk rock is? He's a dead hero, man! Where have you been?"

Dr. Winston sighed and reached for his needle.

"Nurse, could you please hold her down?" he said. "It takes someone like you to make me do this," he said to me as he jammed the needle into my arm.

After that I had a little screaming fit before I sank into oblivion. That's what happens when you wind up a spring too tightly for too long. One day it springs back. And it's not pretty. And besides all that, I don't like people who try to hurt my babies. It's all Babs' fault for getting me upset to begin with. She shouldn't have done that.

Chapter 32

Signed, Sealed, Delivered

And still of a ghostly night, they say, when the wind is in the trees,
When the moon is a ghostly galleon tossed upon cloudy seas,
When the road is a ribbon of moonlight over the purple moor,
A highwayman comes riding--
Riding--riding--
A highwayman comes riding up to the old inn-door.

Over the cobbles he clatters and clangs in the dark inn-yard;
And he taps with his whip on the shutters, but all is locked and barred;
He whistles a tune to the window, and who should be waiting there
But the landlord's black-eyed daughter
Bess, the landlord's daughter,
Plaiting a dark red love knot into her long black hair.

--The Highwayman, Alfred Noyes

Dear Val,

Don't tell anyone about Friday night. I want it to be our secret. Together forever again, where we belong.

Love, Skip

When Didi brought me home from emergency care, I looked in the hallway mirror and almost screamed with fright. Talk about the mummy from tomb four! It looked like someone had pulled out clumps of my hair, stolen my makeup, put fake blood on my face, and wrapped me in ace bandages. My shoulder and my hand were wrapped up and hurt like heck, and they hadn't even given me any decent pain pills. Good thing I had a little stash of my own. I dragged myself over to the kitchen cupboard and swallowed a Percodan. Then I groped in the back of the cleaners and detergents for the little bottle of whiskey I kept for medicinal purposes only. I knocked back a good, stiff belt straight from the bottle.

"Hey, soldier!" said Didi. "I think that's enough pain medication for the next hour!"

"Shut up!" I ordered. "I am not into pain!" I threw back another belt.

"I noticed," said Didi wryly.

I could hardly stop myself from crying.

"There's only one thing I really hate about pain," I groaned.

"What's that?" asked Didi.

"It hurts." I leaned on the counter and put my face in my hands. "Didi, could you check my palms and see if I'm getting the stigmata?"

She giggled.

"That's right. Have a laugh fest on me. Just ignore my moans," I said.

I hadn't felt this desolate since the trial by water gun incident in eighth grade at the class picnic when everyone turned on me and squirted me half to death as punishment for being elected class president and most likely to succeed. Dana the dork Adams snapped my picture and showed it to everyone in class. Everyone gloried in my humiliation, everyone except Didi, of course. She helped me exact a terrible revenge in a book fair bundt cake laced with enough laxatives to kill a herd of elephants. Thank God for Didi.

I swayed across the room like a drunken John Wayne and opened the chocolate drawer. Some situations demand an indiscriminate fistful of M&M's. I tossed some in my mouth without even stopping to sort by color. Ah, that was better. As queen of the house, my next decree would be to banish all mirrors until further notice.

Didi and I settled at the kitchen table with iced tea for the post mortem. I plopped four sugar cubes in my tea and watched with satisfaction as they melted over the ice cubes.

"I like my tea like I like my men," I mused. "Strong, sweet, and cool does it every time." Didi smiled.

"Pain killer starting to kick in already, is it?"

"Sorry I was cranky," I apologized to Didi. "I'm really starting to feel better now. Thanks for being here. You know you're my best friend. I really, really love you, Didi."

Didi gave me a huge smile. She knew how hard it was for me to put feelings into words. Of course, drugs helped.

"I would hug you but I don't want to make you scream. What really put you onto Babs?" she asked, and took a sip of her tea. I settled back in my chair, being careful not to put pressure on any bruised or wounded parts, which included most every part.

"I remembered the case of the dance of the Flowers," I said. "Well, that was how I always thought of them. Remember the Flowers? They had about twelve kids, all girls. The first ones they named Violet, Rose, Marigold, Petunia, and Daisy. Then they moved on to the virtues of Faith, Hope, Charity, and Prudence. Finally they went bonkers with the last ones. They named them Morgana, Starlight, and Precious. Precious was anything but, I assure you. That girl loved to lie, steal, cheat, and forge checks. She practiced identity theft before it became an art. I heard from a cousin of hers that she felt justified in taking money from dumb schmucks, as she called them. I think she ended up in prison."

"And your point is?"

"I'm getting there. Her sister Morgana continued the family tradition when she had kids, but she was into stealing cars so she named her kids Mercedes, Lincoln, and Portia. She just changed the spelling on Porsche because she couldn't spell to begin with."

"How do you know these things?"

"I have my sources."

"So what does all this have to do with Babs?"

"Well, Babs reminded me a lot of Precious; all golden curls and a face like a big fat wad of sweet, gooey cotton candy, but her eyes were vacant and empty. And no matter how much makeup she caked on her face, it couldn't hide the fact that she was mean as dirt. I remembered how Precious pushed Judy Tooley down the stairs after Judy got chosen for homecoming queen. It was just spite, pure and simple."

"Doesn't seem like much to go on."

"But wait, there's more. Also, Babs seemed bitter about not being discovered like Lana Turner in the soda shop. What did she think? Did she expect some Hollywood mogul to pull into the pumpkin patch one day, take one look at her, and say, 'You'll do for the next Hollywood dumb blond bombshell?' I thought about how Precious got greedy with other people's identities and their money, and figured that Babs, running true to type, would be motivated by bitterness and greed. Plus, I went back to Piney Point the day after I got pushed off the cliff and guess what I discovered?"

"I'm afraid to ask."

"I found teeny holes in the ground at the precise spot I went over the cliff."

"So?"

"Those holes were made by spike heels sinking into the soft ground which had been washed with a rain shower only hours before my little accident. Babs never wore anything but high heels. I mean, here we are in God's country and she's walking around everywhere in spike heels twenty-four hours a day like she lives on Rodeo Drive, for Pete's sake.

"And then I saw St. Paul's clock tower in my rearview mirror and realized that ten to two could look just like ten after ten if you saw it in reverse in a mirror, or if you were sometimes just a wee bit dyslexic like Tabby. I realized it had been ten minutes to two o'clock, not ten minutes after ten o'clock, when Tabby went to Babs' house to wash windows and heard her screaming at Scooter."

"So?" said Didi. She slurped the last of her iced tea and poured herself some more.

"So at ten to two, Scooter was already dead in the basement and I had discovered him. Babs had pulled the old trick of making us all think she was screaming at a live Scooter when in reality, there was no one in the house with her. That very one sided argument was staged for Tabby's and the neighbor's benefit. If Scooter was in the house fighting with Babs, he couldn't very well be lying dead in Valerie's basement where Babs had made sure he was locked in with the cats, could he now? It gave her an alibi, didn't it? The only problem was, she didn't expect him to be found so soon, and when I figured out that her timing was off and the fight was staged,

I realized that Babs knew Scooter was already dead. Kind of makes one wonder about her innocence, doesn't it?"

"I guess so," said Didi doubtfully.

"You see, it was Babs, not Scooter, who was the brains of the outfit. Scooter was the marionette and Babs pulled the strings. She directed Scooter to go over to Val's house just before Skip was due at nine o'clock and push Val down the steep basement staircase. Babs knew what everyone would think; that it was an accident. No one would believe that Skip was actually coming for Val that night, and if they did, they would certainly think that if anyone had killed her, it would be Skip."

Didi shivered. "She's really sick!" she said.

"No kidding, and greedy too. Babs knew there was a pile of money hidden somewhere in that house and she wanted the whole pot for herself. Scooter was so used to playing second fiddle to Skip that he didn't mind taking orders from Babs all those years. Babs was the dominant personality and Scooter was the patsy, repeating the pattern played out between Skip and Scooter in their youth. Scooter was weak and malleable. On his own, he probably never would have considered killing Val or stealing the money, but with Babs to order him around and push him, he became a murderer and a thief."

"What a pair of jerks," said Didi.

"And then, Babs got really greedy," I continued. "She didn't even want to share the money with Scooter. She killed him. That story about him leaving her and moving to Florida was so transparent it wasn't even funny. Plus that, a woman like Babs would never go around without makeup and big eighties hair just because her husband left her. When she came to my house without makeup and all pale and weepy, I knew something was false. Talk about a bad acting job!

"And when Scooter turned up 'accidentally dead' in Val's basement, Babs was the one who rushed to judgment, eagerly pinning Val's murder on him. All that talk about Scooter and Val having some mad passionate affair was just hooey! We all know that Val carried a torch for no one but Skip until her dying breath. I think Babs planned to wait a few months until the furor died down and then move out to Hollywood and start a new life with Val's money.

Maybe she thought she would be discovered at her advanced age and play character parts."

"The only part she could play would be in Sunset Boulevard," said Didi. I laughed.

"As soon as Scooter turned up dead I started to wonder about Babs. It was those eyes of hers, flat and dead as two cat's eye marbles. Ick! And besides," I continued, "Who would steal a man's inhalers and lock him up in a basement full of cats, thereby committing murder by allergy?

"I ask you, who except a wife could hate a man so much that she would steal his inhalers and cat him to death? Anybody else would just shoot the poor sucker and run, but not mean as dirt old Babs. Oh, no. LeCaptain may have thought it was an accident, but I could only surmise that a man with a severe cat allergy, no inhalers, a basement full of stray, correction, stolen cats, and an accidentally locked door all added up to one thing; murder in the first degree."

"O.K., Miss Marple. You've got a point there. I get the picture. But you're not so hot, and don't credit yourself on being too clever."

"Why not?" I asked, preening myself in the sunlight streaming in through the window. The alcohol and Percodan combined were giving me a giddy, if temporary, feeling of freedom from pain.

"If you hadn't read all that Agatha Christie, you would probably be back at square one, wondering if the butler did it," said Didi. "And who got you out of the police station before you got arrested for breaking and entering?"

I rolled my eyes.

"Who helped you interview the suspects and point out the errors in your thinking?" asked Didi patiently.

"Which errors are those?" I snapped.

"Who helped clarify your muddled hypotheses, just like I did in chemistry class in 1968? Who supported you, encouraged you, and shone the beacon of rationality on your tortured logical quagmires? Who saved your skin from being shot in a boat and drowned, stranded on a cliff, and discovered in a jail cell with Arden Wasserschmidt? Moi! That's who!" said Didi. "Don't you think it's about time you acknowledged my contribution, Sherlock?"

"Hats off to Didi Spencer, my own dear Watson," I said graciously. After a decent interval of two seconds, I added, "Could we go to lunch now? I'm pretty hungry."

"That is so like you! Half dead and still hungry! Aren't you on a health food diet?" she carped.

"Yeah, so I'll just have a burger and fries and skip the chocolate shake. I'll have a diet Coke instead. Happy now?"

We smiled at each other. I counted myself as extremely fortunate to have a best friend like Didi, who knew when to nag and when to leave it alone.

When Didi and I were young, I was just as skinny as she was. But time, genetics, and chocolate had changed things. Just once in my life, I'd like to be thinner than Didi and not brag about it. Wouldn't that just drive her crazy? I thought about a diet. How hard could it be to lose twenty pounds in a month?

"Why are you staring at me with that squinty, mysterious look on your face?" asked Didi.

"Nothing," I said innocently.

My cell phone chimed out Beethoven's Fifth.

"Hello?" I said.

"Hi, Mom! This is me, Tabby. Krystal just got her driver's license and we're at the strip mall in Shelbyville."

My eyes grew wide with fear.

"Are you in shock?" I said.

"Mom! I'm O.K. I just need to distract myself!"

"I didn't say you could get in a car with Krystal, especially not on the first day she has her license! Especially not after the horrible experience we had today!" I said.

"Chill, Mom! We're just here to buy some midnight blue hair dye and purple passion for our bangs. Then we're coming right home to do our hair. We're sick of being blond sex objects."

"But I didn't even get a picture of you as a sex object," I wailed.

"Mom! You have already scarred my retina enough with all the flashes from all the pictures you've taken of me since the day I was born! We don't have time for pictures. We're going to go ultra-super punk, and the sooner the better."

"Oh, great," I said. "That reassures me. Just make sure Krystal doesn't swallow her tongue stud on the way home and drive off the road."

"Mom! Calm down! I just called to tell you that Jen called from Madison. I told her the whole story about Miss Cooper and said you were a heroine. She said she put a dent in the rear bumper of the car going to a gay rights rally but not to worry, it won't be covered by insurance so no need to report it. She met a cool punk guy her own age with a six inch green Mohawk and she might need some condoms right away. She describes him as a walking, talking, pulsating sex pistol. But she wants you to buy the condoms for her and mail them overnight delivery because she is too embarrassed to buy them herself."

"Whoa!" I said. "None of my children have my permission to have sex until they are thirty years old or I'm dead, whichever comes first! And anyone who wants her mom to send her Pokemon vitamins should not be talking about special delivery condoms! I never slept with anyone but your father and that was after we were married when I was thirty."

Mentally, I made the sign of the cross for telling that whopper. Tabby ignored me and continued.

"Let's see. Oh! And Matt broke his big toe in football practice, but it's O.K. because Kelly moved into the house to take care of him and do all the housework until he feels better. They want to start living together because Kelly is a feminist and doesn't believe in marriage. She thinks it's a patriarchal institution designed by men to keep women down. I like her."

Sigh.

"You what? Jen what? Matt what? I will deal with all of you later, but right now I have something to tell you, too," I said. "I've just met a twenty year old man who is madly in love with me. We're going out to buy some condoms right now. I heard sex uses up eight hundred calories so I plan to have sex about twelve times a day. It's my new weight loss plan. I can achieve drastic weight loss in just three weeks and write a bestseller called *Grandma's Feel the Burn Sensational Sex Weight Loss Program*. Oh, and by the way, my lover boy and I are running away to Hawaii on the next plane where we're staging a free love erotica fest in a nudist colony! I'll be naked on the cover of the *National Inquirer*. Great, huh? You, Jen, and Matt will all have to get jobs and support yourselves. See you on the Internet! Don't call me! I'll call you!" I clicked off.

Didi wagged a finger at me.

"You are so bad!" she said.

"Didi, call Father Dunn and ask him to make an emergency run to the house."

"You aren't going to break down and go to confession, are you?" asked Didi.

"No, I think I need Extreme Unction. These kids are going to kill me soon. Might as well throw in the last rites right away."

"Cheer up. At least they're not running up their college credit card entertaining prospective girlfriends like Jared is doing. He's starting to take after his father."

"God forbid he should turn out like Darin Derwood Darwood, the Yankee answer to Elvis. If Jared starts wearing his hair like Darin, we'll have to corner the market on men's hairspray and start stocking up."

The phone rang again.

"Hello?"

"Yo, Mom! I heard you kicked some major butt! Excellent work, Mom. I'm glad you're on my team! Kelly and I are like, living together now. Hope you don't mind, since it's your house we're living in. Her parents are cool with it and so is Jennifer, so yeah. Well, gotta go ice my broken toe," said Matt and hung up. I related the gist of the conversation to Didi.

"Why do your children constantly try to kill you?" asked Didi sadly. "If you stroke out, I'll have no one to talk to. I'll have no one to fight with in the nursing home."

I decided to ignore that last remark. Personally, I would rather swallow cyanide than do time in a nursing home, but the mere thought of captivity was so repugnant I couldn't even bring myself to talk about it.

"Why me, God?" I asked Didi. "Is it illegal to force your daughters into a nunnery and your son into the priesthood? Just when I was about to declare the next thirty years of my life the *pax* Rhiannon, I get thunked on the head with the realization that motherhood never ends. It just segues into being a grandmother."

"Well, duh!" said Didi. "It took you this long to figure that out?"

"But Didi!" I wailed. "I wanted to grow into a serene marvel of an older woman, a woman with elan, imperturbable and unflappable, whose wisdom everyone would admire. Inscrutably, irresistibly, impeccably me!"

"Fat chance, ducky!" said Didi. "Besides, you aren't a wise old woman. You're an Amazon warrior masquerading as a middle aged mom. When I saw your eyes as you burst up those stairs, I didn't know whether to call the police or an exorcist. I could have told Babs she didn't have a chance of winning, but why spoil the fun? It isn't often I get to see you morph into Attila the Hun. Now that you're in menopause and don't get PMS anymore, I don't have the fun of watching you change from Strawberry Shortcake to Genghis Khan every month."

The phone rang again.

"Hi, uh, this is Stan. Just heard. Wow, you're really something."

I winked at Didi.

"Oh, hi Stan. Yes, I am something and it's about time you realized it." Didi started giggling and choked on her iced tea.

"I fixed the door and the windshield and the right front fender on the Ford and I, uh, well, I'd like to do something else for you," said Stan.

I raised an eyebrow.

"And just what is it you would like to do for me, Stan?" I asked. Didi laughed, rolled her eyes and shook her head. Her golden curls fell over her triangular face, making her look like a well preserved supermodel in a shampoo commercial.

"Well, I uh, heard that Babs cut you in the shoulder and again in the hand and you're kind of bandaged up," said Stan. "Since you can't drive too well, I thought I could be your chauffeur for a while."

"Thanks Stan, and you're right. I can barely drive with two good shoulders and hands. I probably shouldn't tempt fate by driving with one good hand. How about Monday night?"

"Sounds good!" said Stan and signed off.

"I don't think Stan likes to talk on the phone," I said to Didi. A minute later, the phone rang again.

"Hello?" I said.

"Hi, Rhi. Ian here. Can I bring Buddy home now? He keeps fighting with the kids over the soccer ball."

"Guess so, since it's all over and your little sister is the heroine who caught the villainess and set all things right."

"Hey!" said Didi. "I helped!"

"Oh, yeah," I said to Ian. "Didi and I solved it together. This is the second case we've succeeded with. We're going to be famous. We're going to start planning our color scheme for Oprah tonight."

"Good for you. Who did the murderer turn out to be?" asked Ian.

"To make a long story short, it turned out it was Babs O'Reilly, Scooter's wife, who was the evil genius behind it all. She is a socially challenged aging wannabe blond bombshell Hollywood movie star with the manners of a timeshare condo salesman. She murdered her husband Scooter after she had him murder Valerie for her so she could get all the money Val had stashed in the basement. She didn't even want to share the cash with her own husband. Babs kept sending threatening notes to Tabby and Scooter tried to kill me with his truck. Skip committed suicide on Valerie's grave, and Skip's wife Melanie chased me around town taking potshots at my head. Fortunately for me, she was a lousy shot. In fact, she and Babs both tried to kill me more than once. Collectively, I think they all tried to kill me about ten times. And the high school drama teacher complicated things by stalking me everywhere I went. I had about five other suspects in mind but it turned out it was Babs O'Reilly all along. And that is the *Reader's Digest* version."

There was a stunned silence, followed by a sigh of exasperation.

"Rhiannon, you went to this godforsaken village which doesn't even boast a performing arts center. You had the firmly envisioned goal of having a little law firm and living in peace and quiet. And this is the kind of environment you're living in? Sounds like a bunch of deranged half wits run amok."

"I can't argue with that. In fact, that about sums it up," I said.

"Did you say her name is Babs?" continued Ian. "Isn't that short for Barbara? Oh, that must be why Buddy kept crying out in his sleep. He kept screaming, 'Mean Barbie! Mean Barbie! Scooter is bad!'"

It was my turn to sigh.

"Yeah, thanks a lot, Professor Ian. I mean, you couldn't have called me and given me that little clue, could you?"

There was a sheepish silence.

"If I had known it was a clue, I would have called you," said Ian.

"Never mind," I said. "Just send Buddy home on the next bus or run him up here in your Lexus. He's out of danger now."

"Will do," said Ian.

"Hey, thanks," I said. There was no response. "Ian? Ian?"

"I'm on the floor. I might be having a stroke."

"What?" I said, alarmed.

"I'm in shock because you deigned to say thanks!"

"Oh, shut up!" I said and hung up.

"Sometimes brothers can be so dense!" I said to Didi. "Ian had a clue under his nose and didn't even bother to tell me."

"Sounds like something Ian would do," said Didi. "I knew he was dense when we were sixteen and he started dating Trina Schultz. Remember her? She always took her retainer out and set it on her plate before we ate lunch at school. She was obsessed with macrame."

I laughed, recalling Trina and how she had made Ian a macrame belt. That was the worst looking belt I have ever seen in my life.

The telephone rang yet again.

"Hello. This better be good news," I said into the phone.

"Oh, it is, dear," said Eunice's sweet voice. "My sisters, Fayne and Maida, are so happy with you for setting things right for Valerie Cooper's soul that they have made you three dozen Irish scones just the way you like them. Now you won't have to waste time and money burning any more dough. You know, we spinsters don't take too kindly to people being mean to other spinsters, so we felt especially keen that Valerie's soul finds peace."

"Super!" I said. Just like Pavlov's dog at the sound of a bell, I started to salivate at the mention of the word scone.

"And it gets even better," said Eunice. "You just got the Stoegbauer case. We're solvent for another month."

"Well, praise the Lord and pass the potatoes! Rhi Nolan signing off here! Over and out!"

Epilogue

A glooming peace this morning with it brings.
The sun for sorrow will not show his head.
Go hence, to have more talk of these sad things;
Some shall be pardoned, and some punished;
For never was a story of more woe
Than this of Juliet and her Romeo.

--William Shakespeare, *Romeo and Juliet*, Act V,
Scene iii

On Monday night, I looked up from one of my favorite Agatha
Christie mysteries to see Tabby and Krystal come down the stairs in
full punk rock regalia. Tabby's hair was once again bright purple.
She wore a black leather jacket, old baggy black patched clothes full
of safety pins, her black punk rock platform boots, black nail polish,
and black lipstick. Krystal had put her tongue stud back in and died
her hair pink again, but once again, it had turned out orange.

"What happened?" I asked. "Tired of normalcy?"

"I'm tired of being a sex object, Mom," said Tabby. "And I'm
sick of role playing for the satisfaction of the patriarchal male
culture."

"That means sick of trying to look sexy for Todd," explained
Krystal.

"What happened to Todd, anyway?" I asked. "I haven't seen the
androgen wonder around lately."

"Todd started to go out with Ashleigh Kane because she does it
on the first date. That's why they call her Candy Kane."

"Does what?"

"You know, stuff. You wouldn't understand, Mom. It's stuff you
don't know anything about. You shouldn't hear it. I decided Todd

is really kind of a bonehead and I'm not into being gay, either. I've decided being a virgin is like, really cool."

"Hey, I say be cool," I told her.

"Yeah, well, Krystal and I are going to see two punk rock bands at Porcupine Junction. Skewered and Skull Babies are both playing tonight."

I jumped up from the rocker, grabbed Tabby, and gave her a big hug.

"Don't ever change!" I murmured into her glued up purple hair.

"Mom! You're squishing my bones!" she groaned. "You are so embarrassing!"

"Aren't you hungry?" I asked.

"Yes!" said Krystal.

"No!" said Tabby. "We're out of here!" They left and I sighed with satisfaction.

Thank God things were back to normal.

On Tuesday night, an emergency town meeting was called. Everyone voted unanimously that since Valerie left no will except for what she told Skip were her intentions, part of Val's money should be used as a scholarship fund, just as Skip had requested. Valerie's falling down house would be given to her twin cousins, Julia and Pamela of Jubilee. Julia could remain happily stuck in the fifties in Val's house. Luckily, Val's clothes would probably fit her to a tee. And cousin Pamela could go on living life in the sixties to her heart's content.

It was determined that the rest of the stolen money retrieved from Melanie and Babs, minus the part that went to taxes and the lawyers, would be used to create a special memorial in Valerie's name in the park. There would be a shelter and playground equipment with a huge fountain, banks and banks of flowers, and a statue of Valerie presiding over all. I just hoped they got the hair and the figure right. I know Valerie wouldn't want to be remembered as anything less, or shall I say more, than a perfectly preserved size six. I hoped they dressed the statue in a twinset, poodle skirt, bobby socks, and saddle shoes.

I would forever see Val in her 1957 Chev with her cat's eye sunglasses, her red lipstick, and her hair tied back with a pink chiffon scarf, waving gaily at all of us, her romantic dreams intact.

That night I dreamed I saw Valerie and Skip holding hands and running through a fields of daisies together. They looked very young and very happy, and Val wore a divinely pink poodle skirt and twinset with pearls. Skip had on tight jeans and a white muscle tee shirt and he looked mmm-mmm good. They glanced back at me, waved, laughed, and ran away into eternal love and eternal youth.

As the only lawyer in town, I was elected to call up cousins Julia and Pamela and inform them that according to Val's wishes, they had inherited her house. Julia called Pamela to pick up on the extension, a princess phone, no doubt. They both twittered at me with fluting, bird-like voices.

"Oh, sharp!" said Julia. "Pam, we have a house of our very own, and such a beauty!"

"Oh, fab!" sang Pamela. "When can we move in?"

"The sooner the better," I said, and smiled.

I was in Jane's Grocery with Stan on Wednesday night stocking up on M&M's when a bony finger poked me in the arm.

"Ouch!" I said.

"Hey!" said Stan to Pavalik. "Don't poke her! She's still recovering from almost getting killed by that madwoman!"

"Hey, yourself! What are those M&M's doing in her basket? Aren't you on a low carb diet, Mrs.?" asked Mr. Pavalik.

"No! I'm on a refined carb diet. Haven't you heard? It's the newest thing!" I said. "The object is to let yourself enjoy life before it's over."

"Ha! That's what I tell my doctor when he says I shouldn't drink and smoke if I want to live to see ninety," croaked Mr. P. He pulled a cigarette from behind his ear and rolled it between his gnarled thumb and forefinger. "Say, I could have told you the murderer would turn out to be that Babs O'Reilly. We all should have suspected her right from the start. She wasn't one of us, you know. She's one of them Lutherans from Minnesota. Didn't you notice she talked a little different? Ya, hey!"

"I noticed she didn't have the perfect cheese head twang. Her diphthongs were a little different. So?" I said nonchalantly.

"I don't know about them thongs but you never can tell what them Minnesota Lutherans will do. Inbred, you know." He nodded sagely.

And speaking of inbred, ya hey! I didn't know that the not one of us, darling philosophy could prevail here in New Belgium in the modern mobile age, but I should have figured. After all, Babs had only lived here forty years, and you had to have ancestry dating back to circa 1850 to be considered one of the cheese heads. I sighed. Ah, New Belgium! Too bad Green Acres had gone off the air. These folks would be perfect as extras.

"Well, I'm not one of you either," I said in my own defense.

"Whaddaya mean, you ain't one of us?" asked Pavalik. "You been through enough now. You can be an official New Belgium cheese head. You could get elected mayor!"

"Lucky me," I said. "Too bad I've always thought of politics as make believe without the fun."

Stan hugged me and clapped me on the back.

"You're official! You're one of us!" he proclaimed. I winced.

"Stan! Please! I have just been thrown down a flight of stairs, slashed with a knife, and beat up in a cat fight. Watch the shoulder, please!"

"Sorry," said Stan and beamed at me. Mr. P. looked him up and down and squinted.

"He don't look sorry," said Mr. P. "He looks like a man in love. If you play your cards right, maybe you'll get the chance to love, honor, and obey." I bristled at this.

"Obey? What year is this, 1950? How do you survive in post-feminist America? Have you been in a cave for fifty years? Isn't it time for you to go now?" I asked none too gently.

"Hmpf! Touchy as usual. You must be recovering," Pavalik said and shuffled into the dried beef jerky aisle.

"Oh, by the way," I called to him. "I heard you had gallstones but I got mixed up and went down to the Pickle Jar and told all your old cronies that you were stoned all the time so you might have to sort that out."

"Hey, Rhiannon!" called Jane from the checkout counter. "I was at the library and I saw that the book you ordered is in. It's sitting on the counter with your name written real big across it in white tape."

"What book is that?" I asked her.

"Don't you remember? You reserved *The Joy of Sex*," said Jane. Every head in the place turned to look at me and they all laughed. Stan blushed redder than the bag of MacIntosh apples he was holding. I heard Pavalik croak a guffaw from the next aisle. He started to laugh and wheeze so hard I thought he would choke. He is such an old cheese head.

"Great!" I called out. I stared everybody down except Mrs. Drusilla Swinkle. She clucked her tongue at me. I thrust an avocado under her nose, popped it into my basket, and said, "Aphrodisiac!" She scurried away.

One thing about cheese heads; the world for them is divided into cheese heads and non-cheese heads, and cheeseheadism is the only category they recognize. All others are foreigners. Refreshing in a way. Makes life less complicated. Of course, too much cheese will clog up your veins. One should remember to save room for those M&M's.

Look for Rhiannon's next adventure in:

Death in Starched White

Rhiannon goes undercover at Eldermanse, a nursing home on the edge of town, to find a particularly nasty and vengeful murderer. Meanwhile, Rhi's best friend and sleuthing partner, Didi Spencer, tries her hand at writing a romance novel and at matchmaking. Will she write a blockbuster, and even more difficult, find a date for Rhi? Can Rhi ferret out the identity of the crafty killer with the help of the Dunn sisters, Eunice, Fayne, and Maida? All the quirky characters of New Belgium reunite for another baffling puzzle. Hold onto your cheddar. It's another trip through cheese head land.

Ask for the Rhiannon Nolan books by Kathy Buchen at your library or find them on the worldwide web at www.AuthorHouse. com.

And coming in 2006:

Death in A Bad Habit
Death in Down
Death in Mink

DEMCO

Printed in the United States
36167LVS00005B/42

9 781420 832570